SEEING OTHER PEOPLE

DIANA REID

SEEING OTHER PEOPLE

DIANA REID

ultimo press

Published in 2022 by Ultimo Press,
an imprint of Hardie Grant Publishing.
This edition published in 2023.

Ultimo Press
Gadigal Country
7, 45 Jones Street
Ultimo, NSW 2007
ultimopress.com.au

Ultimo Press (London)
5th & 6th Floors
52–54 Southwark Street
London SE1 1UN

  ultimopress

Seeing Other People
ISBN 978 1 76115 257 3 (hardback)

Cover design George Saad
Author photo Courtesy of Daniel Boud
Text design Simon Paterson, Bookhouse
Typesetting Bookhouse, Sydney | 12/17.5 pt Baskerville MT Pro
Copyeditor Ali Lavau
Proofreader Rebecca Hamilton

10 9 8 7 6 5 4 3 2 1

MIX
Paper | Supporting responsible forestry
FSC® C013604

Printed and bound by CPI Group (UK) Ltd, Croydon, CR0 4YY.

Ultimo Press acknowledges the Traditional Owners of the Country on which we work, the Gadigal People of the Eora Nation and the Wurundjeri People of the Kulin Nation, and recognises their continuing connection to the land, waters and culture. We pay our respects to their Elders past and present.

For Maureen

‘meaningful commitment to a love in the world can require the sacrifice of one’s own moral purity’

—Martha Nussbaum, *Love’s Knowledge*

1

BREAKING A HEART can be an act of kindness. Mark missed his opportunity. Not only was his break-up just an accumulation of mistakes, but Eleanor's heart (or whatever part of her brain she'd tasked with feelings) remained decidedly unbroken.

The cracks—an intricate web, perceptible only in hindsight—led at last to a severance, which took place in an open-air food court in Sydney's central business district, on a Friday during the lunchtime rush.

In the food court, the pop songs were depressingly festive, and each window display was obscured by tinsel. Christmas was five weeks away.

They sat at a little table on the end of a long bench. Eleanor wore sunglasses and Mark squinted. She offered to look for a seat in the shade, but he said it would be impossible. Mark had the bin at his left shoulder, and a suited man at his right. Some people looked at him in an apologetic way when they lifted the lid to deposit their lunch scraps. Few paused to separate out their recycling. Each time the bin opened, a thick, not entirely unpleasant smell emerged, like the smoke off a deep-fryer.

Mark tried to shuffle further up the bench, but the table was bolted to the ground.

Eleanor picked at her poke bowl, and pushed her sunglasses up her nose. 'You're not getting anything?'

'I'm not hungry.'

She stopped eating, her chopsticks next to her face, her free hand articulating the frustration he couldn't see behind those dark lenses. 'You were the one who wanted to meet for lunch.'

Mark hadn't eaten since yesterday. Guilt and a hangover wrangled his insides. 'Remember how I told you I went to a strip club last Saturday?'

When Mark had told Eleanor, on the Sunday, she had said: 'I don't know how I feel about that,' in a tone so prim and disapproving it made her feelings explicit. They hadn't broached the topic since. The details of that evening were Mark's to bear, and Eleanor's to imagine.

—

ONE OF MARK'S friends from school was getting married. At twenty-six, he was the first of their group to do so. He had booked an Airbnb in the city for his bucks night. Mark, who was disdainful of both the wedding industrial complex and staycations in equal measure, was determined to be depressed and alienated by the whole experience.

After about eight standard drinks, however, he found the familiar company of his schoolfriends, and his easy dominance in their little group—the way they all looked to him as 'the funny one'—about as depressing as a warm bubble bath.

At the club, he tried to adopt an attitude of respectful admiration, as if he were watching a play. He prided himself on using exclusively desexualised language. *She's particularly talented. Very well-rehearsed. That one's got real charisma.*

His discomfort must have been obvious, though, because a lap dance was procured. Mark kept his hands at his sides, first in fists, then he lay them flat against the seat. He laughed and hoped it made him sound non-threatening. He tried conversation: 'How did you get into this?'

She certainly didn't sound threatened. In fact, she made Mark feel very small. 'Does my backstory interest you?'

She was getting a law degree. He had finished one two years ago. He had worked as a paralegal at a big commercial firm while he was studying. She earned significantly more in her chosen part-time job.

He asked her whether she was concerned about how this job might affect her legal career. Her back was turned to him, and she looked over her shoulder, wide brown eyes mocking him. 'What difference does it make? Your face could also be photoshopped onto deepfake porn if you ever became important enough to, like, cancel.'

He laughed as if the suggestion were absurd: as if he did not, in fact, aspire to become somebody worthy of cancellation. Or at the very least, somebody with a Wikipedia page.

—

ELEANOR PUSHED HER sunglasses onto her forehead and said: 'Do we have to talk about this now? I have to be back in twenty minutes.'

'Obviously, I hated it, and I knew it was wrong—'

'It's not *wrong*.'

'What?'

Eleanor sighed, and speared a slice of salmon sashimi with a single chopstick. She didn't put it in her mouth. 'I'm not mad at you because I think strip clubs are *wrong*. Clearly they're not. And

I respect the women who trade their bodies and their skill for money. It's no different from the way I trade my intellect and time.'

Mark raised his eyebrows on *intellect*: reproaching Eleanor for being so judgemental. As if that wasn't exactly what he was doing, when he looked at her that way.

This expression was familiar to Eleanor—eyebrows up and gaze down and out the corner of his wire-framed glasses; away from confrontation. A little performance of self-control, like Mark was too decent, or considerate, or simply powerless, to voice whatever criticism he had formulated. Usually she'd beg him to tell her—*What? What is it?!*—so that by the time he voiced his judgement she felt the extra shame of having extracted it.

Today, she was multiple steps ahead. She rebutted him before he could speak. After two monogamous years, they had achieved the level of love and intimacy where mere facial expressions invite lengthy counterarguments.

'And don't think,' Eleanor said, 'I'm suggesting that selling my intellect is any more empowering than selling physical talents. In fact, it's probably a lot less, given that our time on this planet is finite, and what my employers take from me, overwhelmingly, is time.'

She paused, looking at a notification on her Apple watch, then continued, 'It's just . . . God I don't know how to put this in a way that won't seriously upset you—'

'Go on.'

'It's just pathetic, Mark. I find the customers—male customers—pathetic. Like, it's very sad that you're paying to leer at women so you can feel some kind of power over them. And it's all the more pathetic because, like, guys sitting in a dark room with stiffies have no power at all.'

'It was quite well lit, actually.' He waved a hand. 'Theatrical.'

Eleanor's face was a vacuum: it sucked the laughter, first from his smile, then right out of his chest.

A man threw an empty plastic sushi container at the bin with one hand, and flicked the lid up with the other. The timing was all wrong. The container landed open at Mark's feet. The man had already turned, exhibiting that city-centre impatience which says more about how highly a person regards themselves than how many appointments they have to keep.

Mark put the dripping container on the tabletop. He looked at his hands, slick with soy sauce. When he looked up, Eleanor was holding out her napkin like an accusation.

He wiped his hands on the napkin, then scrunched it into a ball.

Eleanor broke the silence. 'Please don't make me feel guilty for saying that. I don't want you to build this up into some political stance of mine. I just think it's a fucking lame way to spend a Saturday night.'

Mark's fist tightened around the napkin. He could tell from her sharp intake of breath that Eleanor had already formulated the next thing she would say. When she opened her mouth, he cut in: 'I got with someone.'

'What?'

Mark didn't say anything. From her furious, combative gaze, he knew she had heard him perfectly. And hearing it, she understood how difficult it was to say aloud. So, her stare squeezed him, and demanded he repeat himself. That she was entitled to make demands of him, given what he'd done, only intensified his reluctance. He heard himself swallow.

'On Saturday night, after, you know . . .'

Eleanor's glare was merciless.

'. . . after the strip club, I sort of—well, I didn't, actually, but I *almost*—slept with someone.'

Eleanor laughed. Mark recognised the sound, but found her face newly twisted with it. '*How?*'

—

THEY ONLY STAYED at the club for an hour. Mark spent much of his time in the bathroom. When he left, it was with a drunken tread—all purpose and no direction.

It was a wet night: rubbish flat and sodden against the pavement. He almost missed her face in the rain. The wide eyes, the bleached-white hair.

Time and place poured like liquid over his mind, not sinking in. But someone—he assumed he must have been the one to do it—invited her up for a drink. Because back at the Airbnb, he stood on the balcony and tried to focus on smoking, while those heavy-lidded eyes stared back, and her smile mocked him for finding her so beautiful. He wondered, until she asked him for a dart, whether he was imagining her.

She turned so her back was against the railing, and leaned on it, stretching out. She was wearing a white ribbed tank with no bra. Mark asked if he could kiss her.

'You're not going to romanticise this, are you?' she said. Because he already was, he was delighted.

'You're very perceptive,' he told her.

'You're very predictable.'

Then it was she who leaned in.

Their repartee: the symmetry of it; the dull background noise of voices and music coming from inside the room—he could already parse it like a screenplay. Even when she leaned in, her face was in close-up. But from the moment their lips touched, he lost all sense of himself, and when she pulled away, although triumphant, he felt no sense of narrative climax. He felt, instead, an urge to run his fingers up and down her slender back, and to tell her (which he did) that her skin was smoother than he could have imagined.

—

'So you boys invited one of the strippers back to the Airbnb, and you fucked her?'

'No, that's not what happened.'

Eleanor put her head in her hands. 'Oh god, you haven't romanticised this, have you?'

'We were all very drunk—'

'Mark, please tell me you don't think you had some sort of special connection.'

He started to stammer.

Eleanor straightened her chopsticks, and pushed the cardboard bowl to one side. 'I'm sorry,' she said. 'I can't . . . I'm finding it hard to look at you.'

She cast her eyes around the food court, and he contemplated her face. The long, slightly aquiline nose, the high, round cheeks, her mouth wide and resting at a downturn. When she smiled, her upper lip dipped to a bow shape, her cheeks rose in perfect symmetry, and her nose straightened at the centre. It was her smile that animated her, and rendered her beautiful. In this current state of distress, she looked almost ugly.

'I'm so sorry,' he said. 'Please believe me. I really am. But it's not what you think. I mean, I did sort of *see* someone on Saturday. But it wasn't *fucking*. And it wasn't—'

'I mean, obviously I'm very emotional.' This wasn't obvious at all. Her eyes were dry, and she was talking with her hands, like she was delivering a speech. 'I want to take some time to reflect, so we don't make any rash decisions, but I think it's pretty clear that we'll have to break up.'

'Eleanor—'

'You just cheated on me with someone you met in a strip club. I'm sorry, Mark, but a break-up is the only rational response.'

'It wasn't someone . . . We don't have to rush into anything, we can keep talking about it: about what actually happened. And, like you said, take some time to think about it.'

'Oh, I'll think about it.' Her watch lit up with a phone call. 'Charlie's calling me.'

Mark ran a hand through his hair. He'd grown it out: at chin-length it was the longest it had ever been and he had a habit of tucking it behind his ears. Too short to tie back in a ponytail, but long enough to set him apart from the other men in his office—men who, in all other respects, looked exactly the same as Mark.

Eleanor touched her forehead with the tips of her fingers. 'Her play's tonight,' she said to herself. And then to him: 'Don't even think about coming.'

—

AT WORK, ELEANOR usually left her personal phone in her bag, and only looked at it when she went to lunch, or to the toilet. She could spend up to fifteen minutes in the bathroom on her phone—provided of course that she hadn't gone there to cry. In those cases, she just cried, wiping her nose with toilet paper enough times to rough the skin. Otherwise, she'd sit until her thighs were porcelain-branded: replying to messages; reading group chats with just enough energy to react rather than reply. She marvelled at the efficiency: that whole relationships could be sustained, and invitations to group events secured, just by sad-reacting a couple of times a week, either ironically (*I've got a date tonight!*) or in genuine sympathy (*Why are all men trash?!*).

Today, it was not for one of these soul-numbing administrative spells that Eleanor locked herself in the cubicle. She was there to vomit.

Afterwards, looking at the brown rice grains that floated, facetious, in the toilet water, she gagged—but noiselessly—with no real momentum.

Her mouth still acidic, she put her phone to her ear and rang her housemate.

She had to call twice. As the phone rang a second time, she wondered whether she had ever called Seb at work before. She didn't even have his mobile number. Since they'd met in their first week at university, they had always messaged on Facebook. Today, she rung him via the app, with the blue, throbbing sound that didn't even attempt to recall a phone that might, at some point in history, have hung on a wall, a bell embedded in its stomach.

'Eleanor, are you okay?'

Seb must have left the office to take her call. She could hear the rumble of traffic and picture him—AirPods sleek and cordless—charging around the block while they spoke.

'Hi, I'm sorry—'

'I was in a meeting but I've popped ou—'

'Mark cheated on me.'

'Eleanor!'

'What?'

'I thought someone had *died*. Or the apartment had exploded, or something. I was sitting here wondering whether I'd turned the stove off. I'm ninety-nine per cent sure I did. But you know how, when you try to recall it—like actually conjure up the memory—you just have no idea?'

'Seb. The only memory I'm conjuring is my boyfriend telling me over lunch that he cheated on me.'

'Right. God. I'm so sorry. Do you know who it was?'

'A stripper.'

Seb's skin was enviably smooth, his hair the kind of subtle fade that can only be achieved by fortnightly cuts and gels that come in glass jars. But his teeth—naturally straight and artificially white—were his real asset. These were on glistening display, right down to his molars, when his jaw dropped towards the pavement on Elizabeth Street. 'What? When did this happen? *How?*'

'At this bucks night he went to on the weekend.'

'With a stripper?'

'He met her at a strip club, yes. I think'—Eleanor exhaled; her chest felt heavier for the effort—'I think he thinks it's more than sex.'

'Flay me alive.'

'You don't think it's . . .' Eleanor felt the second wave of tears ache in the back of her throat. 'I'm just so embarrassed.'

'*You're* embarrassed? It's embarrassing for *him*. Not for you or the stripper—or the Other Woman, or whatever not-reductive name we want to use . . . Do we know her name?'

'No, Seb. I don't know her name.'

'Shame. I wanted to stalk.'

Eleanor didn't say anything. She rested her head against the cubicle wall. She found it surprisingly cool.

'God, Eleanor. I'm just so sorry. What a shitty thing.'

'Yeah.'

'Let's get properly fuck-eyed this weekend.'

She smiled. She appreciated the violence of his language. 'Good idea. I imagine I'll be feeling self-destructive.'

'Absolutely. Look, I have to go. Are you okay?'

'Yeah. Go. We can talk about it when you're home.'

'I've said it before and I'll say it again: men are trash.'

Eleanor laughed. She didn't find it funny. She didn't even think he'd said it as a joke. The situation just seemed absurd: that a quote from a meme—a caption they lifted from the internet and bandied about as a way of participating in a cultural moment—might suddenly seem so wise. She supposed it must have been funny at one point, not because everybody was saying it, but because somebody found it true.

—

ELEANOR WAS RUNNING late.

When she'd applied for the Women's Internship at her consulting firm, in her final year of university, she attended a cocktail evening where female graduates listed what they loved about working there. 'Friday nights are sacred,' they said, in cultish imitations of each other's exact tone and turn of phrase. At the time, Eleanor took *sacred* to mean: *reserved for personal use.* Now she knew *sacred* meant: *with alcohol.* From four pm on Friday, it was socially acceptable to help yourself to a beer from the fridge, which, at all other times in the week, sat fully stocked and unlocked. Then you could work on your slides and your spreadsheets between sips until your manager dismissed you from Sacred Time.

In the lift, newly dismissed, her manager asked who the flowers were for. Eleanor's thoughts were so consumed with Mark, the question arrived from a great distance, and she seemed surprised to find in her own arms the unwieldy bouquet she'd bought that morning. She peeped between two proteas.

'My sister. She's in a play tonight.'

'Oh? She's an actress?' He said this in a strangely pitying tone, as if *actress* were an upsetting medical diagnosis. He might as well have said: *Oh? She thinks she's a fairy princess?*

Eleanor lowered the bouquet. 'Yeah, she's very talented, actually.'

'She must love it,' he said, as if being good at something and loving it were the same thing.

They emerged into the lobby, which was almost empty, the revolving door momentarily stalled. Eleanor was alert to the time. But that swelling anxiety—the distractable glances at her phone clock—was dulled by another kind of irritation. She felt a defensive need to resolve the conversation in Charlie's favour. For small talk, it all seemed very value-laden.

'It's amazing, actually,' Eleanor said, 'how passionate she is. Like, each show is a gift.'

'I suppose that makes sense though, doesn't it?' He extended an arm to indicate that Eleanor should enter the revolving door in front of him. Their slice of the glass cylinder was tiny. The more fragile flowers in the bouquet trembled beneath his breath. 'With our kind of work, the correlation between input and outcome is obvious. We work hard, we see results. With actors—with anything subjective—the results, career-wise, are arbitrary. A lot of talented people fail.'

'Aren't all fortunes equally arbitrary, in a world that's structurally unfair?'

He smiled. To her manager, being contradicted was as good as being flirted with. 'Sure. But success in some industries has to be more arbitrary than others. Ours, for example, isn't dictated by subjective tastes.'

'Don't you ever think, though, that it wouldn't be such a bad thing for your life to be dictated by these irrational tastes? Or, I guess, passions.'

'Are you saying spreadsheets don't inspire passion?'

'Your words, not mine.'

He lifted his briefcase, pointing his finger at her, in a kind of wave. 'That's why we pay you.' He said this as if it were a common idiom, or a quote from a famous person.

Eleanor laughed like she recognised it, before hoisting the flowers to a more comfortable position, and walking towards the station.

2

AT THE TENDER age of twenty-two, Charlie Hamor was already living in the shadow of her own potential. If the origins of her acting career were full of promise, then the story so far was of failures to perform.

She was the youngest person in her acting class at the most prestigious drama school in Sydney, if not the country. She had auditioned right out of high school, when she was still seventeen, and been accepted straight away, even though the application form expressly asked about 'life experience' which Eleanor said could only mean: *time spent alive.*

After her first-year showcase, Charlie signed with a well-respected agent—the only person in her cohort to do so. She had a face for screen, they all said. The teachers said this like a compliment. The other students managed to make it sound dismissive. Although she must have had some X factor, because she'd shortened Charlotte to Charlie, and pulled it off.

She had characterful eyes and lips (which is precisely where you want character) while her nose and chin and hair were perfectly impersonal. The hair in particular—straight, thin, dirty blonde—was a blank canvas. Often it was dyed and cut and curled to cast those expressive eyes and that bow-lipped smile in different lights.

Even more importantly, she was tall—over six feet—and skinny, in that thin-legged, flat-chested way that no amount of exercise or healthy eating can imitate. Bodies for screen—female bodies—were teenaged.

In her third and final year this spindly ingenue secured a minor role in a mainstage production. While everybody else applied for casual jobs to subsidise the impending cycle of audition and rejection, Charlie's mind was six months ahead, at her debut. She mentally drafted reviews.

Raw.

A revelation.

A once-in-a-generation talent.

In her mind, other roles flooded in. Then feature articles in the Sunday paper, where a journalist would interview her over lunch and confidently extrapolate her whole personality from whether she did or didn't eat her chips.

Reality, however, proved less thrilling. Charlie graduated from drama school at the end of November 2019. Two years of lockdowns followed, interrupted only by auditions and rejections, and hope that the cancelled mainstage show might be rescheduled. It wasn't.

Then Charlie spent November 2021 rehearsing for a small, independent theatre, wondering all the while whether she'd forgotten how to act.

On opening night, she stood backstage, and listened to the audience file in. So close, their voices were individual, although none Charlie recognised. She took a deep breath and told herself that her fear was irrational—performance was instinct. If drama school had taught her anything, it was that acting couldn't be taught.

—

WHEN ELEANOR ARRIVED at the theatre, a bell was ringing with the intensity of a siren, summoning the audience to their seats. Without pausing to greet anyone, with her arms tight at her side and her footsteps small, she picked her way through the crowd and up a narrow set of stairs.

Finding her row, she slid past seated audience members, apologising to each in turn as she rained petals on their shoes—most of which, unfortunately, were open-toed. She found her seat with ease: three empty chairs at the centre of the row. She sat next to a stranger, with two seats empty to her right, so as to look less alone.

Her mother had called as she was getting on the train. It was crowded, and the man next to her was laughing into a video call, and Eleanor found it difficult to hear. Something about a meeting. 'Let Mark take my ticket.'

Eleanor didn't say that she'd already bought a ticket for Mark, or that she'd forbidden him from using it on account of the cheating. Instead, she thanked her mother, and offered to reimburse her on Mark's behalf. That conversation was a rehearsal, Eleanor thought, for how she would behave when she saw her sister after the show.

If she could get through the evening without having to tell anyone how she was—if their conversation could remain on actors and their characters, and not the real people who so occupied her thoughts—Eleanor might have a tearless night. It was her sister's first show in two years, and her mother had probably had a very stressful week. If she had to cry—although Mark didn't deserve it—she would do it in private.

Determined not to look at her phone (*I'm so sorry—let me know when you're ready to talk about it*), Eleanor stared at the ticket in her lap, and tried to think of higher things.

A Doll's House

Eleanor had studied the play in high school. She remembered all the themes, and how it ended, which were annoying details to recall. A puzzle already solved.

Charlie would be dressed up in the flounciest nineteenth-century European dress the small independent theatre company could afford, and the actor playing her husband would spend the next hour or so treating her like a little doll. Eventually, Charlie would tire of her total lack of agency. Then, she would abandon her husband and her children in a radical assertion of personhood.

If Eleanor were to put her own interests first, she thought, it wouldn't be radical; it would just be obnoxious. She wondered where the line was—the degree of liberation—after which self-actualisation is no longer a political project. She sensed that women like herself had comfortably crossed it. Looking as she did, with her university degree and graduate salary, exercises in self-love could not plausibly be part of some greater liberating project.

Dimming lights and an abrupt hush interrupted Eleanor's thoughts.

The stage was dark, the actors assembling as silhouettes. Black slashes on grey. Eleanor could tell, from the vague stroke of her body, which one was Charlie. She fixed a resolute gaze, and tried to concentrate on her sister. The play might prove a soothing distraction. If Eleanor could just focus on someone other than herself—if she could commit to dutiful sistering—she might forget her own problems. As the lights rose and the play began, Eleanor measured every actor's talent against her sister's.

Unfortunately, this did not prove much of a distraction. It was only a few minutes before Eleanor confirmed what she already knew: Charlie was in a league of her own. She combined two rare gifts: an expressive, elastic face, and a capacity for stillness. Where other actors would flap their hands about—anything to keep them from hanging at their sides—Charlie found a position (one hand on hip; arms crossed in front of her; hands outstretched) and stayed there. Her expressions, too, did not flit from one reaction to the next. She watched whoever was speaking, patiently, often without so much as the twitch of an eye. But in her stillness, the audience could almost hear her blood pump.

Now that the competition for best actor was over, there was nothing to hold Eleanor's attention. Certainly not the play.

Eleanor didn't enjoy theatre. Every time she came to a show to support her sister, she would listen to the audience surrounding her and cringe. She particularly hated those self-congratulatory little laughs which declared: *I get the joke.* Like society's great, glaring inequalities were only perceptible to a particularly cultured eye. *I'm not the problem*, those snickers said. As if to snicker were to be self-aware; as if self-awareness were a solution.

The few times Eleanor had been to the theatre with Mark, he had laughed as loud as the rest. Seated next to him Eleanor had laughed too, and felt the stab of self-betrayal. Eleanor and Mark disagreed on matters of taste so often, and Eleanor relented so regularly, that she wasn't sure she had tastes at all. Mark had worked diligently to paint Eleanor as a philistine, wherever her opinions diverged from his. Movies Eleanor didn't like were just films she hadn't understood. Plays she found indulgent were scripts whose depths she was incapable of fathoming. Tonight, with a Mark-less seat beside her, Eleanor admitted to herself that she never did—and certainly didn't now—care what happened on stage. It was a small freedom, and difficult to enjoy, because it left her trapped with her own thoughts.

Mentally, Eleanor read back through their messages since Saturday night: she'd asked how he was feeling on Sunday, and whether he wanted to hang out, and he'd said he was too hungover to function. A week of post-midnight finishes at work made Eleanor easily avoidable. Finally, they'd settled on Friday lunch. She'd told him she was looking forward to seeing him with a mortifying emoji: the smiley face with the little splayed hands. Now she heard those messages in a toddler's whine and hated herself for them.

She tried to imagine Mark having sex—*almost* sex, he had called it. She wondered how he would move around another body: whether he would be a different person entirely. Her hands (which she eventually sat on) physically ached to reach for her phone, and find the woman online. She traced a path of possible searches. Mark's tagged photos on Instagram to determine where they had been drinking on the weekend. Google Maps, and a one-kilometre radius, to see nearby strip clubs. What if they had caught cabs? A ten-kilometre radius, then. She wanted a face and a name—even a made-up name—to pin with grievances. Someone to stand between her and Mark and carry the weight of the betrayal.

Eleanor was so absorbed in these imagined scenes, she did not stop for intermission. Instead, as the lights rose and the audience stood, her thoughts only intensified. She took her phone and exited to the foyer.

—

ELEANOR LOOKED AT herself in the mirror. Her hands under the hot tap and her phone in her back pocket, her eyes were momentarily relieved from the screen. She looked at the girl on her left and wondered whether they'd met before. Maybe she'd seen her in another of Charlie's plays. Or maybe it was just that her face (the small nose, the dark, emphatic eyebrows) was a type she'd seen a thousand times before. Only a septum piercing—silver beads glinting in each nostril—distinguished it from any other boringly perfect face.

Her blue eyes, looking at Eleanor.

Eye contact in a mirror is always more intense than in the flesh. Still conscious of her own reflection, Eleanor was acutely aware—not only of seeing, but of being seen. She blushed, as if caught in a private vanity.

'How are you finding the show?'

'It's good, the actors are good. It's . . .' Eleanor looked from the mirror to her hands, then back up to the woman's real face. 'Well, it's a play, isn't it?'

The woman laughed, and moved from the sink to the wall. She handed Eleanor a paper towel. 'You don't like plays?'

'I like them, but . . . surely theatre is just TV without famous people?'

'And they don't even let you play on your phone while you're watching.'

'Exactly! It's coercive.'

They threw the used towels in the bin. The woman held the bathroom door open. Eleanor slipped through and, as if in thanks, said, 'So do you know anyone in the show tonight, or do you just love theatre or something?'

'I directed it.'

'Oh, did you?' Eleanor shook her head. Of course she did. 'Fuck you. Theatre is awesome.'

The director was smiling now too. 'Have you tried TV though?'

'I'm actually a very sophisticated person.'

The bell sounded the end of intermission. Eleanor—cheeks still hot—seized her opportunity. 'Well, it was mortifying to meet you. Great job on the play. I'd better . . .'

She'd already started to turn away, when the director placed a gentle hand on her shoulder.

'It gets better in the second half.'

—

THE SECOND HALF ran for fifty-five minutes, fifty-five of which Eleanor spent replaying her relationship with Mark.

When Eleanor and Mark had started seeing each other, they were both in their last semester at university. There were smiles above laptops in the library, long coffee breaks, and average marks in their final exams. They both already had jobs lined up for when they graduated, so they laughed at their mediocrity, as if it didn't matter. Nothing, that summer, seemed to matter. They knew that a chapter was ending: real life was coming. But their future was uncoloured by fear. They couldn't see it; they could only feel it, in the soul-relaxed sensation that their lives might yet turn out any number of ways. All they saw was the present: gold-tinted, as if by a setting sun.

They went to the beach, they drank outdoors, they rubbed sunscreen on each other's backs and said: 'I love you.' In Eleanor's case, the words were an echo—a prayer repeated—following Mark's incantation. She was happy, she didn't want to hurt him, so she said them, reflexively, to make him happy too.

Then they started full-time work, and Mark suggested they move in together. Eleanor said she thought it was too soon, they had their whole lives to live together—although that prospect terrified her, and she wondered whether it was meant to. Instead, Mark stayed over every Friday night and all weekend, and they parted on Monday morning when they alighted the train.

During these stays, Mark would often—any time they had somewhere to be—stop for a kiss at the wide double doors of Eleanor's apartment building, just before they stepped onto the street. A peck at first, and then tongue, and then hands running up and up her legs, her back against the wall. It would be easier, then, to go back upstairs and look at the ceiling and try to forget how late they were. Easier than resisting, and enduring his mood.

'It's always me who initiates,' he'd say, like these grabs at her—timed almost sadistically—were his share of some domestic chore. In cabs or on public transport, too, there'd be petting and neck biting, and fighting afterwards, if she pushed him off too strongly. *Do you know how you made me look?*

When the play ended, as plays often did, with a crescendo of music and then a snap to black, there was that breath-bated silence that can only mean one thing. The audience, despite initial reluctance—their own dramatic sense of anticipation—would end on their feet.

Eleanor stood and clapped with the rest, feeling nothing.

—

'YOU WERE A fucking superstar.'

Charlie's housemate, Mandy, was gripping her shoulders and issuing compliments with the urgency of commands. 'It was so *raw*, Charlie.'

Charlie looked at her feet in a convincing show of humility. 'Every man and his dog has either seen it already or studied it. It's such a cliché.'

'You don't understand. I wept, I laughed. I questioned everything I know. Oh, there's Helen. I must congratulate her. Unbelievable. She must be an actual genius. You too, of course.'

Charlie winced as she was kissed once on each cheek. Her clothes were her own, but her face was still her character's. Through mascara-laden lashes, she scanned the room for her sister. They had identical bow-lipped smiles. Now, they showed them to each other across the theatre's foyer.

Eleanor hugged her and quietly—privately, so as not to embarrass her—whispered congratulations.

'Are you with Mum?'

'She got stuck at work,' Eleanor said. And then, because lies were always improved by proximity to truth: 'Mark did too.'

'Oh.'

'They were both so upset to miss it.' Eleanor handed her sister the bouquet. 'But well done. You were a fucking superstar.'

Although she was obviously quoting Mandy, Eleanor did not speak with her usual facetious tone. It sounded to Charlie like her voice might have cracked. A joke in form only: the substance flooded with sincerity. 'Eleanor, are you alri—'

'Anyway'—Eleanor's face sealed suddenly with a smile, tighter than the one she had worn to congratulate Charlie—'how *is* Mandy? Still Sydney's best up-and-coming comedian?'

They both turned to look at Mandy. She stood a few metres away, her white shirt cropped to reveal a flat torso. She was bouncing in a pair of green snakeskin boots while saying very loudly, as if addressing the whole room: 'You're the best actor I've ever seen.'

Charlie turned back to her sister. 'She's fine.'

'Sorry, I shouldn't be so harsh. Standup is a tricky medium.'

Remembering Eleanor's thoughts on the genre ('too didactic to be funny; not clever enough to be a lecture'), Charlie tried to end the conversation. 'It's not for everyone.'

'Yeah, and you get what you pay for.'

'She gave us those tickets for free.'

'As I said.'

There was no time to laugh. As soon as she'd said it, Eleanor caught sight of something behind Charlie that made her take a panicked step back.

'Mandy! How are you? Great set the other night. Really funny.'

Charlie made room for Mandy at her side, and quickly studied her face. From its blank politeness, she satisfied herself that Mandy hadn't heard Eleanor's comment.

Eleanor, meanwhile, was overcompensating. 'I liked the bit about . . .' She rotated her hand in the silence, like a compliment was loading.

Charlie remembered her sister laughing, once, in shock at an anecdote about Mandy's Cambodian mother. Deciding that it would be awkward to bring up Pol Pot, Charlie said: 'You liked that bit about Mandy being hot.'

Mandy boasted superhero proportions: a concrete stomach, pert little breasts, and thighs that, although thin, were so densely packed with muscles they didn't wobble or fold but moved as if locked in rigor mortis. Tonight, she had strangled her long dark hair into a high ponytail, and from her naturally round face had conjured contours. Her lipstick—red—ever so slightly overspilled the bounds of her human lips. Those red slashes now moved in a furious blur, as Mandy launched into an explanation of her standup routine.

'For a few years I was the only woman of colour in most line-ups, which is obviously, like, a much bigger problem. But then when they started to have women-only nights, or the club owner got woke or whatever, I was just like: if the next girl gets up and makes reductive jokes about their immigrant parents, or tells us how crazy she was when her boyfriend dumped her, I will scream. It was like we finally got a spot in the room, and all we could do was apologise for occupying that space. So I decided: I won't talk about my identity—I won't even talk about sex. But I *will* talk about what it's like to be perceived as a sex object.'

'Sure,' Eleanor said. 'And being an attractive woman shouldn't preclude other personality traits, like being funny.'

'Exactly! Hot *and* funny.' Mandy smiled: a wry red line. 'Revolutionary.'

Eleanor looked lost, as if the revolution had come full circle, and was now back at its starting point. After opening and closing her mouth twice, she settled on: 'That's very Hannah Gadsby of you.'

Mandy looked like she was trying to swallow bile, so Charlie changed the subject. She put a hand on Eleanor's arm. 'Are you staying for a drink?'

'No. Thank you. I'd love to. But I should go.'

'Just one drink. I want you to meet Helen. You'd love her.'

'You have to meet her,' Mandy said. 'She's so talented.'

Eleanor turned to her sister. 'Which one was she?'

'She wasn't in it. She's the director.'

'The director!'

Charlie couldn't understand Eleanor's sudden panic. 'Don't worry, it's very chill. She's our housemate. Like, she's our age.'

'Sorry. I've had a huge week.'

There was that tone again: a timid, cracking voice that Charlie didn't recognise. Already dreading what she'd find there, Charlie tried to interpret Eleanor's face: head tilted down, eyes avoidant. Eleanor flapped a hand in front of her eyes, as if drawing a curtain over them. 'You go. Have fun. You should be so proud.'

Even though Eleanor's expression was closed to onlookers, Charlie thought she could make out a betrayal written there. Her stomach twisted and her throat fraudulent, Charlie put a hand on her sister's wrist, and leaned in, so no one else could hear.

'Eleanor, is everything okay? Where's Mark?'

What Eleanor did next confirmed Charlie's worst fears. She flung her arms around her sister, the bouquet crushed between them and burst into tears.

3

AT THE PUB after the show, Charlie was so happy she worried it was a moral failing. She had been sad, certainly, to see Eleanor cry outside the theatre. Her own eyes had even moistened when she brushed a tear of Eleanor's with her thumb. But here, at the pub, sitting next to Helen, a jug of beer bubbling between them and the applause still fizzing in her veins, she felt nothing short of joy.

The actress who played Charlie's nanny in the play had been delivering a long monologue with two seemingly contradictory themes: 'Charlie should enjoy her success now, because it's probably a long descent from here,' and, 'It was never too early to start worrying about fertility.' Now Charlie had extracted herself and was sitting on a table with the crew, most of whom—like Charlie—were in their early twenties.

At Charlie's side, Helen said something quietly, and was asked to repeat it. The whole table laughed. Helen was the director. She and Charlie also lived in the same sharehouse. Working with her and living with her, Charlie had grown accustomed to social environments that were essentially competitions to win Helen's approval. It doesn't matter how robust the egalitarian principles, how well-intentioned the stance against social stratification: in any group of people, hierarchies always form around beauty.

Apart from her colouring—mahogany hair, and harsh dark arches for eyebrows—Helen's features were unremarkable: thin lips, blue eyes, a small, straight nose. But their arrangement on her face, in such fine balance, was striking. She wore a septum piercing: a horseshoe shape with little silver beads suspended in each nostril, which twinkled and advertised her symmetry.

When Charlie first met her, she thought that Helen's charm came from her obliviousness. When Helen joked about being an ugly and awkward teenager, although it was difficult to picture, Charlie believed it. Only because her eyes were so outwards-focused—no hint of a mirror. Unlike Charlie, who had long drawn stares and taken selfies and confused likes for love, Helen's appearance was incidental to her character. Charlie was almost envious—not because she was pretty, but because she was charming first, and pretty later.

Indeed, Helen's charm resided in her ability to resist admiration. Despite her strikingly clean, intelligent sentences—words like *problematic* and *obtuse* that reminded Charlie of her sister—Helen always spoke in gentle tones, and accepted any interruption with a patience that amounted to gratitude. As if the actors were always contributing, and never cutting her off.

And when they weren't working, Helen used that single-file style of social interaction that is reserved for the very attractive. Whether at a large table in a pub, or in a rehearsal room, she would pull one person aside and grant them total attention. Her voice was deep, her eyes probing, so there was always a sense, when she was speaking, of being drawn in. And just when you were close enough to touch her, she'd look away, laughing at a joke across the room, and shine her light on someone else.

Tonight Helen's eyes were—for the moment—fixed on Charlie.

Charlie had told the whole table that she was 'wigging out' because her sister had just broken up with her boyfriend of two years.

The rest of the table had moved on, but Helen still had questions.

'Did you see it coming?'

'I didn't think they were that well suited, but, you know, I thought I'd probably be at their wedding in the next five years.'

Helen seemed amused by this. She took a sip of her beer and rested her elbow on the table, so her body was open to Charlie. 'Why?'

'Oh, I don't know. Ideas of themselves, or something.' Beneath Helen's gaze, thoughts that Charlie hadn't previously been able to articulate suddenly revealed themselves. Flowers turning their faces to the sun. 'Eleanor's a very good person. She's hard on herself, so she can seem very, I don't know . . . closed. But that's only because her sense of self is very much based on being dutiful, and supportive and whatever. Like, she basically raised me.' Charlie swallowed. 'And Mark—he's very sensitive, and just the type that needs a lot of support.'

'A coalescence of flaws!'

Charlie laughed, and threw her head back to show she wasn't laughing just to be polite but really did find Helen neck-snappingly hilarious. 'Exactly.'

'What more can you ask for? In a long-term relationship.'

'God that's grim.'

'To monogamy!'

Charlie raised her glass, she hoped with some irony. 'To monogamy.'

Helen placed her beer back on its coaster, and reached across Charlie for a chip. 'And what does your sister do?'

'She's a business analyst. Investment analyst? Something with numbers. She can count, basically. One of many differences between us.'

'So she likes helping people *and* mining companies.' Helen raised her eyebrows at the end, but didn't say it like a question.

'Is that what business analysts do?'

'You really don't care, do you?'

'Who cares about anyone else's job?' Charlie said. 'Everyone's just doing their own thing, thinking about themselves.'

'Everyone cares about actors.'

'Except *my* job. Obviously.'

It was Helen's turn to laugh. Charlie reached for the jug at the centre of the table and refilled her glass. The head was foamy-thick and pleased with itself.

'And what about this boyfriend? Why did he need so much support?'

'He wants to be a writer.'

'Ah,' Helen nodded: a septum-piercing flash of understanding. 'And he's what, a business, numbers person as well?'

'He's a corporate lawyer.'

'Of course he is. Nice private school boy, is he?'

Charlie nodded.

Helen was smiling again, but their conversation had none of its former levity. 'I've thought about this a lot,' she said. 'I think that high-achieving, type-A sorts of people are sometimes the worst suited to artistic careers.'

'Because they're used to everything being handed to them on a platter?'

'I actually think it's more basic than that. Like, I'm perfectly prepared to accept that this heartbreaker . . .' She held out her hand, as if Charlie were about to place something in it.

'Mark.'

Helen nodded. 'Right. I'm prepared to accept that Mark's a hard worker and self-motivated and whatever. I just think that for people who are, like, smart and wealthy, they're not equipped to fail. Like, they're used to doing everything for pretty clear results.

They sit an exam, they get a good mark. They apply for jobs, they get one. They work hard, they get promoted. I don't know how someone like that could take a draft and show it to someone for the first time, and risk them saying: *You know what? This was a total waste of time. No rewards. Start again.*'

'Are you saying it's a hard time for rich white men in the arts?' Charlie hadn't intended to sound facetious, but noting the smile that accompanied Helen's scoff, she made a mental note to try it again some time.

'Hardly! It's just easy in a different kind of way. Woke boys are profiting from the low bar set by, like, all of human history. Like, they used to get applauded for just existing, now they get applauded for pointing out how unfair it was in the past when they got applauded for just existing.'

'They can't win, can they?'

'No. They *always* win. That's the point.' Helen emptied her beer glass and looked around the table.

Just when Charlie thought she had been dismissed, Helen turned back to her with a smile. 'Although it's obviously reductive and probably quite meaningless to discuss men as a collective. We might as well say: *Women! They're an emotional lot, aren't they?*'

Charlie had thought that talking about people as a collective was Helen's style. She always seemed to operate at an abstract, theoretical level that reduced people to demographics and situations to social issues.

Helen turned her attention to the person seated on her other side, and Charlie, confused, did not know how to reclaim the conversation. With Eleanor as her sister, she was familiar with the suffocating sensation of your intellect being overwhelmed. She felt that saying anything more to Helen would be as eloquent and incisive as screaming underwater.

—

WHEN CHARLIE WAS in her first year at drama school, Helen was in her final year of a master's in directing. The admiration Charlie had for her was the kind that requires the support of entire institutions. She felt about Helen the way schoolgirls feel about prefects, or adults about celebrities. Four years older than Charlie, Helen's existence was aspirational: she represented a future life; goals Charlie might one day achieve.

Her peers were always whispering about how *smart* she was, in tones so resentful it must have been true. All the directing students were very intense: they had to produce portfolios and have artistic statements. For many of them, their artistic statements were also statements about their identity. They were interested in race and representation; in queer stories and music theatre; in challenging patriarchal metanarratives. Helen, in her corduroy pants and Doc Marten loafers (who was, incidentally, both queer and female) resisted any such statements. She was interested, she said, in theatre.

Once, during Charlie's first and Helen's final year, they kissed. They attended the same birthday party—a mutual friend—and ordered each other alternating rounds at the pub. At a club afterward, they hooked up on the dance floor and then, mortifyingly, dry-humped in an alleyway behind it, until a chef from the neighbouring late-night kebab shop interrupted them. He stood with a knife in one hand, garbage bag in the other, and said, 'Are you serious?'

They went back into the club after that and Charlie was too embarrassed to ask Helen if she wanted to go outside again. So they never confirmed whether they were, in fact, serious.

A few weeks later, Charlie started seeing a boy—another actor in her class. She worried that Helen might think their kiss had been a cheap, single-use experiment, and not the sort of constant, throbbing memory Charlie later fantasised about, when her handsome face-for-screen boyfriend was inside her. Against the backdrop of that relationship, Charlie was always looking for ways to perform her identity—from auditioning for queer roles to adding rainbow emojis to her Instagram bio. She wanted Helen to know bisexuality wasn't just something Charlie did at parties for attention. Not that Helen was necessarily watching.

In the years that followed, their friendship consisted of Charlie fire-reacting social media posts about whatever plays Helen was directing, and sending her one of two messages:

Yes queen!

Or

Go you good thing!

That was until a few months ago, when Helen posted a picture of a spare room in her sharehouse. Charlie responded:

Very! Interested!!

—

CHARLIE GROANED AS her forehead hit the table. She mimed bashing it several more times, until she felt Helen's hand between her shoulders. Just the fingertips, no palm, like she was typing.

'What's up?' This was not the voice Helen used for issuing directions. It was a tender tone that claimed no responsibility.

'My laptop,' Charlie said. 'I left it in the dressing room.'

If Helen had asked why Charlie had brought her laptop to the dressing room, Charlie would have had to groan and bash her head again. The answer was: so she could watch Netflix during intermission.

But Helen didn't ask. She removed her hand—with a quick, spine-tingling slide down half of Charlie's back—and told her not to worry. Then she led her out of the pub and back to the theatre.

According to their stage manager, the magic of theatre depended on the magic of workplace health and safety. Prop knives and fake guns—even the ones with tinsel at the end—were locked in a safe, in case someone tried to rob a bank with them. Backstage, every surface was outlined in blue tape. Most importantly, master keys were the director's responsibility, and *strictly* for emergencies.

Charlie was usually oblivious to such rules. Nonetheless, she felt a cautious exhilaration as Helen stepped back and held the door open. Like a student drinking on campus after hours, one eye saw the darkness as a threat, the other as invitation.

Maybe it was the sign above the door, which spelled the name of the theatre and lit Helen's face: flat and stark. Maybe the standing ovation, which Charlie could still hear and still feel, like air, in her lightened chest. Maybe it was the thought, echoed in that applause, that her actions *mattered*: lockdown was over; theatre was back; the show was *on* again. Charlie felt, for the first time in months, that her life might *mean* something: each event would impact the next. There was a plot, and she was a character.

Backstage, the brick walls flashed white beneath fluorescent bulbs. The dressing room was clammy—air stiff with hairspray and stale sweat. After a few more performances, Charlie wouldn't be able to smell it. Tonight, she raised a hand to cover her nose.

When Charlie returned to the door, laptop safely underarm, she couldn't find Helen. The lights in the foyer had been turned on. It was a summer night, and the air conditioning in the foyer was off, but something about the room's stillness rendered it cool.

Charlie found Helen, and stood alongside her in the green glow of an exit sign, just to the left of the bar. Helen was holding a great black door ajar. Charlie stepped through it, and tried not to breathe audibly. She knew that they were standing at the back of the theatre in the last row of seats. But in the darkness, she could not make out the stage.

'I can't see shit.' Helen was close. 'I'll get the lights.' Her words tickled Charlie's neck. When she moved, she placed her hands at Charlie's waist, so she could brush past without tripping.

With a click, the lights were on, and the space seemed to contract. Charlie thought how small it was with no people in it.

'We've come a long way since drama school,' Helen said, and her voice sounded very loud.

Charlie looked at her, but Helen's eyes were fixed on the stage. Charlie couldn't be sure what Helen meant when she said *drama school.* The phrase trembled with possibility—it might be an arrow, pointing down an alley behind a club, smelling like red onion and tasting like traded drinks. It might be another allusion entirely. Or it might go no deeper than its surface: signifying nothing.

'It was a long time ago,' Charlie said. 'I guess we were different people then . . .'

Helen took Charlie's hand gently in her own, and, under the full glare of the house lights, they kissed. It was tentative at first, and then Charlie stepped forward, so that not only did their lips touch, but their whole bodies stood flush together.

When they pulled apart, they swapped smiles that could only have one possible meaning.

Because she was drunk, or because the theatre impregnated her with a sense of climax, or because it was true, Charlie couldn't help but say: 'I've thought about this for a long time.'

4

IN ENMORE (OR Newtown, depending on who was asking), on a street that followed the trainline, a row of terraces sat sandwiched between an apartment block and a warehouse conversion. In Bethel Street, the most derelict terrace was number 93. For more than three years, with bond-compromising hilarity, Mandy, Kevin, Helen and—more recently—Charlie had occupied it.

Helen loved everything about that house: the large, overgrown lawn at the back, which Kevin mowed every six months with shirt-off relish; the kitchen with its mustard-coloured tiles; the purple bathroom; even the plastic roof that covered the side alley, over which possums ran so loudly it sounded like they were hoofed. The hot water was temperamental, only one of the burners on the stove worked, and the decorative cornices didn't quite distract from the constant creep of mould. But, if it weren't for its flaws, 93 Bethel Street would have been too expensive for inner-city artists to rent, and too clean to soil and restore every weekend. As it was, they only needed to pick up empty bottles (cigarette stubs would be pedantic) and give the visible surfaces a wipe.

Kevin had lived there for five years. He was from Singapore, where his parents still lived. They owned several hotels, and whether or not they subsidised Kevin's rent was a constant subject of speculation. Whenever Kevin was drunk or high, Helen took the opportunity to interview him on the topic of his finances. In these bi-weekly interrogations, he would remain silent, and speak liquidly on any other possible topic. This struck everyone else as normal and basically polite, and Helen as deeply suspicious.

Helen's evidence was as follows.

First, there was the obvious family money. Kevin and his older brother had both gone to a country boarding school from the age of twelve (this couldn't have been cheap).

Then there was the lack of any fiscal—Helen didn't use the word *responsibility*—*coherence* on Kevin's part. He was a DJ, with a seemingly pathological aversion to regular employment. Side gigs abounded: he checked continuity on music video sets; he handed out water at festivals; he weeded gardens via Airtasker. If he worked anywhere for more than three months, he'd quit. He was so reliably unreliable that, at Bethel Street, time was measured by Kevin's job cycle. They would clean the bathroom as soon as he quit. When did they last bomb the oven? Four jobs ago.

Finally, there was the generosity. It was *always* Kevin's shout. And if asked for bank details, or implored to split the bill, he would respond: 'Have you no sense of poetry?'

Even though Helen said behind his back that he had no sense of reality, she loved Kevin: both for his quirks, and for his flashes of self-awareness—the impression he gave that, although his life was a joke, it was at least for his own amusement.

When their old housemate moved out in June, they were all determined that the friendship not be tested. They interviewed Charlie, and Kevin told her that they weren't interested in people who wanted somewhere to live: she had to want a lifestyle. They hosted a lot of parties—fairy lights on the Hills hoist and Kevin's decks on the balcony. They did their own composting. They owned a bunny called Petronella.

Charlie salivated.

'What we're asking,' Helen said, 'is can you get kumbaya about the whole sharehouse thing?' She was teasing, but with an air of invitation rather than superiority. Her smile was all-inclusive.

To date, Charlie had been good to her word. She had proven, by how late she stayed and how much she drank, that she loved a sesh as much as any of them. And in the sober daylight hours, she was brightly conversational—thoughtful details remembered—but never so talkative that moods or hangovers weren't respected. Friendship, until recently, had been no more tested than a summer day by a fresh sea breeze.

—

HELEN WOKE THE morning after opening night in a strange and familiar room. The ceiling looked the same as her bedroom—decorative cornices and a low-hanging, old-fashioned light—but the sheets were softer than hers, the walls closer, and the floor strewn with someone else's clothes. She swallowed—her tongue so dry it almost itched—and remembered. She'd slept in Charlie's bed.

Her hangover began, as it always did, with indignation. Then Helen started counting how many drinks she'd had at the pub. When she reached seven, she stopped counting, and had to concede that she'd done this to herself. A twenty-six-year-old woman who gets drunk and sleeps with her colleague. Housemate too, but colleague, in that sticky morning sun, seemed more shameful.

Helen's headache was rendering consciousness a chore, and convincing her that life would just get harder and more complicated until she eventually died. So she took the only known cure.

A shower was cleansing—in that comforting, metaphorical way: washing away her sins. Perhaps more importantly, it tricked her into thinking that the day might not be a waste. Like she had some control over her own life, and was capable of making good decisions.

Helen had never slept with an actor before. She had never wanted to. At work, she was so used to seeing each performer as a piece of a larger whole: thinking about how they related to each other and to the play. Actors, and their relentless insistence that they *were* the artwork, not just a late step along the way, infuriated her.

Charlie was different. Now Helen thought about it, she hadn't behaved like an actor at all. She was sensitive to other people, whether crew or fellow performers, fitting to the shape of their ego. Talking to the costume designer, she was quiet and polite. With the older actors, she was a young student, always asking for advice. And her co-star would probably describe her as 'fun'. She did impersonations of the rest of the cast, took silly selfies in the dressing room, and laughed when people forgot their lines—loudest when the fault was hers.

And with Helen?

With one hand wet against the purple bathroom tiles, Helen leaned forward and started to see a picture that—like all hungover reconstructions—positioned herself at the centre. Charlie moving in because of Helen. Charlie auditioning for the play when Helen asked her to, not just because she needed the work, but because it felt good to do what Helen said. Or perhaps it was less impulsive—part of a plan to spend more time with Helen: work with her, get to know her better, develop a rapport.

Charlie seemed so young, suddenly, and Helen so stupid.

A gentle knock at the bathroom door interrupted her thoughts.

Although she couldn't remember whether she'd shampooed her hair, Helen rinsed it and turned the shower off. Hair dripping, and a towel tucked modestly under her armpits, she returned to Charlie's room.

Charlie was sitting cross-legged on the bed. She smiled at Helen as if at a friend across a room full of strangers. A smile that held secrets, and promised not to tell.

Helen wasn't up to games, or even up to her usual irony. 'I'm not having a good time,' she declared.

Charlie said she felt fine, actually, and made space on the bed.

'You're only twenty-three—'

'Twenty-two.'

'—so of course your hangovers are a picnic.'

Helen did not make it back to bed. She returned to the bathroom, where she proceeded very loudly—loudly enough to amuse her housemates for several days after—to not have a good time at all.

—

ELEANOR WAS FINDING the weekend unbearable. She'd cancelled her plans to go out with Seb. Instead, she spent Saturday at home, where even simple acts, like getting out of bed and into the shower seemed monumental.

Unlike her sister, who was a connoisseur of suffering, Eleanor had never acquired the taste. Whenever she felt anxious—even about legitimate problems, like climate change or her parents' divorce—she also felt guilty for being self-indulgent.

On Saturday night, Eleanor lay in bed with the curtains drawn. Seb was out, the apartment was silent, and she was engrossed in the only thing that seemed to help: stalking Mark online.

She was looking at his Facebook profile picture: a photo she'd taken in the very early days of their relationship. He was holding a pink cocktail and grinning. At the time, they'd made some joke about men and pink drinks. Eleanor couldn't remember anything about it now, except how much they'd both laughed. Looking at the picture, Eleanor felt a sting of doubt. Breaking up, she thought, was a little like going mad. She questioned all her judgements. Perhaps that was never funny; perhaps Mark had never been endearing, and her friends had been too shy or too intimidated or too uninterested to tell her.

She couldn't identify which was upsetting her more: Mark's betrayal, or the fact that she was taking it so badly. All attempts at reason—*we were never that well suited, I would have broken up with him eventually anyway*—only made her more wretched. She could cope with the idea that their relationship was over. What humiliated her was that she hadn't been the one to end it. She hated that he had the power to hurt her: that she could behave perfectly, and treat him with respect, and still emerge undignified and small. No choice in how it ended, or how to feel about it. Just tears, hot and mocking, betraying her further still.

She placed her phone on the bedside table so she could wipe her eyes. When they were dry, she picked it up again. First, she looked at his tagged photos on Instagram. Then she went to the profiles of his friends and looked at *their* tagged photos, just in case Mark had hidden a picture from his profile. Finding nothing, she turned her attention to the accounts Mark followed. She scanned the list, looking for new names.

She was looking for some evidence—a photo, a new contact—of what happened the night that Mark betrayed her. Somewhere between attending the strip club and returning home, a line had been crossed. Eleanor was taking a scalpel to the past, and trying to draw that line: the exact point at which Mark's conduct went from unsavoury to unforgiveable. She felt—not small and misused—but outraged and superior, when she thought of him paying to look at women's bodies and paying extra to touch—trading people like chattels. In a room full of other men doing the same, surrounded by security guards, in a nod to the threat of violence that he—all men—represented. Their break-up was an allegory: the physical and economic dominance of every man over every woman. From that moralistic viewpoint, Eleanor didn't need to engage with any intimate, inconvenient truths. Like the fact that she'd never really loved him, and said she did because it seemed the kinder thing to do. Or that she'd let him depend on her, and, in her own way, in spite of herself, had come to depend on him too.

Somehow, she'd ended up looking at the Instagram account of the girlfriend of one of Mark's schoolfriends, when her phone vibrated. She started so violently she dropped it from the bed and had to climb out to retrieve it.

A text from Mark filled her screen:

Hey just thought I'd check in. So sorry about yesterday and really hope you're okay
Let me know when you're ready to talk

Eleanor took a screenshot and sent it to her sister. Charlie had been in constant contact all day: text messages, links to unhelpful pop psychology articles, and actually helpful TikToks of a beguiling Russian dwarf called Hasbulla.

Charlie replied immediately.

Want me to come over later?

No no I'm fine

How not-fine are you?
On a scale of one to mum

Haha dw not full mum
Just slowly going insane
wondering what happened
Like who where when etc.
I want DETAILS

One sec let me call

Eleanor picked up on the first ring. 'Hey. Don't you have the play?'

'It's intermission.'

'Oh cool. Well go when you have to.' Eleanor hadn't spoken in hours. She hoped her voice didn't sound too wobbly.

'So what are you going to reply?' Charlie asked.

'I'll try to meet him next week or something.'

'What? Why?'

'He'll be expecting me to. He still owes me an explanation. I need to know what actually happened.'

Charlie was silent.

'I'm going insane.' Eleanor's voice was distinctly wobbly. She covered her mouth with her free hand.

'Eleanor, I'm so sorry,' said Charlie. 'You deserve so much better.'

While her sister went on, Eleanor pulled the phone away and wiped it on the sheet. She then wiped both cheeks with her sleeve. By the time she returned the phone to her ear, Charlie had progressed from condolences to advice.

'He'll just want you to forgive him,' Charlie was saying. 'Men always want that. They need to get you off their conscience. But you don't have to, you know. It's not your *job* to make Mark feel like a good guy.'

This scene was familiar to both of them: one sister broken, the other picking up the pieces. Only this time, their roles were inverted. Charlie was adapting to hers with grace and growing more assertive with each sentence. Eleanor, meanwhile, remained silent.

'Don't let him beg,' Charlie concluded. 'You're entitled to your boundaries.'

Eleanor was suspicious of psychobabble. To her, terms like *boundaries* or *needs* were emotionally ostentatious. She was, however, fluent in entitlements. In this case, she had been thinking of her own entitlement to truth: to the whole story. It was only now, when her sister pointed it out, that she realised Mark might want the opportunity to explain himself. The prospect of denying Mark—even if it meant denying herself—seemed deliciously empowering.

Eleanor thanked her sister, wished her well for Act Two ('I think it actually gets better in the second half') and typed out a response to Mark. Drafting the message was like pressing on a bruise: there was pain, but also pleasure from the sensation of control.

After everything you did

Here she paused. She was factually correct—this text was a direct consequence of his actions—but she'd rather be righteous than right. Better to put it gently, so as not to appear vindictive.

After everything that's happened, I think
I'd rather not see you in person again.
I think we're better off just making a clean break.

Typing that word—*break*—and pressing send was more than just communication. Like taking a vow, or signing a contract, the words were action.

—

ON MONDAY EVENING, the occupants of 93 Bethel Street congregated in the garden. Monday was the only day of the week that Charlie did not have a show. Over the weekend, Helen had avoided her without effort; she worked both days, and Charlie performed both evenings. Charlie texted though, regularly, and Helen always replied with an apology, even if only half an hour had passed.

Sorry! Didn't see this!
Hey, sorry
Wow my bad just checked my phone

It was as if Charlie were a delicate object that Helen had dropped and lightly cracked. So she apologised, and apologised again—not knowing whether that first light crack might lead to a break beyond repair.

But that Monday in the garden, they sat as they often did—Helen with a film camera in her lap—and enjoyed a four-cornered conversation. Helen talked and took pictures and thought, for the first time, that everything might be exactly as it was.

This was Helen's favourite time of day to photograph. The sun had lost its heat, and the grass sloped languorously up to the evening sky. In the far corner was the Hills hoist, and opposite it a rocking horse which Kevin had acquired on a night out. Mandy was straddling it while she ate chickpeas out of a can.

Helen sat at the wooden table. Her lens was on a shirtless Kevin, who sat next to her, his legs long in cotton pyjama shorts. He was shovelling cold pad thai out of a plastic container.

Helen smiled. 'Good breakfast?'

A noodle slipped from his fork and rested in the rivets between his abs. Helen clicked the shutter.

'Did you go out last night?' Mandy spoke louder than the others, so she could be heard from the rocking horse.

'No.' Kevin paused and wiped his mouth with the back of his hand. 'I just woke up super late. But you know what I realised?

As soon as I finished up that last job, I was *so* tired. Like, in my soul. Just total exhaustion. And I thought: is this the condition of late capitalism—to be tired all the time?'

Mandy had finished her chickpeas, and started to rock back and forth. 'Sometimes a girl's gotta nap.'

Helen frowned. Kevin's jobs were difficult to keep track of. 'When you say *that last job*, are you talking about the drug trial?'

'Yeah. Five days, no symptoms. I think they gave me the placebo.'

'You don't think fatigue might be a side effect?'

'It's not the drugs, Helen.' He smacked his plastic fork on the table in a performance of outrage. 'It's systemic oppression of the human spirit. I've diagnosed myself. It's not healthy—all this emphasis on individual flourishing in the face of mass inequality and suffering. And consumer choice, and surveillance capitalism, and whatever.'

'Now you're just saying words.' Helen patted his knee, all white in the evening light. 'I'm sure it's nothing a lie-down can't fix.'

Charlie, who had been in the kitchen taking a phone call, returned.

'Any luck?' Mandy pulled the horse to a stop. Phone calls, she knew, were usually from Charlie's agent.

'No, no.' Charlie waved a hand. 'It was just my sister.'

Helen's elbows were on the wooden table, her camera in her hands. Seeing it, Charlie lowered her sunglasses from the top of her head and leaned against the wooden pole, adopting a comfortable position for the conversation. Not quite posing, just adjusting to the camera's presence.

The shutter clicked, and Helen returned the camera to the table. 'She okay?'

‘I invited her to New Year’s.’

‘What?’ Kevin’s fork stalled halfway to his mouth.

Charlie had sounded unresolved, but her tone hardened beneath Kevin’s challenging stare. ‘To New Year’s. She just broke up with her boyfriend so I think she’ll need company.’

‘How long did they go out?’ Mandy asked.

‘Like, two years.’

‘Statistically’—Kevin’s mouth was full—‘most couples fall out of love after two years. So, you know, she’s not anomalous.’

‘I’m sure that will be a great comfort,’ said Helen.

‘We’ve already got so many people.’

Kevin had been planning this party for months, never with more attention to detail than when Sydney was in the darkest days of lockdown. His vision for the event was an all-day rave. He’d foraged dozens of milk crates from Enmore’s graffitied back streets, finessed the line-up to the second, and put in an order for a more-criminal-than-usual supply of drugs.

‘It’s one more,’ Charlie said.

Mandy and Helen chimed their support.

Kevin stood and rapped his empty plastic container on the table as if it were a gavel. It didn’t make a sound. ‘Right. Charlie, you can have your sister, because we feel sorry for her. And then that’s it, okay? That’s *it.* Charlie’s sister is the last plus one. Plus none from now on. We can’t get shut down.’

Whether his eyes were glassy because of his recent drug trial or because the sun was setting in them, Kevin cut a vulnerable figure. The three women nodded their agreement.

Kevin and Mandy went to the kitchen to wash up, and Charlie sat down next to Helen, who was still holding her camera in her lap. They were sitting side by side, and Helen was very conscious of the distance between their knees. No more than a few centimetres. It made sense, Helen thought, that a space like that contained whole constellations of particles. Not like the wooden garden table, or the rusty Hills hoist. These were flat and finite. Charlie's body and the spaces around it—the distance between them—seemed fraught with possibility.

Their proximity rendered Helen witless. When she spoke, it was polite, as if she didn't know Charlie at all. 'I'm excited to meet Eleanor.'

'Yeah?'

'It'll put you in context.'

'She probably won't come.'

Charlie was smiling, so Helen took one last photo before the sun set.

—

'I'VE THOUGHT ABOUT it . . .'

'Yeah?'

'And I'd love to come.'

Charlie was making dinner. She lowered the gas, so her pasta water wouldn't bubble over, and sat at the kitchen table, her phone at her ear. 'Really?'

'Yeah. It's so nice of you to invite me.'

'Because there's no pressure, of course. Like don't feel like you have to come to be polite or whatever.'

'No, no, that's not it. I want to come. Really.'

In the week after texting Mark, Eleanor had busied herself doing all the things people were supposed to do when they were going through a break-up. She had googled it, and found a confusing mix of distractions (exercising; socialising) and pleas to avoid distraction (grief-sitting; time-taking). Because the latter seemed oblique and inefficient, Eleanor had launched herself into the former. She would exercise daily—she was currently walking home from a boxing class so intense, the pressure of holding her phone to her ear was inducing a cramp in her shoulder. And she would go to Charlie's scary druggy orgy.

What had occupied Eleanor's thoughts was not whether she would attend, but the manner of her attendance. 'Do I have to take drugs?' Eleanor asked, moving the phone to her left hand so she could rotate her throbbing right shoulder.

'It's like anything in life, Eleanor.' Charlie was using her 'worldly' voice, where she sighed whole sentences in a single exhale. 'You don't have to take drugs, but you'll probably have more fun if you do.'

'That can't be true of *anything* in life. There are a lot of experiences that aren't improved by stimulants. Like, I don't know . . . sleeping.'

'Whatever. All sweeping generalisations have exceptions.'

'What about that one?'

'What?' Charlie was looking at the stove. Small blue flames lapped at the pot, and bubbles pushed up beneath the lid.

'Never mind,' Eleanor said. 'Thanks for the bait. I appreciate it.'

Charlie removed the lid and watched the bubbles dissolve. She prodded some penne with her fork. 'No worries.'

'Really. Lollies you.'

It was one of those family phrases that changes over time, obscuring its own origins. It was years since their mother had confused *laugh out loud* with *lots of love*, but her abbreviated *LOL* lived on, first as a private joke, and now as a declaration, invoked only with the greatest sincerity, when the word *love* couldn't cover that particular affection felt by one sister for the other.

'Lollies you too, Eleanor.'

It was because Eleanor thought of parties as inconsequential—distractions from the business of living—that she made the decision so lightly. And, like a traveller heading down the wrong road, it was not until long after she took the turn that Eleanor would realise: she was lost.

5

ALTHOUGH HELEN HAD given Charlie her car keys and told her to split the cost of the beers, Charlie still felt a heart-fluttering sense of trespass when she sat in the driver's seat. She had been a passenger in Helen's car several times since they'd lived together but she had never driven it alone.

Helen was working a box-office shift at Sydney's largest theatre company, where she was casually employed and hoped, one day, to enter into a more serious relationship. Charlie, who had nothing on before that evening's final performance, had offered to pick up gear for kick-ons.

Charlie hated driving. Perhaps it was because she usually worked with made-up situations, that the stakes of driving—the possibility of running someone over—seemed unbearably high.

Nonetheless, Helen's car felt intimate, and driving it seemed more thrilling than dangerous. It was more intimate even than a bedroom, which can usually, by the simple act of making the bed, be dressed for strangers. This car and the debris that had washed up in it seemed to reveal its owner's secrets. There were old coffee cups jammed into the doors and scripts on the floor of the passenger seat. Across the back lay a tennis racquet, some rolled-up posters, and a picnic blanket with blades of grass—now dead and brown—still sticking to its fluff. There was a red tube of papaw ointment in the middle console, which made Charlie smile, because she also used that brand, though she didn't know what it was for or when she'd picked up the habit. Charlie was vulturous for these intimate scraps—little details that might bring her closer to Helen.

After their kiss, four weeks ago, and the night that followed, Charlie had spent many hours reflecting on the show. The rehearsals, in particular, she saw through a new filter. Perhaps Helen's professionalism—the way she issued directions, and gave notes, and, in a warm-up, touched Charlie's back to straighten it—was not generic professionalism at all, but something more like *restraint.* A willed control: a submission of desire to convention.

For directors, the job finishes when the show begins. They usually only attend opening and closing night. It seemed calculated, then, that Helen kissed Charlie on opening night—mere hours after their working relationship had ended.

Many times in the play's four-week run, Charlie had rehearsed imagined conversations with the other cast and crew. In these, Charlie was always coy, as if privacy were something she valued.

The other actor would start with an allusion, like: 'You and Helen . . .'

'We've known each other for years.' Charlie's tone would be light—innocent even—but just unconvincing enough to nod to the other sense in which she *knew* Helen.

'And how long have you . . .'

Here Charlie would blush. 'Only since opening night.' A laugh. 'All very above board.'

'I can't say it's come as a surprise.'

There these imagined conversations ended: with confirmation that what Helen and Charlie were doing was predictable. As if the plot had already been so carefully crafted that this was its only possible resolution.

Except, after opening night, nothing happened.

In the four weeks that followed, Charlie performed in the evenings, slept late in the mornings, and, when she saw Helen at home, gave her a report on the show. A prop forgotten, a seam split, a line bungled. In these conversations, Helen was all smiles and questions, and it felt, sometimes, like flirting. But then Charlie would watch Helen with their other housemates and realise that this was precisely her charm. When her attention was on you, it was so devoted it *had* to be personal: a credit to you—the way she felt about you.

Stopping at a red light, Charlie squeezed some of Helen's papaw ointment onto the pad of her index finger. The tube was greasy with regular use. Charlie applied the ointment, then rubbed her lips together. They had the texture of a paste. The furry, apple sauce flavour bled into her mouth. Charlie smiled. That's why, when she'd kissed Helen, she'd tasted so familiar. Later—months later—that taste would make Charlie sick.

—

LIKE MOST WORKPLACES, people in theatre only really light up when they happen upon a mutual acquaintance they can bitch about. More than art, or taste, or aesthetic sensibility, nothing bonds them quite like finding the same person difficult to work with.

The afterparty was full of these conversations, and kick-ons at 93 Bethel Street even more so. About twenty of the cast and crew were gathered in the living room, beer bottles crowding the coffee table. Everybody was excited to award 'most insufferable' and 'least talented', if only because, for these sorts of prizes, the judges are never in contention. Everybody except Charlie.

In a spongy armchair in the corner of the room, tucked just behind Kevin's expensive speakers, sat the costume designer, Jacinta with Charlie perched on the armrest.

Helen leaned in the doorway, her camera in her hand, and watched their conversation for the length of three photographs. Jacinta had a shaved head and large eyes. Her earrings were made of cork. When she spoke, she was so focused that the corks didn't move. They could have been plastered to the wallpaper behind her. Charlie, meanwhile, was animated. Every few seconds, she would touch Jacinta's shoulder and look down at her with horror. Helen found something comical, or at the very least aesthetically interesting, in their asymmetry. Charlie's limbs like water, her expressions fluid, and Jacinta stone-faced and still-corked.

Feeling pleasantly protective, Helen approached and whispered to Charlie something about a drink. Charlie leaped up but Jacinta remained seated.

'Was she telling you about her ex?'

Helen had led Charlie into the kitchen and was talking—very loudly—into the fridge. 'Here, I thought I should save you. You're welcome.'

She pressed a cold beer towards Charlie. The glass was wet to the touch. Helen offered her a bottle opener from the back pocket of her jeans. Charlie opened it, and Helen stuck out her hand to collect the lid. When Charlie let it fall from her palm to Helen's, their hands almost touched.

'Did I end up transferring you for those?' Helen's dimples were cheeky.

'He sounds awful,' Charlie said.

'Who?'

'The ex-boyfriend.'

'Oh, that.' Helen took a sip of her beer. 'He's a stage manager. I did a show with him earlier last year, and he was going through the whole drama at the time. He took out an AVO out against her.'

'What?'

Helen needed little encouragement. She launched into her story. 'So she was stalking him. Like, knew where he lived obviously and kept turning up. And the police said they couldn't do anything, and no community legal centres would deal with him because they only deal with women, which is, like, totally fair enough. And then one night he comes home and she's let herself in and *she's in his bed* and is, like, ready to seduce him, but—and this is the best bit—he'd been out all night *with a date* and brought her home.'

Charlie's head was in her hands. 'There's just no way to explain that.'

'The optics aren't good. Then again'—Helen smiled—'he could have seen it as a marvellous opportunity.'

Charlie didn't laugh. She was scratching at the neck of her beer. 'Poor girl.'

'I know. I mean, she would have assumed he was springing a threesome on her.'

'No, I meant poor Jacinta.'

Normally, Helen loved conversations about other people. She found it confessional, describing someone else's flaws. It revealed her own values—what she saw as right and good—and invited someone else to say: *Yes, I see things the same way.*

But tonight, trying to discuss Jacinta, Charlie seemed to stiffen. She was looking at Helen in quiet panic, as if she were watching her recede.

Charlie didn't see people the way Helen did. She didn't need to judge, or even think: it was enough to just respond. She could love them, or be delighted by them, or walk right past them—each a fresh painting in the same gallery. Criticism didn't interest her. She went on: 'It's just, when I hear about people doing mad things in love, I hear it in my stomach.' She motioned to it. 'I sort of think, we've all got that in us. I can imagine myself unhinging like that.'

'Really?'

'I don't know—madness doesn't seem such foreign territory to me. It's a place I can really see myself. Maybe my grip on reality is more tenuous than yours.'

Helen smiled at that. 'Don't beat yourself up. I suppose we're all mad, in a way. Like, I think everybody exists in their own private reality. That's why we do what we do, right?'

Charlie's smile was benign, like she had no idea what Helen was talking about.

'This play,' Helen said, and drew an arc with her beer bottle. 'Plays generally. We create a shared reality.'

'Like, on stage?'

'And for the audience.' Helen was no longer yelling over the music but speaking at a normal volume. She stood close enough to make out the little black specks of mascara that had fallen around Charlie's eyes. 'Everyone experiencing the same thing at the same time, you know? That's real. While it's happening, if they all believe it, it's real.'

Once again, Charlie looked at Helen like she was far away, and when she spoke—with a small step forward—she was gentle and deliberate, as if trying to coax her back.

'Helen? Can I ask you something?'

Helen looked at the half-drunk beer in her hand, and then out of the kitchen, down the hall. She must have known what Charlie was about to say, because she knew to look away.

'On opening night, when we . . . we still haven't talked about it. I guess I just wanted to ask whether, well why we didn't. Whether you thought it might happen again?'

Helen passed a hand over her face. 'I—I'm . . .' She blinked slowly and, when her eyes were open, started again. 'I didn't mean to make things weird. I was your director. We live together, you know. I didn't want to . . .' This time, when Helen trailed off, she looked at the floor. She was suddenly conscious of how much taller Charlie was.

'Right,' Charlie said. 'Sure.'

'God,' Helen covered her face with her hand and placed her middle finger and thumb on the outer edges of each eye. She pulled them apart until she could feel them stretch. 'I'm nearly thirty.'

'Aren't you twenty-six?'

'Exactly.' Helen looked straight at Charlie. She was standing very still, and Helen was reminded of the way she stood on stage.

Charlie seemed determined to keep the conversation personal: small enough to hold. She kept stepping closer—away from theories, or theatre, or other people—until there were only centimetres separating them.

'What would you have said? If we had talked about it, what would you have said?'

Helen shook her head. 'I . . . it . . . God.'

Charlie was looking down at Helen from a sharp angle. 'I could start?'

'It was lovely. You're lovely, Charlie. And very talented. And I love living with you. I wanted you for the house. I mean, the others did too, but I was the one who was like: she's cool, we have to have her. And I think because we live together, and, you know, we might work together again—'

'Should you be so lucky.'

Helen smiled, but did not admit the joke. She felt she had been—however inarticulately—working up to a point. 'I mean, living together, working together, sleeping together. Does it get more psychosexually entangled?'

Charlie raised her eyebrows. 'Psychosexually entangled?'

Helen gave a breathy, self-deprecating laugh. The air between them relaxed, as if after a cough in an audience. Perhaps, Helen thought, the stakes were not so high. They could laugh about it already. They did not work together anymore—had not, since opening night. Maybe, Helen thought, she was taking herself too seriously.

Charlie laughed then too, and when she spoke, it was difficult to hear above the music. But her lips rounded around it. 'You seem to have given this a lot of thought.'

'Yeah, well. What would you have said?'

Charlie's head was still and her gaze steady, as if she were very sure: 'I think we're both adults, and if we both agree it's just casual, then it'll only be as weird as we make it.'

'Right.'

'So let's not make it weird.'

They were standing close, with Charlie leaning closer, so Helen's words were barely more than tickling breath on Charlie's neck. 'Yes, let's.'

For a moment, soft lips, and the shy sliding touch of tongues. Then, as soon as they pulled away, Helen contemplated a joke about how silly she had sounded—the assonance, the hissing sibilance. *Yes. Let's.*

She looked at Charlie, and chose instead to respect the moment, not to colour it in jest.

—

FOR THE REST of the night, they moved, it seemed, not as individuals through a crowd, but as two limbs on the same body, making shapes with their motion, existing always in relation to each other.

Helen knew when Charlie was looking at her, and met her gaze as if she had been summoned. She could tell, too, when Charlie moved, and would turn and track her progress across the room—across the dance floor, then onto the couch. And when Helen left the living room, she knew Charlie was following her.

They stood for a moment in the dark and damp-smelling laundry. Outside, the fairy lights flickered and people sat around vaping. Music reached them from the living room: the heavy, steady thump of the bass. But here, with toilet paper stacked precariously above their heads, all was dark and blurred, and their whispers were stark against the tiles.

'I was just gonna get some air.'

Charlie slid her palm down Helen's arm and took her hand. She squeezed. 'I might dance for a bit more.'

There was no reason why their touches need be secret and their conversations whispered. The show was over, professionalism no longer a concern. On the dance floor, two of the cast members kissed, and out in the yard, hands were on thighs and eyes holding eyes all around the table. But if, when they were in public, Helen and Charlie each held something back—kept something for each other—it made their public selves a performance and what they shared in private, by contrast, real.

It seemed important, before they parted ways, to acknowledge this secret they were sharing; the game they were playing. Helen extended a single finger, like a key into a lock. It slid over Charlie's t-shirt, which, in turn, sat over her bra, so she could have scarcely felt it, but she groaned, audibly, and seemed to have no ownership of the sound.

'I'll find you,' Helen said, before exiting to the yard.

The music switched to a playlist of pop songs that most people at the party would never admit to liking: songs they nonetheless knew all words to and mouthed along with, as if the lyrics were urgent, the rhythms vital.

Some left to go home or to other parties. Others, high off their own rapport, insisted on sitting outside and reminiscing about the show, as if it had ended years ago—when they were different, more naive people—and not that very evening. Eventually, when there was no phone attached to the speakers, and only one guest remained, Jacinta the costume designer was encouraged to sleep on the couch.

Helen and Charlie didn't touch again until the door closed on Charlie's room. There was no discussion that it should be Charlie's room. Hers was closest to the stairs.

—

AFTERWARDS, THEY LAY atop the sheets. Helen was quick to speak. 'That had to happen.'

Charlie wasn't sure if it required a response. 'Mm.'

Despite the heat, Charlie shivered once—violently—with her whole body. Helen pulled a sheet over both of them.

Although Helen's own bed was only a few steps away, neither of them contemplated that she might leave this warmth, this tender bubble, and sleep elsewhere.

All night, Charlie held Helen and did not sleep. She leaned her head forward, so her face touched Helen's hair. The smell was not entirely pleasant. Charlie knew, from sharing a shower, that Helen used Head & Shoulders Clean & Balanced anti-dandruff shampoo.

Underneath the bland soapy smell, it was almost as if something were burning. Charlie lay there, breathing slowly through her nose, and thought about all the ways she knew Helen—all the domestic indignities they shared—and felt an urge to squeeze her tighter. But she didn't want to wake her.

Eventually Charlie dozed, her thoughts acquiring the lucidity and independence of dreams without ever surrendering to them.

When Helen stirred, Charlie let go and stood to open the blinds. They both sat up, the pillows stacked against their backs, and talked.

Helen sat with her knees up to her chin, her dark hair obscuring her face. The morning sun had no heat yet—it was just light, tender light, holding them.

'I'm glad you stayed,' Charlie said.

'Too expensive to Uber.'

—

IN THE KITCHEN, Mandy raised her eyebrows. She had just got them done. They were shaped, already, as if she were surprised, so Mandy expressed little by raising them.

Charlie said nothing. She proceeded to make toast, and only turned when she heard Mandy's laugh.

Helen was leaning against the doorway, wearing only a t-shirt and underwear, as she often did on a Sunday morning. Except this Sunday morning, Mandy assaulted them both with laughter, and Helen smiled back. A tight, twisted smile that looked, to Charlie's horror, a lot like embarrassment.

'Fuck me.' With a shake of her head, Mandy confirmed that—whether she'd seen them touch across a crowded room, or heard them through the wall—she knew.

Charlie was about to tell her that she didn't understand. She wanted to reclaim the privacy they'd found at the party: the sacred space that was only theirs; the space that was as wide as Charlie's bed, and as quiet as the morning light. But then Helen's smile—the strained line of her lips—snapped, with a laugh.

By letting Mandy in on the joke, Helen rendered the events of the night a joke after all. How random and impulsive and hilarious, for two housemates to sleep together.

'I cannot *wait* to tell Kevin,' Mandy said, like it was already an anecdote, with a beginning, middle and end. Not like it was the start of something, and not like Charlie had—in those hours of sleepless contemplation, in which Helen neither laughed nor smiled but breathed quietly in her arms—imagined the rest of the story.

How could Mandy tell Kevin—how could she tell anyone—that?

6

FOR THE HAMOR sisters, Christmas was always the same. Every year, their mother entertained visions of hosting an Orphan Christmas: a lunch for anyone who had nowhere else to go. This year, just like all the previous years, they attended the Wayside Chapel street party in the morning, before retreating home a lonely trio, to sit on plastic chairs at a plastic table in the car park of an apartment block.

Home always felt empty and purposeless after the morning's benevolent frenzy. They'd grown up in the two-bedroom apartment—Eleanor at the desk in the living room, and Charlie on a daybed in the sunroom, where the light was almost always good for selfies. The building was halfway between Coogee and Maroubra beaches, and although it was not walking distance from either, the apartment's carpet was always sandy. At the back of the car park was a patch of grass and flowers, which their neighbours tended as militantly as their mother maintained the communal library in the front lobby. In the corner was a stone cherub lifted from a fountain. At one time in its little life, it wept moss. These days it just pouted around dry, cracked lips.

This Christmas, the sisters had agreed to meet at Eleanor's apartment in Potts Point. From there, they could walk up the hill to Kings Cross and meet their mother in the crowd. Among the homeless and the community-minded, sweating between steaming aluminium trays of food, Mary would be in her element. Because she'd spent her working life in aged care, Eleanor speculated that she was most comfortable in environments that smelled like industrial quantities of hand sanitiser: nursing homes, hospitals, shelters. Charlie thought she liked living for someone other than herself.

When Eleanor opened the door, Charlie thought her sister looked decidedly Christmassy. She was wearing her holiday expression—Eleanor approached the day like a medical procedure: with grim resignation, and faith that it would somehow be good for her.

'You're late.'

'Sorry.'

Eleanor left the door open and returned to her kitchen, where several punnets of berries were open on the counter.

In the middle of a chopping board sat a very flat pavlova. Despite being no higher than a pancake, it still managed to sag in the middle. Charlie leaned forward to inspect it, and was slapped away.

'I'm almost done.'

Charlie reached for a punnet of blueberries. She was slapped away again, so she sat on the couch at the other side of the room and watched.

Eleanor always cooked like someone had asked her to do it, even though nobody ever did. Measurements were precise, results were invariably imperfect, and stress levels ran high. It was stressful, too, for those who had to eat her creations. They would smile even as they chewed, because they could tell—no matter how many times Eleanor said, 'The recipe is surprisingly easy'—that her sanity had been diced very finely by the whole ordeal.

'It looks great, Eleanor.'

Eleanor threw a blueberry at the sink, then immediately picked it up and placed it in the bin. 'No it doesn't. I've fucked it.' She looked at her watch. 'And we're so late.'

The constant movement: the pacing, the watch-revealing roll of her wrist, the lurching grab at her phone to triple-check the recipe, these were all the normal motions of Eleanor in the kitchen. It was when she stalled in front of the cake, hands on hips and head dejected, that Charlie leaped up to help. She had never seen her sister so defeated. That familiar wide-eyed stare, so capable of criticism, now looked inward, making Eleanor appear, not hard, but *brittle*. Charlie stood next to her, and gently—so as not to break her—nudged Eleanor out of the way.

On the surface of the cake, Eleanor had arranged the fruit in concentric circles: blueberries, raspberries, blueberries. She had run out halfway through a ring of raspberries. Charlie halved a passionfruit, and spooned the insides over the cake. 'There,' she said. 'There's no pattern to ruin.'

Eleanor inspected her sister's work. Her silence suggested she couldn't think of any criticisms. She sighed then, and placed the cake in a large Tupperware container. It still had a sticker on it. Charlie wondered whether Eleanor had bought it for the occasion.

'Let's go,' Eleanor said, with as much impatience as if Charlie had held her up.

And Charlie, who had been ready to go since she arrived, repeated her much-used, childhood refrain: a cry that scrambled to keep up, and affirmed Eleanor as leader.

'Coming!'

—

ELEANOR WAS ELEVEN when their father left. Charlie had recently turned nine. As adults, they looked back and reflected that what their mother experienced—understandably—was a breakdown. At the time, Eleanor and Charlie just knew their mother was taking some time off work. For Charlie, this involved listening to a lot of music on her iPod shuffle. For Eleanor, it meant walking her sister to school and adopting her mother's turn of phrase (*Hurry up, I'm always late because of you*), making sure they had enough cash to share a tuckshop lunch, and fixing everyone dinner. Eleanor's scrambled eggs grew more watery and more complicated each week. By the time she had invented canned tuna, frozen peas, and barbecue sauce flavour, their mother's sister flew down from Queensland and stayed for one weekend. Their mother shot out of her bedroom with defensive haste. Eleanor and Charlie hadn't seen their aunt since.

The three of them—mother and daughters—never spoke about that period, though Charlie spoke to a therapist, after her drama school teacher told her she wasn't cut out for screen acting, because she was insufficiently connected to her inner child. On stage, apparently, this wasn't such a big issue, but you couldn't lie to the camera.

It was unclear whether the ten government-funded therapy sessions improved Charlie's acting, but they certainly improved her vocabulary. She left with a more sophisticated language for articulating all kinds of resentment. Strangely, Charlie didn't use this new vocabulary in conversations with her parents—neither the father who'd left indefinitely, nor the mother who'd stayed forever and just taken a few weeks to cope. Instead, she did what she'd always done, ever since he left: she confided in her sister.

In the early years following the separation, when their father still lived in Sydney, he used to come to the apartment on weekends and take Charlie and Eleanor out for pizza in Randwick. Eleanor would sit up straight at the table, and try to rise to the occasion by talking about current affairs. Sometimes she mentioned her friends at school, and her father nodded and smiled and asked questions which were polite but revealed he had no idea what Eleanor was talking about. Afterwards, Charlie would complain that the whole evening had been about Eleanor.

He came to Sydney when Charlie graduated drama school to watch her end-of-year showcase. The play was very sexually explicit, and Charlie swore a lot, and they were all worried about how he was going to take it.

At dinner afterwards, he couldn't stop smiling, and kept repeating his favourite bits, even doing some of the voices. Their mother laughed at all of his jokes behind her hand, like she was trying to hide it. When he went up to the counter to pay, and Charlie went to the bathroom—to text, presumably—their mother stared at her crumpled paper napkin and looked like she was about to cry.

'What a nice night,' Eleanor said, while her mother raised the napkin to her face. 'We're all so proud of her.'

'I thought, sometimes'—her mother wiped in one rough stroke, pulling her skin to reveal the red and fleshy underside of her eye—'I thought maybe I'd imagined that man.'

—

MARY HAD THE double distinction of a career that was both objectively socially necessary and not very well paid. Twenty-five years old, and in her second year at a prestigious consulting firm, Eleanor already earned more than her mother did as an administrator of an aged care home.

They found her by the barbecue—black slacks and a white shirt, sleeves rolled to the elbows—distributing slices of ham among paper plates. When she saw her daughters, Mary put down the tongs and hugged them both.

Apart from the hair—Eleanor's long and natural brown, Charlie's short and bleached white—they had their mother's features: the same mouth and deep-set hazel eyes, though Mary's lids were heavier, bearing greater burdens. But when all three were assembled, Charlie was the odd one out. Standing next to Charlie, the other two suddenly had proud noses, and their bodies seemed short and squat. Fittingly, at almost three years older, Eleanor looked like the first draft.

'I'm sorry we're late,' Eleanor said.

'Late? I didn't know you were coming. It's wonderful to see you.'

Charlie went for another hug. 'You too, Mum.'

'We come every year,' Eleanor said.

'And you've brought a cake!'

Eleanor adjusted the Tupperware under her arm. 'It's for the three of us.' She resisted the urge to add: 'Like every year.'

'And in this heat!'

'Yeah, can I put it in the fridge or something?'

But their mother had already turned her attention to the other side of the barbecue. Somebody was asking about a first-aid kit. She handed Eleanor the tongs. 'Do you mind?'

Eleanor put her Tupperware container down a few metres from the barbecue and continued her mother's task of distributing ham. Charlie stood next to her and started piling the plates with the elegance of a waitress—or an out-of-work actor.

The sun beat down on the laneway and bounced off the bricks. Eleanor's feet were already starting to sweat-slide in her mules. They clacked, officious, on the concrete, while Charlie was lithe in her ribbed singlet, and lime green TNs. Down the length of the laneway, Charlie padded between white trestle tables. Eleanor watched her slow progress, stopping with every plate for a chat that almost always ended in a hug.

For Eleanor, whose natural mode was analytical, the idea of 'common humanity' seemed an oversimplification. She observed people from a studied distance, trying to appreciate their intricacies—all the ways they were particular. But Charlie *felt* her way through every interaction, so at ease with her own emotions. She was unguarded, she shared too much—although maybe it was just enough, and maybe people didn't need to withhold at all, when the prospect of connection was so real.

When Eleanor's job was done, rather than head towards the tables, she sat on a low brick wall, and watched. Eventually, Charlie joined her.

Eleanor was always amazed at her sister's ability to materialise a vape, seemingly without even reaching into a pocket or bag. Now, Charlie took a tentative sip. 'Sorry,' she said, blowing smoke through her nose. 'Sorry, this is random, but before we go home and, like, do the whole Christmas thing, there's something I need to tell you about Mark.'

Eleanor shielded her eyes with her hand, so she could look at her sister. The glare was punishing. She steadied herself with her spare hand, as if to brace herself. Charlie's face was scrunched too, although she was looking down away from the sun—tight, perhaps, with guilt. Eleanor suspected then, with a dread so thick it almost amounted to certainty, that Charlie knew who Mark had slept with that night.

'He emailed me this morning.'

'About what?'

'I haven't really read it. But'—Charlie looked at her sister—'I guess he didn't tell you.'

Eleanor was wearing a thin cotton dress. Her bum was warm against the wall. She pressed her bare calves to the brick. The heat flared and then dulled, spreading across her skin.

'Not all the time'—Charlie exhaled, long and indulgent, in a cloud of sweet-smelling smoke—'but we've had a pretty consistent chain of emails back and forth for most of the time you guys were going out. He shares his drafts and tells me what he's working on, and we recommend stuff for each other to watch or read. It's a wank, basically. But yeah, I thought you should know, because it can be quite personal. It's quite an intimate thing, to show your work to someone.'

Eleanor might have been more outraged had she not expected a juicier revelation. 'Right.'

'And, um, yeah. He's just sent me another email.'

'Okay?'

'It's a Merry Christmas kind of thing, I guess.'

'How festive.'

Now, Eleanor was working her way to outrage. It *did* sound quite intimate: a different kind of infidelity to the one she'd feared, but a betrayal nonetheless. Not least of all because—Eleanor recalled with a lightning stroke of righteousness—*she* had been the one to set Mark and Charlie up in the first place.

When Charlie was in her final year of drama school, she'd devised her own performance. Eleanor had said: 'The boy I'm seeing is super smart, and a writer. I haven't read anything he's written, but he's read everything. Literally, everything.' (Which Charlie knew meant: more than Eleanor.)

From then on, Eleanor had always thought that Mark and Charlie were only slightly better friends than one's partner and sibling usually were: polite interest in each other's lives, phone calls ahead of Eleanor's birthday for advice about what present to buy. Occasionally, Mark would call or text Charlie to congratulate her on a performance. If this seemed sycophantic, Eleanor had always assured herself that *she* was the sister being sucked up to.

Now, she lifted her legs from the wall and kicked it with her heels. The air cooled on her sweat. 'So how long have you been pen pals?' she said. 'Since he tutored you?'

'Sort of. It picked up last year in lockdown.' Charlie was still looking at her lap. Eleanor said nothing, willing her to elaborate.

'It was a hard time, Eleanor. All my friends were having a terrible time. And Mark was really nice about it. I think, you know, he had the emotional energy, because he hadn't lost his job or anything and was just working from home. So I got into this habit of telling him about my days. It was just, like, something to do. In the morning, I'd go for a walk and tell him what I saw. Little, stupid things. Like a baby that looked shocked when I smiled at it. Or a friendly cat that was always in the same spot, like it was waiting for me. And I guess it went on long enough that I could admit eventually that I was going for these walks so I'd have something to talk to Mark about. Those emails quite literally got me out of bed.'

To Eleanor, her sister's speech had a premeditated eloquence. Like there were lines lifted from one of these emails. She sighed. It was all so *Charlie*. Not for the first time, Eleanor thought: *She's too beautiful for her own good.* Charlie would be worried that if she didn't reply to Mark, he'd be hurt. She'd feel that injustice keenly—not just her own guilt, but his pain, both compounded by the fact he'd been so nice to her. She was so depressingly *optimistic* about people: she thought each relationship was special and pure in its own right—that you could love without hurting, that it wasn't all a dreadful, complex mixture.

For all of this, Eleanor was able to muster genuine admiration. What irritated her was the sense that beneath the surface of all that optimism, lay a current of manipulation. *A terrible time. He had the emotional energy.* With each assertion of her own weakness, Charlie gained a little power. Her needs *mattered*, she was saying—they mattered more than Eleanor's.

'What about these "boundaries" you recommended I establish? So, I'm not allowed to even ask Mark for an explanation because

I need to set up "boundaries" but you can chat to him whenever? Is that the situation?'

Eleanor was incapable of using any therapy-adjacent terminology without first dunking it in sarcasm. Each time she used it, she put bunny ears around the word *boundaries*, just in case her tone wasn't explicit. Although it was a familiar trick, Charlie still flushed like a chastised child.

This must have been the reaction Eleanor wanted when she made the remark, but upon seeing it she felt no satisfaction. She wanted to babble apologies, as if she had stepped on a puppy's tail. Except she'd done it on purpose.

'I think it's important that we both do what's right for us,' Charlie said, very quietly.

'But you're asking my permission? To reply to him?'

'I guess.'

They sat in silence while the question hung in the air.

Eleanor knew she would probably give her sister what she asked for, because she always did. But she wanted to let the tension last a while. After Charlie's little speech—her assertion of victimhood—Eleanor felt it was her turn to claim some power. And Charlie, with her head hanging and her vape idle, seemed to relish her own wretchedness.

It was because Charlie seemed to be enjoying herself so much that Eleanor finally said, 'You know, Charlie—'

'That Mason is a character. What were you talking to him about for so long?'

Both sisters sat up straight. Their mother stood before them, an exhausted smile bolted to her lips and the long sleeves of her white shirt rolled back down to her wrists. Apparently, it was time to go home.

'Um . . .' Charlie tried to recall the conversation. 'I think he was saying he liked my shoes?'

Their mother started to laugh.

'What?'

Mary wiped her eyes with her fingers, and then the sweat from her forehead with the back of her hand.

'What, Mum?'

'Well, you know, Charlie, you do dress like a homeless person.'

'Are you serious?'

'A beautiful street sleeper, don't get me wrong.'

'No, I mean, do you have *any* sense of where we are?'

Eleanor slid off the wall and stood next to her mother. 'I was thinking, actually, it would be a good theme for a fashion blog type thing: *On trend, or on crack?*'

Charlie said nothing, even though she knew that her failure to participate would be seen by her mother and her sister as a failure of character. Like she wasn't robust enough.

Now Mary turned her maternal, mocking smile to Eleanor, who always rose to the challenge. 'Mark didn't want to come today?'

'I'm not seeing him anymore.'

It was almost comical, the speed with which Mary dismantled her smile. 'You didn't tell me. Are you okay? What happened?'

'I'm fine. It was very mutual.' Eleanor could feel Charlie's eyes on her.

'Oh, I'm sorry to hear that.' Mary reached out and put a hand on Eleanor's wrist. 'How did it happen?'

Charlie sat completely still.

'He . . .' Eleanor swallowed. 'We just weren't that well suited.'

'His hair was always a bit stupid, wasn't it?'

Charlie's protest—*Mum!*—almost drowned out Eleanor's cackle. Eleanor found it more therapeutic than if her mother had taken her grief too seriously.

Mary continued. 'It was always so, I don't know . . .'

'Like Lord Farquaad?' Eleanor offered.

It was Charlie's turn to laugh. She brought both hands up to her ears, imitating Mark's habit of tucking away his long hair.

'Okay,' Eleanor said, when her stomach hurt and she was so full of mirth that she was starting to feel guilty. 'Let's go. I just need to get the cake.'

Eleanor nodded to the Tupperware container she'd left pushed up against a wall. When she'd placed it there, it had been in the shade. Now it appeared to be sweating.

Mary gasped. 'Oh no, Eleanor, not your lovely cake. Why don't I put it in the fridge while I finish packing up?'

Cradling the container in both hands, Mary took a few steps away, then turned and said over her shoulder: 'I was never convinced he'd be a particularly good writer. He didn't strike me as very observant.'

This time, Charlie was barely audible because she and Eleanor spoke at the exact same time: 'He's talented!'

'I'm sure he's above average.'

'Yeah, above average,' Charlie said.

Their mother had already walked off.

Eleanor resumed her seat next to her sister. The two of them together.

Eleanor was not sure that she knew how to be fragile in front of Charlie. She had needed her recently—she had been hurt; rejected. But never broken. She had accepted Charlie's recent help with a kind of magnanimity. *Isn't this big of me, to be so vulnerable with you?*

'You don't have to, like, cancel him,' she said. 'And I didn't know you relied on him so much. Just let me know, will you? If he says anything stupid, or if an accident befalls him.'

Charlie laughed and reached for Eleanor's hand.

Charlie didn't know that Eleanor had in fact taken an online test earlier that week because she had been shocked by how acutely she wanted Mark to suffer, and the specificity of her fantasies in that regard—the least elaborate being a collision between a jogging Mark and a bicycle in Centennial Park, resulting in the surgical removal of one testicle. The online test had confirmed that, as far as sociopathy was concerned, Eleanor was 'within the normal range'.

But as soon as she'd said it, and with Charlie's hand on hers, Eleanor realised she didn't feel quite so strongly anymore. It was a pleasure, she thought, to be so forgiving. It felt big and gracious, giving her little sister permission.

Then, as if offering a gift of thanks, Charlie said exactly what Eleanor needed to hear.

'Thank you so much for making that cake.'

7

ARRIVING AT CHARLIE'S New Year's Eve party, Eleanor saw no one she recognised but a type she was familiar with. They seemed to her one single person: bare skin and clothes cobbled together, usually arranged by colour. A purple tulle skirt underlining a bare, chiselled chest. Red flared jeans, belted at the waist, and a red bikini top. Black underwear, black tape on the nipples, like Xs on a treasure map, and a black, crocheted sheath that, Eleanor supposed, could be generously described as a dress.

Conformity, Eleanor thought, was depressingly inevitable. All these people—baring their unique individual snowflakeness in the fearless flash of naked cheeks, nipples, chests—looked, to her, interchangeable.

As the only nearly dressed person at a party full of the nearly naked, it was difficult to know who was more exposed. This was exactly what Eleanor had feared when she'd dressed that morning.

'How do I dress like I'm pro recreational drugs?' she had wondered aloud. Seb, her housemate, motioned to himself. Chinos and a shirt.

'Not cocaine,' she clarified.

'Oh.' He nodded his understanding. 'Like you go to festivals?'

'Exactly.'

He waved his hand. 'Crop tops and little sunglasses and shit. Just dress like you love yourself sick.'

In a black denim skirt, a white crop top, and pink sunglasses with slits for lenses, Eleanor's cowboy hat was doing most of the legwork. She was not so much wearing it as suffering it, with a head-bent attitude of apology. Nonetheless, she hoped it made her look sure of herself, or something.

She'd entered via the back lane, and was standing by the door. A few metres away, Charlie was perched on the end of a long bench, two people on the ground at her feet. She had a VB in one hand and a cigarette in a comically long holder in the other.

Eleanor felt—as she often did when she saw Charlie in a crowd—the sisterly stirrings of pride. With her cropped blonde hair, a strapless green top, and a very short green skirt, she was fairylike: elegant and irreverent. She was telling a story, or perhaps impersonating someone—Eleanor saw her pull an un-Charlie face and flap her hands, while her audience of two laughed so hard they leaned on each other for support.

Charlie had always been cooler than Eleanor. It was her beauty—her long-limbed elegance—as well as her natural warmth, which meant she could be cool without being exclusive. And although she envied her, there were also times—like now, when Charlie saw her from across the yard, and leaped up to embrace her—that Eleanor felt cooler by association.

They exchanged the same wide smile, which made their faces fall into what looked like their intended shapes: their cheeks rounded on either side; their noses drawn into a straight line.

'Let me get you a beer.'

'I brought some.' Eleanor held up a reusable grocery bag.

'A nang then?' Charlie motioned to a fold-out table on the other side of the grass. Hanging from the back fence was a wooden board carved with the words: *Nangs Station.*

'Nice sign.'

'Kevin made it. He's really talented.'

Eleanor squinted. The sign was certainly legible, she had to give him that. 'Evidently.'

Charlie touched her arm. 'Come on. I'll introduce you to my housemates.'

'I'm sure I'll love them.'

—

BEFORE THE PARTY Charlie had told Eleanor two things about Kevin. First, he was a DJ. Second, he was 'a lost boy'. The second, Eleanor had snapped, could be intuited from the first.

Meeting him in person, Eleanor surprised herself. She found his *lostness* charming, as if he had unfulfilled potential, which she, through insight and attention, might help him claim. He was wearing a ballerina skirt and a fanny pack draped over his shoulders like a sash. His eyes were liquid black, and his lashes thick enough to give the impression of a child or a great, docile beast.

He had said: 'You must be Charlie's sister,' and, when Eleanor nodded, said the 'sartorial resemblance' had tipped him off. Eleanor, realising he probably meant *sororal,* felt suddenly powerful. Like she was playing chess and had just thought of a brilliant next move.

It was not long before Kevin had manoeuvred them into the alley that ran down the side of the house, and had manoeuvred the conversation to the topic of a rave he had organised in the new year.

'Of course, we'll provide earplugs.'

'Because the music will be so loud?' Eleanor shouted this question, smiling at the irony, over the thud of techno music. Her skin crawled with sweat—both hers and other people's. Her hat long discarded, she had been brushing up against Charlie's guests for several hours now. The smell, like the throb of the bass that could be heard all the way down the street, attested to the party's success.

'Is that why you need to provide earplugs?' Eleanor asked. 'Can't you just turn the volume down?'

'No,' Kevin shouted. 'Because people won't be able to handle it.'

'How do you mean *handle*?'

'It's, like, unfathomably dirty. Such a hardcore sound that you actually *cannot* listen to it.'

'Or what?'

He smiled, like she was being deliberately obtuse.

'Or what?' she repeated, irritably enough for him to stop smiling.

'I don't—'

'What happens if you hear this un-hearable music?'

He paused. 'You'd just like, die.'

'Just die?'

'I know it sounds crazy—'

'No, it just sounds like you've sort of forgotten the point of live music. People can "not hear" anything at home.'

He started to say something that included the words *protest* and *donk*. Eleanor, while nodding, wondered what was so wrong with the pop music that she—and millions of others—liked to listen to. She felt the twinge of a headache—probably from dehydration, she thought, as she surveyed the scene.

They were standing in italics, leaning against the brick wall that separated number 93 Bethel Street from the next terrace. To her right, Eleanor could see to the back of the garden, where a rosemary bush and tomato vine were not so much growing as sinking feebly into the ground. To her left was the dance floor. In the tanned curve of hundreds of shoulders, Eleanor saw the colour of a long hot summer. All these artists with their protests and their tiny sunglasses. Resisting capitalism—or whatever it was they were resisting—was like trying not to trip on the deck of a sinking ship.

Kevin, realising perhaps that he had lost his audience, nudged Eleanor and excused himself for his set. Eleanor checked her phone. It was too early to leave; Charlie would be upset. She looked at the faces thronging the yard and wished she hadn't finished her beer.

'Have we met before?'

Her voice was deep and glamorous. Eleanor turned and saw that she was short, and was looking up at Eleanor with a face so full of intelligence it made her feel as if she were the subject of an elaborate joke. Eleanor recognised her immediately, although she couldn't remember her name: the director of Charlie's last play. She was relieved at first to see her, remembering how much she'd enjoyed their conversation in the bathroom. Then, remembering how it had ended, she was freshly embarrassed.

'I'm not sure?' Regretting her upward inflection, Eleanor tried to cover it with talk. 'But maybe we have, you know, in a different context. It's hard to place people out of context.'

She regretted the talk too. As she said *context* she motioned to the woman in a way that, given her outfit, implied another meaning entirely. She was wearing thin black underwear, black tape on her nipples and a dress that appeared to be made out of a very open-weave fishnet.

'Out of context or out of clothes?'

Eleanor laughed, while the woman pouted around her vape, her mouth forming a very deliberate circle—anything but a smile.

'Anyway, I'm Eleanor. Charlie's sister.'

'Oh *you're* Eleanor. It's so nice to meet you.'

She leaned over and her lips brushed Eleanor's cheek. Eleanor resisted an urge to touch the spot after she pulled away.

'I'm Helen.'

'Helen!'

With her name, it clicked: the woman she'd met at the play, the director, was also the woman Charlie was seeing.

Yesterday, Eleanor had texted Charlie to ask if she could bring anything to the party (or as she called it: *your depraved function*), like dips or chips. Charlie had said no, don't worry, and—because she could see the real purpose of the text—she'd tried to assure Eleanor that she might actually have a good time.

I really want you to meet Helen

Which one's Helen?

The housemate I'm seeing

Housemate? Seeing?
Charlie!

It's casual!

It sounds complicated . . .

She's chill you'll really like her

Eleanor had thumbs-up-reacted this last message. Then, feeling guilty about being sceptical—especially when her sister was making such an effort to include her—she'd added:

Really looking forward to it!!

. . . And a TikTok of the Russian dwarf, Hasbulla, poolside and sunglass-shaded, his tiny arms hugging a bowl of chips.

Now, as Eleanor looked at Helen's perfect, symmetrical face, she couldn't see anything complicated at all. Of course, Charlie would have a crush on her. Dark hair, wide insightful eyes, and a pair of teasing dimples.

'I saw Kevin boring you,' Helen said.

Eleanor smiled. 'On the contrary, he's very entertaining.'

'He's a parody of himself.'

'I did think that if he wants to create a truly un-listenable experience for this rave he's planning, he could play his own conversation on a loop.'

Helen laughed at that, tossing her head back. 'I always think that.' The dimples were back. 'He's always going on about how we'll need earplugs during his set. And I'm like: what about right now? Where are my earplugs now?'

Eleanor, matching Helen's stance, stopped leaning against the wall. She stood upright. It was almost golden hour. The sun no longer burned but soothed, casting the party in a nostalgic glow that rendered the day most beautiful, their youth most perfect, even as it dwindled.

Helen leaned over, so her lips brushed Eleanor's ear. Her dark hair fell across her shoulder, and she raised a slender hand to flick it back. 'This is his set now.'

The bass that had thumped all afternoon was now so loud it had acquired the pressure of a heartbeat. Eleanor was reduced to shouting into Helen's ear, and felt that conversation, in a place like this, just wasn't worth it. Helen started to dance then, on the spot, which was the most natural thing to do. For Eleanor, that kind of unselfconscious movement—connecting your body to the world outside of it—was difficult.

She shuffled her weight: left foot then right foot, marching out an attempt at participation. Helen moved closer and leaned forward, shouting into her ear: 'Water?'

Eleanor nodded. She followed Helen inside, trying to look at the back of her head and not the straight black arrow of her G-string.

In the house, the bass was less oppressive, although the air was so thick with sweat the walls glistened.

They stopped in the kitchen, where Helen reached behind someone for mugs, filled them with water and handed one to Eleanor. Helen drank hers in one, her head tipped back. Eleanor watched her throat rise and fall with each gulp.

She slammed the mug on the counter and wiped her mouth with the back of her hand. 'Fuck me, I was thirsty.'

Eleanor smiled and sipped her water. It was lukewarm. An arm brushed against hers. Charlie, emerging through the crowd, squeezed herself between Eleanor and the fridge.

'I see you've met Helen.'

Eleanor admired Charlie's indifference—how coolly she tossed off the name. In private conversations between the sisters, Charlie said *Helen* like a prayer. She said it again: 'Helen, this is my sister. Remember, I was telling you about her break-up.'

'*I* did the breaking up.'

Charlie's smile was insufferably sympathetic. It accused and indulged Eleanor at the same time, like she was fibbing, but only because she was too fragile for the truth.

'So who did you dump?' Helen asked.

'You wouldn't know him.'

'I hate him already.'

In gratitude, Eleanor gave her the name. 'Mark Chapman.'

Helen put a hand to her mouth to stifle a laugh. 'You're kidding. I know him. Oh god, did he break your heart?'

'Not really.'

'Good. He's a bit of a cunt.'

Charlie laughed. 'Helen!'

Helen was assertive; her dancing hands illustrating the thoughts that spun across her face. 'He wasn't like malicious or anything.

Like, I don't think he would *think* he's a cunt. He was just . . . Being a tortured artist was very much his brand.'

'How do you know him?'

'Oh, I barely know him at all.' Helen and Eleanor faced each other now, and Charlie watched from the side as their profiles bent towards each other. They spoke loudly, but their pose was that of a whispered conversation, as if secrets were being traded. 'I was at uni with him.'

'You went to law school?'

'Dropout.'

'Good for you. Half the law students I knew aspired to drop out.'

'Why didn't they?'

'They lacked the commitment. And the drive. Dropping out is hard.'

At Helen's laugh, Eleanor felt triumphant. Charlie laughed too, although hers was unconvincing.

For a long time, Charlie had wanted to introduce Helen to her sister—her sharp, unsparing sister, who was effortlessly impressive, and so difficult to impress. In Helen, Charlie had recognised her sister's habit: observing everything and holding nothing back. And although she found them cruel sometimes—poking at people incessantly with the long stick of their wit—she was proud of them too: her clever sister, and her brilliant friend. Now, as she watched their easy, fluid conversation, she wanted, like a child, to take back what she had gifted.

Charlie kissed Helen on the cheek. Her pupils were dilated, and she was moving on the spot as she said, 'Helen, we need to drop.'

Helen didn't say anything. She cocked her head to the side, letting her hair slip down her shoulder.

'Mandy and Kevin did it hours ago. We should drop for the rest of Kevin's set.'

'I'd rather have earplugs for Kevin's set.' Eleanor looked at Helen as she said this, continuing, faster, when she didn't see her smile, 'I don't want to be chemically enhanced just so I can experience more of his self-proclaimed "un-hearable" music.'

Helen looked at her quickly, with a smile that expressed nothing. Eleanor turned to Charlie. 'Now?'

'Yep. You want some?' Charlie was rummaging in her bag. She didn't look at Eleanor, and started to say something about the previous time she bought from this particular dealer, when Eleanor interrupted.

'Are you sure you've got enough?'

Charlie turned, her mouth wide, her eyes gaping. 'What?'

Eleanor blinked at her. She had considered saying something less passive like, *Count me in.* On Helen's lips, it might have sounded ironic.

'Why not?' Eleanor said, which only made Charlie's mouth hang wider. Eleanor's shrug felt unconvincing, moving through her stiff shoulders. She could only imagine how it looked. 'Treat yourself. Isn't that what you'd say?'

—

ELEANOR'S EXPERIENCE OF being high was one of constant self-diagnosis. The revolving coloured lights on either side of the decks were hypnotic, and bright even when she closed her eyes. Sensitivity to light, she told herself, was a common response to taking MDMA. Her heart rate was quick—also due to the MDMA, she thought, although it could also be due to the dancing. Her feet moved constantly and her arms were pumping to the beat as if entirely separate from her, and separate from her mind, which told her that the dancing was likely a symptom of euphoria.

The sense she felt, when Helen grabbed her arm, that her skin was one continuous surface, and touching part of it was the same as being touched all over—the sense, at the same time, that her skin was scarcely there at all, and that she was bursting out of it, pouring through it . . . MDMA's street-name was *ecstasy* for a reason.

Charlie laughed to see this dancing Eleanor. She flattered herself with images of Eleanor in a few hours' time, when her pupils slackened, her dancing slowed, and she felt the night creep in—a chill all over. Charlie would be kind to Eleanor and show her what it felt like to be seen through non-judgemental eyes. She felt premature pride at the prospect.

At midnight, after everyone counted down and cheered, Charlie put her hand on Helen's hip, the curve soft beneath the rope of her dress. She told her, without letting go, what a privilege it was to start a new year with so much to care about.

'So many times last year,' she said, 'I just felt like my life was empty, that I was friendless and would never go anywhere or do anything. All those things normal people felt if they were, like, alive over the past two years.'

Then Helen kissed her, and Charlie's lips were tingling so much that it was all she could think about: her own lips.

They danced, sometimes two of them, sometimes all three, and then each on their own, drifting through the crowd, only to find their way back with a smile and a touch, or just a look.

They did not notice when Kevin's set ended, and the next began, and they did not notice when Kevin joined them, passing around a little bottle of amyl, that made Eleanor feel like she was floating and, at the same time, falling. When she kissed him, her hands locked together behind his neck. She did not think of the lips as being his; she just wanted to be touched.

Eventually, police were called, and the party moved inside: several groups—hands cobwebbed together—all agreeing vehemently on everything, most especially their mutual conviction that:

This was the closest they'd ever been to another human /

They'd never see each other again.

Like debris floating above this sea of common humanity, Kevin took Eleanor's hand and led her to the master bedroom. It was at the front of the house, and the sucking sound of their lips was punctuated with the chatter of departing guests, then the rumble of cars, and then, eventually, when Kevin slowed to sleep, with silence.

Eleanor lay in the fetal position, strangely grateful for the stranger's arms that held her, and her mind ran rabid, snatching at repeated themes. Her mother's despair, if she became a drug-addled junkie; how desperately sad her funeral would be. Mark would probably want to read a poem.

When she did, at last, slip into half-sleep—still awake but thoughts incoherent—her vision seemed filtered, as if through a rippling black net.

—

ELEANOR WOKE WITH eyes stinging from the light that streamed through Kevin's open windows and a stomach full of shame. Her clothes were flung across Kevin's room, which seemed to be furnished entirely with milk crates.

She pulled them on hurriedly then retreated downstairs to the kitchen. Charging her phone by the toaster, the knots in her stomach only tightened, and she sensed that she was experiencing more than a chemical regret.

The kitchen bore signs of the subtle student squalor that she had only recently left behind and therefore couldn't help but catalogue fastidiously. The tabletop was sticky, there were crumbs under the toaster, the wall where she inserted her phone charger was flecked with what looked like pasta sauce. It rendered her more shameful, she felt, to stand in this sharehouse with her hangover and the delusion that she was somehow *different*. It made her feel as if adulthood was just an affectation and her commitment to it tenuous.

Eleanor was startled by a noise behind her. She turned and saw Helen, wearing tiny boxer shorts and a thin black singlet. Beneath it, her breasts looked larger than they had in her fishnet. The singlet stopped just short of the waistband. Eleanor forced herself to look away from the vulnerable flush of skin.

'You hung around.' Helen's voice was rich with glee. Eleanor checked her phone screen. Still black.

'Just charging my phone.'

'Oh *that's* why you're here, is it?' Helen's amusement wasn't situational—the comic surprise at finding someone unexpected in her kitchen. It was personal. Like she knew that being so compromised—wearing last night's make-up and someone else's smell—was unfamiliar for Eleanor. And knowing that, Helen took particular delight in maximising her discomfort. 'Good night?'

'Why not.' Eleanor pressed the side button on her phone. The screen remained dark.

Helen was eating a nectarine. The bite she took was loud, and she wiped a drop of juice from her cheek. 'I imagine Kevin's a very generous lover.'

Eleanor couldn't tell whether it was she or Kevin who was being mocked. Strangely, she wished it was her, so they might laugh about it, and Eleanor might confess herself out of her depth, and they might know each other better.

Eleanor pressed the side button at a ferocious pace. Her heart, too, quickened. 'What makes you say that?'

'He's a feminist. I'm surprised he didn't tell you.'

'It's always a red flag, isn't it, when they have to tell you.' Eleanor was relieved that this time, when she pressed the side button, the screen lit up. 'I'd better head.'

Eleanor was suddenly embarrassed by her lock screen: a picture of her local harbourside pool on a sunny day. All blue and basic, if it said anything about her personality, it was that she didn't have one.

'What are you on?' Helen was looking at the screen over Eleanor's shoulder. Ever so gently, their hands brushed when Helen took the phone and tilted it towards her. 'You don't want to stay until you're in the green?' Barely a brush; perhaps just the thin hairs on their hands. The tiniest touch of heat from standing so close.

'Eleanor?'

Charlie didn't know which one of them—Eleanor or Helen—took the bigger leap. They both moved so fast.

'Still here?'

There was a cruelty to Charlie's laugh: brief and high-pitched.

Eleanor yanked her phone from the wall. The cord came with it. She rolled it around her fingers and placed it on the bench before making her way to the front of the house. 'Thanks for last night,' Eleanor called over her shoulder as she opened the door, fumbling with the latch.

Charlie was quick to call, 'No worries,' but it was Helen's voice—softer, deeper, more amused—that stayed with Eleanor as she made her way home.

'Happy New Year.'

8

THE RESIDENTS OF 93 Bethel Street had made sure they weren't working on New Year's Day. 'Start the new year right,' Mandy said, in the affected voice she used to acknowledge when she was lifting a joke from the internet. Like her sense of humour was more sophisticated than just quoting things other people had said online. In this instance, *right* meant *languidly*.

Charlie was starting the new year in the manner she had fantasised about for weeks. After Eleanor left, Charlie and Helen retreated to Helen's room, where they'd woken that morning in a sweaty tangle.

Charlie scrolled through pictures of the previous day on her phone. In crowd shots, taken from above by someone standing on a chair, she zoomed in on herself. Her face was always in motion: talking, laughing, chewing. Next to her, Helen sat up with her legs crossed, her own phone in her lap.

'Your sister was nice,' Helen said.

Charlie had been lying flat. She sat up, so she was level with Helen. 'We're very different.'

'I feel like Kevin's not really her type.'

'Not at all.' Charlie smiled, but Helen was still looking at her phone. 'I'm going to hold that over her forever.'

'He'll be so pleased with himself.' Helen made the *o* in *so* long. 'It's infuriating, isn't it?'

Helen threw her phone to the foot of the bed and flopped back down, propping her head up with her right hand. She looked at Charlie. 'You know, it's weird. He's so infuriating, you're right, but I always feel, I don't know, like *maternal* towards him. Is that problematic?'

Charlie matched Helen's position. Their faces were very close. 'I think we all do. He's got that learned helplessness. Like, we're always picking up after him and whatever.'

'But all that domestic bullshit makes me feel murderous towards him, not maternal. I more meant that I wish him well. Why are you laughing?'

'I just think that's putting the, you know, *tidal* force of a mother's love extremely mildly,' Charlie said. 'You can wish a total stranger well.'

'Okay, not maternal then. Maybe I just mean that I hate him less than other people.'

'Do you really *hate* other people?'

The ceiling fan rotated, slowly; outside the day was breezeless. Helen blinked once and looked for a moment like she was considering her answer. Then she leaned forward and, with stale morning-after mouths, they kissed.

Their hangovers turned desire to intimacy—kissing fell to holding, and, in the new year light, they wallowed in each other's arms.

—

WHEN CHARLIE WOKE, the light outside was afternoon-bright. Her nausea and her tender head felt suddenly satisfying. She watched

Helen sleep: the blank canvas of her back, and wondered whether she, too, felt the same sense of rest. A deep calm, as if after a long cry.

Helen stirred. She rolled onto her side, facing Charlie, and mumbled, 'We should—' The rest of her words were muffled by her pillow.

Charlie moved her head closer to Helen's. 'What?'

'It's hot. We should go to the beach.'

Charlie tried to keep a grip on her jubilation. 'I'll get my stuff.'

—

CHARLIE LOCKED THE door of the bathroom she shared with Helen and Mandy. Standing with one leg on the closed toilet seat, she took a rusted razor to her bikini line. It was strange, she thought, that she groomed with such urgency, given that Helen had enjoyed a very close view of that area last night. But Helen would probably bring her camera, and it was one thing to see it under a sheet, another poking out the sides of a polyester costume.

In her room, Charlie packed a tote bag with a towel, sunglasses, and a water bottle. She eyed her bedside table critically. Next to the lamp, in a position so untouched it had become less a novel and more an extension of the furniture, was *Anna Karenina.* On top of it was a slender new release with a colourful cover about a young female narrator self-actualising via zany sexual experiences. Several more of these volumes in similar colours sat well-thumbed and dog-eared on her shelf. Charlie chose the tome. It was so big it would surely inspire a comment. There might even be the opportunity for a relatable, self-deprecating joke about how pretentious she was. *I don't really understand the hype. Why am I doing this to myself?* That type of thing.

Despite her newly heavy beach bag, Charlie still felt like she could float. One drunken sexual encounter might well be a mistake. Or, worse, a regret. But *three*—opening night, closing night, and New Year's Eve—three looked like a habit. Now they would go to the beach, and talk and lounge all afternoon, and know each other in a different way.

Charlie knew from experience that the ocean was as intimate as it was immense. A perfect summer's day was a special thing to share, and never more so than at the start of a newborn year.

Back in Helen's room, Charlie found her phone amid the bed's fond disarray. Her screen was awash with notifications from their house group chat. Photos of lost property, most of which they would rather keep than return (several vapes, a pink cape, a clown mask), and Kevin asking more than once if anyone had seen his fanny pack. When she scrolled all the way to the bottom, Charlie saw the most recent message. It was from Helen, and it said:

Beach thots??

Two love heart emojis confirmed the intrusion on their privacy. Disappointment hit her right in the back of the knees. Charlie sat on the edge of Helen's bed and felt the clammy hands of her hangover take her by the neck, and squeeze.

—

HELEN HELD THE wheel between her thumb and forefinger, and they all laughed, like driving on a hot day was a game they'd invented. Charlie looked out the open window, let the wind stroke her face, and tried to pretend that Kevin and Mandy weren't in the back seat.

At an intersection, Helen took her top off and wordlessly handed it to Charlie. It was still warm. Charlie turned to see her slouching stomach, the curve of her shoulders, the tan line on her neck. She soaked it in with willed attention, like these were already treasured memories.

After much deliberation, they settled on Gordons Bay. They could park on the cliffs and Kevin could smoke his joint when they found a good spot.

The day had almost escaped them. The sun was already sinking below the rocks, the cliffs casting long, even shadows across the bay. At the very edge, just where it curved to Clovelly, a shaft of gold warmed the water. The rest was flat and purplish, shimmering like oil.

On the rocks, they spread their towels in a clearing among the crowd. Everyone looked about their age, and similarly party-worn. Movements were slow and talking soft.

Mandy made a joke about the rocky discomfort being very European. 'Who needs Positano? The sand isn't soft here either.'

Charlie laughed and rolled onto her back, sucking in her stomach.

Mandy was standing over them, lovingly covering her thighs in sunscreen. She looked down at where Charlie and Helen lay, Charlie with *Anna Karenina* splayed across her face like a very heavy hat, and Helen with her hands at either side, one of them almost touching Charlie's.

'So, are you guys going to move into one room, or what?' Mandy said.

Charlie didn't remove her book. 'Excuse me?'

'If you're going to sleep in the same room'—Charlie could hear the flesh-slap sound of Mandy applying more sunscreen—'we might as well move someone into Charlie's room and all cop cheaper rent.'

Neither Charlie nor Helen could formulate a response.

'I'm just fucking with you,' Mandy said. 'But it'd be so much better, financially.'

Kevin, who had been focusing all his attention on rolling, now lit up. 'Please,' he said. 'Just sleep together every night.'

'So you want us to . . . what?' Helen rolled onto her stomach, her head up like a lizard, so she could face the others. 'Should we take monogamy for the team?'

'Why not?' Kevin exhaled in a pungent cloud. 'You're friends. You're housemates. You're fucking.'

Charlie was relieved that her book was still covering her face. She lay perfectly still, and tried to concentrate on the beat of the sun on her front and the hot jagged rock at her back. Like she was in a sandwich press.

'Think about it,' Mandy said. 'We could source some private school bloke—some friend of Kev's—who works in a soulless corporate job and needs his weekends to, like, make him feel alive. He moves into Enmore, pays more than you do now, we all absorb the difference.'

'Very romantic.' Helen always underplayed her sarcasm.

'It *is* romantic. It's fucking romantic,' Mandy said. 'All romance is real estate.'

'Surely,' Helen said, 'we'd absorb most of the difference, because we're doing all the work.' Charlie wasn't sure whether she was flattered that this suggestion was being seriously entertained, or annoyed that their relationship had somehow become classed as labour.

'You two are getting laid, in this scenario.'

'The woman's a genius,' Helen said, turning as if speaking to an imagined audience.

Kevin, who had been making his way through the joint, let out a long, irrelevant laugh. It was a jagged sound that cut across the bay.

Charlie removed her book. It smacked the rock with a thud. For a moment, her vision was all white. Her eyes gasped at the brightness.

'I'm going for a swim.'

—

IT WAS DIFFICULT to get into the water. Charlie, barefoot and cautious, put first one hand on the mossy rock, then both, until she was crawling on all fours. In the cracks beneath her, she caught the occasional sinister scuttle of a crab.

When she reached the water, she kicked out, trying to keep her body as flat as possible, so she didn't skim the rocks. The sea was flecked with brown algae. It ran through Charlie's fingers like ash. Charlie held her breath and kicked as long as she could without breaking the surface, wondering how long she would have to remain submerged before Helen started to worry that she'd drowned. When her kicking became frantic, and the air pressed at her lungs, she broke, gasping and thrashing.

Charlie looked back at the rocks. She could see Helen was sitting up, her shoulders hunched over her phone, and Mandy climbing down towards the water. She decided it was time to get out.

Back at their towels, the smell of weed was increasingly cloying, and a dog—tiny and fluffy like a slipper—had started to yap. For Charlie, the smallest things—a cloud or a speck of alga—were enough to spoil a mood. Every moment was fragile.

'It's not art, though, is it?' Helen was saying. Kevin laughed, but not in response.

Helen turned to Charlie with a frustrated sigh. 'We're talking about Mandy's comedy.'

'And you don't think it's art?' Charlie picked up her towel and hugged herself with it.

'Yeah, like it's funny. She's a funny woman. But she's not an *artist*.'

It distressed Charlie, the confidence with which Helen delivered these assessments. It made Charlie feel, as a conversation partner, that she lacked conviction as well as taste. And as a potential object of analysis—the future subject of these declarations—she was terrified.

'I don't think she claims to be,' Charlie said.

'You're right.'

Charlie's insecurities retreated. But then Helen added, 'She just wants to be famous, I think.'

'Don't we all?'

Helen laughed, acknowledging Charlie's obvious attempt at irony. Although, Charlie wished it wasn't, in her case, true. The distinction between Charlie and Mandy wasn't in the wanting; Charlie had just given up actively focusing on becoming famous so as not to feel too defeated every day.

'Still,' Charlie continued, 'Mandy has more integrity than an Instagram influencer selling skincare products. Like, there's some craft to it.'

'Sure, but it's just: *Setup, punch. Setup, punch.* No actual storytelling. Like, there's a ceiling on how invested people can get, you know. Or how successful she'll be. Her ceiling is, like, a Netflix special.' While Helen was talking, she was squinting through her camera, occasionally pausing to photograph the bay. She started suddenly, and stood, pressing the camera closer to her face. 'We were talking about you!'

Mandy's hands emerged first, as she crawled over the lip of the cliff. 'Oh yeah?'

When her head followed, Helen's shutter clicked. 'We were just talking about your standup.'

Mandy was still panting from the exertion, but she pulled her face into a ravenous smile.

Helen fiddled with her camera. 'I literally just said to Charlie that you're on track for a Netflix special.'

It was cruel, the way Helen could say this with so much warmth that Mandy took it as a compliment. It seemed to mock her twice. For not being in on the joke, and for being so predictable: for relishing the flattery.

Charlie lay on her back and opened her book, which proved too heavy to absorb her. She just stared at the pages, comprehending nothing, while her arms ached with strain. Nobody commented on what she was reading, or spoke to her, until they decided it was time to head home.

—

IN THE CAR park at Clovelly, Mandy and Kevin stood back to let Charlie take the front seat, as if by right. When they were pulling into Bethel Street, Helen put a hand on Charlie's thigh.

They went straight up to Helen's room, where they exchanged salty kisses. Charlie's lips were forceful, as if asking for an explanation. When Helen drifted into sleep, Charlie lay awake and watched.

The sky outside was starry now. Helen's movements, in the dark, seemed louder. Charlie prodded her awake. 'Hey.'

Helen stirred.

'I was just thinking, I don't think a Netflix special is anything to make fun of.' Charlie tried to whisper, but her voice was loud. A voice that could break something.

'What?'

'How you told Mandy at the beach that she would have a Netflix special. I don't think that's something we should be mocking.'

'Of course not.' Helen rolled onto her other side, her back towards Charlie. 'It's a huge achievement. More than I'll ever achieve.'

Charlie watched Helen's shoulders move as she slipped back to sleep. Charlie could have laughed. It would have been a manic, frustrated sound.

Helen flitted so naturally between her smiling self—the generous one, who handed out compliments and took her friends' achievements seriously—and this other, stranger girl, who traced thin-fingered shapes and cut their world into harsh little sketches. The Helen that lay in bed—who buried her face in Charlie—was she either of these, or a different person?

Charlie's hangover was in its second wave, and her brain felt twisted and dripping, like a dirty sponge.

In the dark, Charlie inched closer, and slid her arm under Helen's neck. Beneath Charlie's ear, the pillow was damp. Charlie smiled. Helen dribbled when she slept. It would have taken a fraction of a movement to wipe the wet patch. But Charlie lay still. She soaked Helen in, and squeezed her, as if to confirm that what she held was a real, physical thing—too solid to slip through her fingers.

—

THE NEXT DAY, Helen awoke in a square of golden sun, and Charlie took a photo on her phone.

An angel, bathed in light, her black hair like handwriting on the bed around her.

When Charlie composed her Instagram post, she put that picture third. The first was a live picture of the water at Gordons Bay, lapping the rocks. The little video shimmered, suspended on a loop, the same three seconds of sun and sea and sparkle, playing over and over again. The second picture was a paddle-pop that had been dropped on cement. It was banana-flavoured and the light yellow made the road look slate-coloured, almost navy, rather than grey. The third was the picture of Helen. The square of light; her rippling hair. Her eyelashes were luxurious, the little smile that played on her lips so private, to look at it was to walk in her easy dreams.

—

HELEN DIDN'T SAY anything about the photo.

'Did you see my gram?'

'Yeah, it was cute.'

'So you don't mind?'

'Not at all. I looked great.'

Charlie did not ask what she really wanted to know, which was: *Did you mind that I depicted you as mine?*

9

HELEN LOVED JANUARY in Sydney. The days were long, and if anybody worked, it was without real effort. Sweat was reserved for the backyard and the beach—it dripped down the neck of a beer, and it dried, salty, on backs bared to the sun. Plans were made and unmade—footprints in the sand—and people drifted between gatherings without urgency, like they never had anywhere else to be.

This January, so far, was no exception.

Christmas with her family had been the usual affair, with love so thick it compressed her chest. Helen had sat on the floor for hours, playing games with her nieces and nephews. Later, in her childhood home, her parents had looked more tired than she'd ever seen them. As always, the TV was garrulous, while they said nothing at all. On Boxing Day, her father was up early for work. She worried, as she did every time she drove away, that those silences only intensified when she wasn't there to share them.

In Sydney, especially in January, love was not so weighty. It was all cheek kisses and midnight declarations. Even with her housemates—even with Charlie—there was nothing like intimacy: just easy empty exchanges.

The first few times they'd had sex, they were drunk, or high, and they had snatched and bitten, as if each were trying to prove themselves hungrier than the other. Then, on New Year's Day, they were both sober. Helen was even more sober than sober. She felt as if she were missing a layer of skin. Light was brighter, the beach crusted her tongue, and the cool breeze was a gift on the back of her neck. Everything hurt, and nothing escaped her. In this mood, she worried that Charlie might need her—that she too was tender—and that they might pour into each other.

But they lay together in near silence, except for the odd comment from Charlie about something on her phone. And when they fucked, it was without that famished sense of purpose of the previous times. Charlie's eyes remained closed. Like a child who covers their eyes in order to hide, Charlie scrunched hers up—the smallest, hardest version of herself. Each of Helen's touches seemed to wash over her without penetrating—skimming her surfaces.

Even at the beach, when Mandy had joked about them being a couple, Charlie said nothing. She made no attempt to claim it—to correct Mandy, or even to assert herself as part of the joke. Instead, she lay there, as still as the rocks.

Helen looked from herself to Charlie, and where she once saw a rope, thick with associations—*director, housemate, older, lived here longer, more connections in the industry*—she now saw a very thin thread. There was Charlie, with her long limbs and her smooth face and the smile that cracked it open. And there was Helen. The thread was scarcely perceptible, and very long, so each could move where she wanted. If it ever snapped, neither would feel it.

It seemed, to Helen, deceptively simple—that two women might work together, and admire each other, and live together, and sleep together, and that none of it would, in Charlie's words, 'make it weird'. And on the second day in January, when Helen woke, and Charlie showed her an Instagram post in which Helen lay like a beach towel—an accessory to the summer—and made Charlie look chill, or happy, or however she wanted to look, it seemed there was nothing weird at all. It seemed that they could try each other on, like clothes they didn't own; that they could give pleasure without pain, and fuck without anything changing.

So Helen told Charlie that she thought she looked cute, and Charlie laughed, and Helen slipped out of the house and didn't think to tell her where she was going. After days of socialising, she felt giddy in her solitude. Like her mind was all the world, and other people just characters in her imagination.

She was so savouring this sense of anonymity that she decided on a longer drive to a place where there was no risk of seeing anyone she knew. The beach would be quicker and she wouldn't have to pay for entry, but she had a particular harbourside pool in mind.

She drove to the pool in such deep contemplation that, when she arrived, she couldn't recall having taken a single turn. She could, however, track the progress of her thoughts. There were three stages. First, Helen thought how lucky she and Charlie were not to have made anything weird. Second, that she didn't want to hurt her. And finally, that she didn't really *want* her, which—as soon as she thought it—she realised had been the starting thought all along. And with that, Helen came to her destination. To preserve their current state—unhurt, untethered—she would take care not to sleep with Charlie again.

—

ELEANOR SPENT THE first day of the new year oscillating between intense, vibrating anxiety, and an exhaustion so profound that it took all her energy just to keep a blink from turning into a nap.

The anxiety, at least, was stimulating. Her thoughts sped up. She chased herself around the New Year's Eve party, recalling every word and movement in an unsparing light. Eleanor longed to reject that former self, dismiss her as another person entirely, rather than have her walk around in the minds of Charlie and her friends, misrepresenting the brand *Charlie's older sister*. Eleanor saw that girl—that version of herself—through the eyes of Helen, standing in the kitchen, eating a nectarine. As Eleanor chewed through these memories, the juice sprayed everywhere, mocking her. Except when she was too tired to think. Then, she lay on her bed and scrolled on her phone, her eyes itchy and her limbs far away.

On the second day, her anxiety had only intensified. Eleanor googled the after-effects of ecstasy, in order to get a better sense of what she ought to be feeling. The effects of coming down were—with a symmetry so perfect as to be boring and predictable—the inverse of coming up. Where she had been energised and elated, she was now exhausted and deflated. Of course.

Eleanor lay in her bed with the curtains drawn for the second day in a row, a whole week stretching ahead before she had to go back to work. She browsed Netflix. She opened a list of recommendations she kept in her phone's notes, found that she read most of the titles in Mark's voice, and then spent two hours on the internet. The first of these was spent on Mark's profile, and the profile of his friends. Still, there was no information about that night or who the woman was. Eleanor feared that the trail was growing cold. So she spent the second hour reading the news, and tried to normalise the idea of living with a mystery.

Feeling no more relaxed, or decompressed or even *herself* for all that me-time, she closed her eyes and napped.

When she woke, she was disappointed to find that only twenty minutes had passed. It seemed she couldn't achieve anything at all.

She resolved to procure a better mood. To that end, she packed her bag and headed to the pool. If she turned time into fitness—if she optimised her leisure by improving her body—then her day could not be said to be a waste. This thought alone cheered her.

There was purpose in her stride as she walked past the wharves, the great navy ships docked squat and humourless on her right.

From this aspect, Sydney seemed another city entirely from the one she'd grown up in. It was larger, more ambitious. It took itself seriously. Skyscrapers topped with cranes, reaching always a little higher. Sandstone buildings and statues on horseback. Even the pool—light chlorine blue—was framed on two sides by the harbour. A pool on top of a pool.

The women's changeroom was never crowded: just the odd sag and flap, feet spongey against the tiles. Judging by the bodies that dotted the wooden deck around the pool, Eleanor could only imagine that the men's changeroom was tightly packed. Each lounging figure was uncompromisingly beautiful. They, too, took themselves seriously. Their neon-coloured budgie smugglers were often patterned like a challenge—cacti, eggplants, elephants with cartoonishly enlarged trunks. With their scowls, and the tight clutch of the polyester against their most important—and also most comic—parts, they dared you to laugh.

Eleanor did not go in for lounging. She coiled her hair beneath a lemon-coloured cap, which left a mark across her forehead. Her goggles had lost their suction, so she bashed them into her skull, one fist at each eye. Her face would be ringed for hours.

She always dived headfirst, her body a graceful arch from fingertips to toes. Given the end goal was total submersion, testing the waters seemed silly. Better to leap and take the shock of the cold everywhere at once. She saw people sitting on the edge, their feet flirting with the water, and saw how they were paralysed with choice. Deliberation was agony. This tortured, writhing dance:

the illusion of control. As if you could make the water warmer by thinking about it.

In the water, which was mild, Eleanor's thoughts splattered. She didn't think in sentences, or even images, but in rhythms. *One, two, three, four.* Every now and then, she would overtake the swimmer ahead, or race someone in the next lane. But even that brief relation to another person was soon consumed by the water, which thundered in her ears, and fogged her goggles, and brought her back, relentlessly, to herself. *One, two, three, four.*

At the end of her tenth lap, Eleanor didn't dive for a tumble turn but stopped, one hand clinging to the edge of the pool. She was in the deep end, and rested one foot on a slim ledge. With her other leg, she kicked to steady herself.

For the last four laps, she had become aware of a pain behind her left eye, like a wedge between the eyeball and its socket. She told herself it was the water in her eyes and ears that made her more aware of her own body. But when she removed her goggles, the pain intensified. It was a screwdriver now—thin and persistent. The sun was screaming at her, and seemed to appear in several places in the sky at once—bright white against the blue. She shut her eyes against it. When she opened them, the suns had joined, and the whole sky was white.

Eleanor pulled herself out of the pool, dragging her stomach behind her arms. She stumbled across the wooden boards to the fence opposite and crouched there, her back against warm glass, her head on her knees.

A hand was on her shoulder. She breathed heavily, and hoped it would go away.

'I'm fine,' she said. The sound was muffled through her knees. Her body an echo chamber.

The hand went away.

Eleanor tried to focus on her breathing. She adopted the same rhythm she had in the pool.

One, two, three, breathe.

One, two, three, breathe.

When the lightness in her head had receded, although the pain behind her eye was even more acute, she opened her eyes. There was one sun, and it was behind her. The pool was all primary colours: blue water, yellow lifeguards, red flags. She took another deep breath and stood. She became suddenly conscious that she was still wet, and looked at the puddle she'd made on the ground. Then she turned, leaned over the glass railing, and vomited.

She didn't hear it splash, but she saw it floating on the harbour below.

The hand was back on her shoulder. More tentative this time—just the pads of the fingers.

'You might have overdone it.'

Eleanor turned, squinting against the blinding brightness, and saw a face she recognised.

'Helen! Hey.'

Helen didn't remove her hand from Eleanor's shoulder. 'Are you okay?'

'Yeah, I'm fine. It's just a migraine.'

'Oh no. Are you sure you're alright?'

'I get them all the time. With my period. I normally take these hectic prescription painkillers, but I don't have any on me.'

The grip tightened. 'Where are they?'

'At home.'

'I'll drive you.'

'What? Don't be stupid.' Eleanor's back was flush against the glass fence. Beyond it, the harbour dropped at a distance of several metres. She was dizzy again and stretched her neck out, her head rolling back. To the sky, she said: 'I'm fine.'

Helen seemed unconvinced. 'It's no trouble.'

As Helen put an arm around Eleanor and walked her away from the fence, Eleanor said, 'Really. I live close. It's a short walk. You stay. Enjoy your day.'

'I am enjoying it.'

Eleanor was leaning on Helen more than she would like. She noticed that Helen was dry, and found her own dripping skin suddenly shameful. She gestured weakly to the water. 'But it's so nice here. It's such a nice day.'

'How's that sun going for you?'

Eleanor laughed. She had been walking gingerly, her eyes scrunched so tight against the sun that they were almost closed.

They reached the benches, and Eleanor pointed to her blue bag. She removed her towel and felt the sting of tears when Helen draped it around her shoulders and rubbed her dry. Like a toddler after a swimming lesson.

'Seriously,' Helen said, 'I'll drive you.' When Eleanor started to protest she spoke over the top of her. 'I'm not doing anything today. We're not all out here training for the Olympics.'

'What?'

'I saw those tumble turns.'

Eleanor smiled. 'I like to keep my rhythm.'

'At the risk of disturbing your rhythm, why don't I take you home and you can get some sleep.'

Eleanor looked at her feet and rubbed her eyes. Then she rubbed the goggle marks around her eyes to make it look less like she was crying.

—

IN THE CONFINES of the car, the sun was more discerning, and Helen was close enough to Eleanor to make out the white skin on her wrist where her watch usually sat. For the first time, Helen saw a stranger. Charlie was in her smile, but Eleanor wasn't smiling now: after telling Helen her address, she'd leaned her forehead against the window, her mouth downturned, her shoulders hunched. Her body wasn't Charlie's either. It was rounder and softer and, although it took up more space, it commanded less attention.

Helen recalled that she'd only met Eleanor once before. Twice, if the kitchen could be counted as a discrete encounter. Her own forced politeness as she turned the keys and tried to start a conversation spoke to their unfamiliarity.

'Do you swim here often?'

'Yeah. A few times a week.'

At these staccato sentences, Helen said, 'Sorry. You don't have to talk.'

'No, it's good. It's distracting. I'll close my eyes if that's okay but I'm listening.' Eleanor leaned her head back against the seat. As if to prove that she really was paying attention, she said, loudly now, 'And what about you? Do you go there often?'

'Not really, actually. I felt like it today. But normally I find it all very intense.'

'It is intense, isn't it? Too many Adonises.'

'Exactly. I feel like I'm on the set of *Olympia*.'

Eleanor laughed and, in her mirth, seemed to find genuine distraction. When she spoke again, it was in a softer voice, like she'd forgotten to pretend that she wasn't in pain. 'So where do you swim then?'

'The beach.'

'Beach girl!'

Eleanor's tone was tentatively teasing. Helen mocked herself, by way of encouragement. 'The tan's natural,' she said. 'Thanks for asking.'

'Which beach?'

'Wherever, really. I went to Gordons yesterday. I love it there.'

'Gordons. God, I haven't been there since high school.'

'Is that where you went to smoke doobies?'

This time, when Eleanor laughed, she opened her eyes, and turned to look at Helen. 'This might come as a shock,' she said, 'but doobies weren't really a feature of my high school experience.'

Eleanor didn't criticise herself in the usual way, snatching the joke off the shelf before someone else could take it. It seemed an invitation. So Helen said, 'But Charlie's so . . .'

'She's much cooler than me.'

'Didn't you go to school together?'

'Yeah, she was in the year below. People couldn't believe we were related. I was more into praise from adults than peers.'

'I'm sure that's ripe for psychoanalysis.' They'd stopped at a red light, which allowed Helen to face Eleanor. Even though her eyes were closed again, Helen persisted. 'Do you reckon that's still true? I mean, do you think you like to be seen as trustworthy and whatever?'

The silence was long enough that, to Helen, it seemed contemplative. Then, in a child's whine, Eleanor said: 'I don't know, I'm having a migraine.'

Although she'd clearly said it as a joke, Helen took her point: she was vulnerable enough. Helen felt a sudden urge to hug her, this girl who closed her eyes and leaned her head back in pain and then made jokes at her own expense so she wouldn't seem uncomfortable. To be so self-aware, so richly responsible for who you are and how you appear to others, rather than fumbling in the gap between them—no wonder she had a migraine.

Helen slowed the car to a crawl, and felt warmly towards every pedestrian who stalled their progress. They all looked summery and hopeful. 'Is it always this busy?'

'It's the most densely populated suburb in the country.'

'Get any *Rear Window* type action?' Because Eleanor didn't respond, Helen added, '*Rear Window*? The Hitchcock movie?'

With her eyes still on the road, Helen could see Eleanor's hand rise to cover her face. Worrying that her migraine had intensified, Helen placed her foot over the break, and turned to look at her.

Eleanor's eyes were open, and she hadn't moved to block out the light. Instead, her hand was at her mouth, stifling a laugh. 'My mind went straight to a different kind of rear action,' she said.

'Clutching my pearls!' It was Helen's turn to laugh. 'I would never. And *I* can't be blamed for your ignorance of a classic. It's amazing—you should watch it. It's about densely populated living and being too intimately acquainted with what your neighbours are up to.'

'Pre social media, obviously. Now we're all too intimately acquainted with what everyone's up to.'

'Social media isn't intimacy. People can control how they're perceived. That's performance.'

Eleanor pointed at an apartment building. Brown brick and thick wooden double doors. It looked like every other building on the block. 'Just here.'

Helen indicated. 'Sorry. Recommending Hitchcock films. Dissecting social media. What am I, a Soft Boy?'

'Soft Boys have good taste, though. Isn't that their charm?'

They had pulled over. Helen's gaze moved across Eleanor's face, drawing a triangle between eyes and lips. 'I wouldn't know,' she said.

'I just broke up with one. Take my word for it. Good taste was where the charm began and ended.'

With that, Eleanor got out of the car.

Even though the street was busy, Helen didn't drive off. She watched as Eleanor climbed the steps and entered her building—still watching for several seconds after she was gone and the heavy wooden doors had closed behind her.

—

ELEANOR WOKE HOURS later from a foggy-headed sleep. With cringing clarity, she reflected on the day: Helen's kindness, her own quick exit from the car. She hadn't even said thank you. Instead, she'd botched a joke and rushed upstairs to take her painkillers, before Helen had time to pity her any more. Even worse than this rudeness was the recollection of her poolside vulnerability, all wet and pathetic.

In an attempt at distraction, she picked up her laptop from the empty side of the bed and started browsing for something to watch.

Once, Mark had told Eleanor that a sure way to tell whether you were 'into' someone, or 'tuning' them, was if you took up their recommendations. Our lives were so content-saturated, he said. If you recommend something—a book, a TV show, a movie, a song—and the other person accepted that recommendation, they may very well want to sleep with you. The shorter the time between recommendation and uptake, the more carnal the intention.

One of the most uncomfortable things about looking back on that first hot week of January—worse than the guilt—was that Eleanor had to credit Mark with some insight.

That night, Eleanor watched *Rear Window*.

10

'YOU'RE CHOPPING.'

Charlie must have looked blank, because Helen felt the need to repeat herself. 'You're chopping.'

'I . . . um . . . should I take it from the top?'

'Yes. Less choppy.'

'Right.' Charlie paused. This audition was not going well.

Charlie had asked Helen to help her film a self-tape. A sheet of blue cardboard was stuck to the wall behind her; Helen and a ring light were in front, both glaring. Charlie wasn't sure which of the two was casting more judgement.

Like a New Year's resolution, Helen and Charlie's entanglement reached its climax on the last day of December and had been weakening ever since. It was now the third day of January, and Charlie had barely seen Helen since they all went to Gordons Bay. Helen's absence from the house—out all day, home late—only cemented her status at the centre of Charlie's psyche. Schemes to be alone with Helen dominated her thoughts.

First, Charlie toyed with the idea of 'losing' Petronella. She could imprison the bunny in a shoebox under her bed. A large one, with holes in it, so it would only be a little bit like being buried alive. Charlie suspected that she was plagiarising this plan from something she'd seen in a film—kidnapping a pet and enlisting a potential love interest to rescue it had a derivative sound to it. She was pretty sure it featured in a favourite teen movie. While, in principle, there was nothing wrong with treating her life like a movie, Charlie would prefer it to be a classic. Or, at least, a film about adults.

So Charlie held herself to a higher standard than a horny teen, and now adopted an uncharacteristically rational approach. Treating passion like a science experiment, she was trying to replicate the original test conditions. Helen's interest in Charlie was first aroused, it seemed, when they worked together on the play. Perhaps Charlie just needed to present as a pliant object to be directed—but in a sexy way.

So that was how Charlie came to be in her bedroom—her face at once sweaty and flaky with make-up—with twenty takes under her belt, and nothing but an iPhone suspended on a tripod separating her from Helen.

The takes were bad, though, and Charlie was feeling more deluded than desired. It seemed the most pathetic, useless pastime in the world: to act, and fail to convince. All the more so because the audition was important. It was for the lead role in a new Australian play, commissioned by the biggest theatre company in the country. So, by all usual metrics—prestige, size of role, quality of script—it was important. More relevantly, it was important to Helen.

The play was being produced by the same company that Helen worked for, except she worked in the box office, and wanted so desperately to work in the theatre. When Charlie had messaged Helen about the audition, she'd said (with lots of exclamation marks) of course she would help. They'd arranged a time, and Helen had texted to confirm, all of which seemed very formal, given that they were meeting in their own home. When Helen knocked on Charlie's door, and Charlie asked whether her outfit was okay, Helen said she looked beautiful, in a tone of professional neutrality, like it was an objective fact.

From there, Charlie's plan unravelled.

Charlie had never been able to act in front of Helen, or in front of any of the people she loved. Helen, Eleanor, her mother—she could only perform if they were faceless behind the glow of the stage lights. Perhaps it was impossible, always, to exist as a vessel for other people, after being held, gently cupped, cradled in a particular embrace. Charlie could not cloak herself in a fictional personality while Helen's probing eyes stripped her to her essential, inescapable self. And as if to emphasise her failings, after each bungled take, Helen said, 'I really want this for you.'

Now she said, 'When you're ready.' Directors only said this when *they* were ready.

It really was extremely hot. They'd opened the door for airflow, but sweat still clung to Charlie's skin, like she was rolled in Glad Wrap. Helen's forehead was shiny, and the gap between Helen's finger and her phone screen was tiny and impatient.

'Okay, I'm ready.' Charlie hoped that saying it aloud might make it true. This time, she told herself, the take would be perfect.

'I hope you're sitting down. You're going to shit an absolute brick—'

Helen cried out as the bedroom door swung back, hitting her in the arm. Mandy stopped talking as soon as she saw that they were filming. Her ponytail was so tight, it was enlisting the rest of her face into a stressed expression.

'You okay?' Charlie dropped her hands to her sides, out of the position she'd assumed for her last, perfect take.

'Oh yeah, it's good news. About the comedy festival.'

Charlie felt a little kick of disappointment, and then shame, like backwash, for taking her friend's success so badly.

'So I was talking to my agent—' Mandy's agent was a staple in any anecdote. She couldn't go to the toilet without bringing her agent into it.

Helen coughed. 'Mandy, just before you rip in, do you mind if we get this last take? Charlie's doing an audition.'

'Oh, don't worry.' Mandy sat cross-legged on the bed and looked up at Charlie. 'You'll get it.'

'Thanks.'

Helen found Mandy's support for women in the arts so immediate and undiscerning as to be unprincipled. 'You don't even know what the audition is for. She could be auditioning for King Lear.'

Mandy lay back, her shoes on the bed. 'A girl can manifest. Also, if it's for King Lear'—here she waved a hand in Charlie's direction—'he's a lot sluttier than I remember.'

Charlie was wearing her usual audition outfit—a white ribbed singlet with no bra. Her collarbones were eloquent, turning thinness into a fashion statement. It was also simple enough that, if she didn't get the part, she could always console herself by saying that she could have tried harder.

'Can we just get it over with?' she said, looking at Helen.

Helen clapped once, with authority. 'Last take, let's go.'

'You won't even know I'm here,' Mandy said, just in case anyone had forgotten her presence.

Charlie took a deep breath, while Helen whispered 'come on, last one' with all the confidence of a prayer.

'Have you guys seen my fanny pack?'

'Seriously?' Charlie had only just stuck her courage to the camera when Kevin's head popped through the door Mandy had left open.

Helen's hands were on her hips. 'You're kidding.'

'We're filming something,' said Mandy, as if only an idiot would fail to notice.

'It's important.' Kevin closed the door behind him, and lowered his voice to a whisper as if to prevent someone overhearing from the next room. Given that every resident was now crammed on or near Charlie's bed, this struck his housemates as a bit paranoid. 'That fanny pack is chock-a-block with diccy-bickies.'

'I think I saw it in the fruitbowl.' Mandy stood, her ponytail swinging ferociously. 'Let's look.'

When the door closed behind them, Helen looked from the iPhone to Charlie. 'We've probably got enough, don't you reckon?'

Deciding that obliging Helen would impress her more than doing a really sensational final take, Charlie repurposed her camera smile. 'Sure. Thank you.' Helen removed Charlie's phone from the tripod and placed it on the bed.

Now that they were alone, the room felt smaller and the silence loud.

Helen broke it: 'That's exciting for Mandy—that she's got some comedy festival gig.'

'Yeah,' Charlie said, although *exciting* wasn't really the word. She was responding in her usual way to a friend enjoying success in the arts: by concentrating very hard on not wanting to die. She sat on the edge of the bed and tried to give the impression of being normal and mature. 'I wonder what it is. Maybe she's got a solo gig or something?'

Helen remained standing. 'Who knows.'

A vibrating purr distracted both of them. Helen pulled her phone out of her back pocket and looked at the caller ID. The smile Charlie had been looking for all afternoon appeared.

'You should get that.'

'All good,' Helen said. 'I'll reply later.' She folded the tripod, then picked it up, tossing it and catching it—a little exclamation mark. Although it sounded sincere, her goodbye was muffled because she was already halfway out the door and didn't turn to look back at Charlie. Instead, she said to the empty corridor: 'I really hope you get this one!'

—

THE PREVIOUS NIGHT, when dusk revealed herself—all pink and creamy—Helen had messaged Eleanor.

Are you alive?

Helen found her on Facebook, via Charlie's friends list. As the hours passed and there was no response, Helen reminded herself that messages from strangers went into a separate inbox. It was entirely plausible that Eleanor hadn't seen it. It was plausible, too, that she was ignoring Helen.

It was not until that morning, when Helen was helping Charlie with her audition, that her phone vibrated with a reply.

All better, thank you! Drugs are glorious!

Helen read the message as soon as the notification appeared on her screen, but she waited until she was alone in her room to open it in the app. It wasn't shame that compelled her to hide the text from Charlie. She was motivated by desire. The message made her feel like a plucked violin string and all she wanted was to savour it in private.

Sitting cross-legged on her unmade bed, she typed out a reply.

You've changed your tune

The little circle confirmed that Eleanor had opened the message. Then Helen saw the three dots dance.

I was addicted to opioids in high school

THAT'S what you were doing at Gordons Bay!

It's a beautiful spot to shoot up

Helen replied with a photo from her phone of Gordons Bay, taken from the cliffs. The rocks hugged a turquoise sea. Eleanor love-heart-reacted.

Ugh! I miss it. I should go while I'm still on holiday

When do you go back to work?

Next week

Tomorrow?

No like the week after
Next Monday

No I meant do you want to go to Gordons tomorrow? It's meant to be super nice weather

The seconds before Eleanor replied were the silence that anticipates a bang. The three dots moved, indicating that Eleanor was drafting a reply. It took so long, Helen had time to re-read their conversation from the top. The last few messages—inviting her to the beach, then spelling it out a second time—made her cringe. But Helen knew from experience that it didn't pay to be coy about your desires—especially when those desires pertained to women who'd recently dated men.

Great idea

This was difficult to interpret. It was polite, unpunctuated. It recalled the hollow click of the passenger door; how quickly Eleanor had leaped out of Helen's car. Just when she'd told herself not to overthink it, Eleanor double-texted.

Keen!!

One exclamation mark might have been polite. But two! Two induced a popping, world-righting fizz in Helen's bloodstream.

—

MEANWHILE, IN HER bedroom on the other side of the wall she shared with Helen, Charlie sat at her desk, an email open on her laptop.

Unlike Helen's room, where the window was always ajar and sun streamed in, Charlie's was dark and breezeless. Her laptop cast an eerie light.

The email subject line read: *Seasons Greetings etc.* The body was a description, in several hundred words, of Mark Chapman's Christmas plans. He didn't mention the break-up, or Eleanor, except to say that his relatives kept asking after her. He skewered his family, but saved the most eviscerating observations for himself. His thoughts didn't flow, exactly. There was too much punctuation for that: brackets, and asides, and caveats. But Charlie didn't mind that the care he took was undisguised. It seemed designed to flatter and entertain her at the same time. Like she was worth the effort.

The email had been with her for days. She felt its presence whenever she was alone, even when she wasn't on her laptop or her phone. Another creature in the room, staring at her. Before the break-up, Charlie would start drafting her replies to Mark as soon as she received an email. It might take her several days to press 'send' but she'd clutch the draft to her chest, stroke and pet it, until, with a thrill, it was time to let go.

She never once told Eleanor what she and Mark were doing. In hindsight, that secrecy looked sneaky and self-serving. But it was less deliberate at the time. Their correspondence was so intensely private, it was as if it existed in another world. Like dreams or thoughts that are not voiced, it seemed impossible that it could impact anyone—even Eleanor. Sure, it meant a lot, because their writing was intimate and sincere. But it also meant nothing, because they wrote in that strangely formal, anachronistic medium, which allowed them to draft on their phone at any time of the day and edit closely on a computer later. Or to scroll back through the whole chain and quote their former selves, as if each new email competed with those that came before. In this way, they never just had a conversation: they were always playing a game.

In the days following the break-up, however, those emails took the very real shape of Eleanor's distress. It seemed obvious now that they'd never achieved privacy at all. There was no fantasy world of their own making: not when Eleanor was real and good and trusting. She'd been present all along. And although they hadn't, in fact, betrayed her—not in the way she'd feared—Charlie still felt implicated. They might not have acted on it in the basest, most obvious way, but they felt things for each other, and though they hadn't seen each other naked, they'd certainly stripped bare. The sadder Eleanor seemed, the more Charlie and Mark's secrecy soured, until on Christmas, she'd confessed. And in the days since, *Seasons Greetings etc.*—open but undeleted—looked out from her inbox with an accusatory stare.

It was only now, on the third day of the year, when her room was hot and dark and she was too lonely to think beyond it that she finally got around to drafting a reply. She wrote about Helen.

By the time she'd rearranged the sentences, deleted some adjectives and found synonyms for others, Charlie had a clearer picture of her than she'd had when they'd stood together in the same room on either side of the tripod.

She had not written how her stomach turned when Helen entered the room, how her mouth dried, and how her voice sounded distant and her body felt far away. How Helen's every movement registered physically in Charlie's skin—her feet shuffling between takes; her head tilting as she watched; the soft underside of her wrist exposing itself when she reached for the phone.

Instead, she'd told Mark that she liked herself best when she was with Helen. It was only natural, Charlie wrote, that their relationship would intensify, and complicate into the new year, because Helen's wide, curious eyes rendered Charlie intelligent, and full of multitudes, when they looked her way.

And once she'd written it—and pressed *send*—Charlie started to believe it might be true.

Mark's response was very quick. It came within an hour. Charlie had not left her room.

He was very interested, he said, that Charlie liked herself best around Helen. It was interesting because, for a long time, he had thought of love as concentric circles. At the centre—very tight—was care for yourself. He wondered whether loving someone else romantically meant pushing that smallest circle outwards, or whether it was just a case of letting someone else into it. Maybe we love people, he said, because they become extensions of ourselves.

Then—because that was his style—he began to doubt himself. That theory of love didn't cohere at all with his theory of sex, he admitted. (Uncharacteristically, he neglected to mock himself for having a theory of either.)

Mark wrote that when he had sex with someone he loved, there was always a moment when he focused so intently on his own body, he actually forgot who he was—as a *person*, he said. *It's like I don't exist—I don't have a self—I'm just a physical thing.* He asked her whether she thought that was true; whether that's what they really were: physical things.

Initially, these musings thrilled her. It was as if their correspondence had justified itself. It felt so good, it couldn't be wrong. When Charlie wrote to Mark, she could leap and know he'd always catch her. And, like a dance, although they comprised the conversation—they were its constituent parts—it also existed on its own terms: as a work of art. It would be like squandering a talent, not to email Mark anymore.

After a few days, although she was still thinking about it often, she deleted his last email. Because it occurred to her that when Mark spoke of love—of sex—he must have been talking about her sister.

11

ELEANOR FOUND THE experience of messaging Helen—even just about their plans to go to the beach—at once sickening and thrilling. Like standing at a railing, peering over the edge. If it was fun, it was only because it was somehow wrong—scraping the limits of control.

It was greedy, she thought, to leap into this fray when Charlie was already involved. Eleanor had seen them together on New Year's Eve: the touches, the way Charlie looked at Helen, how beautiful and slim they appeared—two champagne glasses that chimed when knocked together, and would shatter under pressure.

It was no comfort that Charlie had described their relationship as 'casual'. If 'casual' meant *transactional*—which, to Eleanor's mind, it always did—then Charlie's problem was that she traded too much. Eleanor knew how hard her sister fell: how she always seemed, in a dramatic, aesthetic way, to admire the shape of her body, squandered at the bottom of the pit. Like slowing down to look at the site of a collision—to mark the colour of blood; how far one wheel has spun from another—Charlie always had time to admire her own pain. Therefore, Eleanor had no doubt that hanging out with Helen would hurt her sister. She just wasn't sure that it *should*—whether, objectively, Charlie was entitled to feel that way.

It was true, Charlie liked Helen a lot. But liking someone wasn't the same as owning them—it didn't preclude other people liking them too. Maybe, Eleanor thought, she shouldn't bend to every feeling Charlie had, only to the reasonable ones. What was the alternative? The tyranny of sensitivity.

Instead of avoiding Helen for Charlie's sake, Eleanor decided to pursue Helen, and avoid getting caught. She could see that lying to Charlie—at least, by omission—probably made her a bad sister. She thought she could live with that: she could cope with the knowledge that she *was* a bad person, as long as nobody else *thought* she was.

With this unsavoury realisation, Eleanor told herself that she could still cancel. She was only peering over the railing. She hadn't jumped yet.

Not wanting to cancel, not wanting to tell Charlie, and not wanting to do the wrong thing, she didn't reply to Helen's message:

> *What time in the morning?*

Eleanor resolved to respond after dinner. A full belly and wise counsel might make the decision for her.

—

THE BULL & HORN in Redfern opened every day at noon. The same family had owned it for decades, and had watched the university campus creep closer and higher—the locals replaced by stray students and, during the holidays, empty chairs. These days, a weekday shift in January was guaranteed to be slow and depressing. Sunshine did the Bull & Horn no favours. It washed out the light from the pokies—an anaemic yellow stain on the carpet—and it rendered the rest of the interiors strangely fraudulent.

Wooden booths with cracked leather cushions. A bar with a sheen that looked like wood polish, but to the accidental touch felt like several years of overspilling foam.

So it was not unusual that, at seven pm on an offensively sunny Monday, there was only one customer in the Bull & Horn. What was unusual, however, was that the customer was a priest.

The bartender did not know this, because the priest was not wearing his dog collar—just chinos and a button-up shirt. But his manner may have given him away. He spoke in that calming cadence of the cloth—as hushed as a whisper, but audible in the very back pew. Even the words, 'Just a jug of Tooheys, please. Three glasses,' managed to convey a spiritual authority.

He waited with the empty glasses and the full jug for several minutes. It would be rude, he thought, to start without them.

The beer was starting to look particularly golden, and the bubbles inviting, when Eleanor walked into the bar. She was wearing a linen dress and carrying a jacket. She saw him straight away.

'Hi Dad.'

He kissed her on the cheek. Or attempted to. She turned away, so they glanced off each other.

He looked older, she thought, than the last time she'd seen him. The skin around his neck sagged.

'It's so good to see you, Eleanor.' He spoke with his hands, palms wide and open to heaven. It seemed an unnecessary, proselytising motion. As if either of them needed to be convinced.

'You too.'

Eleanor sat down and let the situation structure their interaction. They were sharing a meal. There was a program to get through.

'Is beer okay? You're sure you wouldn't like a wine?'

'Oh no, don't be silly. Thank you. Let me know how much I owe you.'

'Nonsense.'

Then they sipped their beers, looked down at the menu, and her father asked, although she'd never been there, whether she knew what was good.

Eleanor began to relax. Drinks in hand, she and her father could talk about nothing—each as polite and attentive as the other—protected by pleasantries from their mutual fear: that they had nothing to talk about.

With their careful cordiality, they more closely resembled strangers than family. Eleanor told him the bare facts of her life, uncoloured by personal reflections. They traded stories about other people; the world around them. Whatever opinions they expressed, they held their own lives at arm's length, so if they argued, it was without stakes.

'And how's Mark?'

'Oh, sorry,' Eleanor tipped her glass back, finishing her beer, and reached for the jug. 'I probably haven't told you. We broke up.'

'I'm very sorry to hear that. The ends of relationships are awful.'

Eleanor's gaze remained on the jug. 'Honestly, it was fine. It was for the best.'

Her father nodded slowly. He rubbed his lips together, his mouth thin and inexpressive. From his sharp intake of breath, Eleanor anticipated a sermon.

'I always thought he had the hair of a man with a bad conscience.'

Eleanor's laugh surprised her while she was taking a generous gulp of beer. She coughed. 'Am I supposed to know what that means?'

'That hair was trying to atone for something.'

They were both laughing now. He always managed to laugh without emitting a sound: his lips pressed together, shaking shoulders betraying him, his amusement accompanied by a look which made the joke very private, as if laughing were an indulgence, and you, having tempted him, were now in on the secret.

Eleanor struggled to remember a time when her affection for her father, and his for her, was not expressed with such reserve and politeness. If he were more paternal, she might have been more filial towards him: emotionally manipulative; demanding; resentful. As it was, he taught her how to love from a studied distance, and what she felt, overwhelmingly, was a sense of duty. She didn't see her father as a personality but as an ego—an idea of himself—which it was her responsibility to protect.

—

WHEN HER PARENTS were still together, Eleanor's father was the head of English at a school where everything was crested, from socks to the carpet outside the auditorium. Eleanor won a scholarship there starting from year six, and Charlie changed schools too. At the time, it made perfect sense: where Eleanor went, Charlie followed. As she grew older, Eleanor realised that Charlie—not having a scholarship—was probably there by virtue of her sister and her father: a staff or sibling discount, or some combination of the two. Oddly, this fact made Eleanor sick with guilt.

Together, wearing backpacks almost as large as they were, and with their fussy socks and ribbons in their hair, Eleanor and Charlie and their father took a bus and a train to school every morning. There were four routes to choose from. On the way home, Charlie was allowed to choose. On the way there, they never had the time.

At some point—bus, or train, or both—Charlie cried, and she spent every lunchtime looking for Eleanor, because she didn't like her sandwich and wanted to swap. The sandwiches were always identical.

In the afternoons, they were allowed to go and wait in their father's office until he'd finished for the day. The office was full of books, which Eleanor liked to pull down and say: *Have you really read this one? What about all the ones at home?* Yes, he'd say. Those too. And in answer to the question: *Which one's the best?* he'd say, Read it Eleanor, and tell me what you think.

At the end of their first term there, Eleanor's father lost his job.

Eleanor knew the reason, because the apartment wasn't large, although her parents thought they were whispering. He had been watching porn on the computer in his office. Eleanor googled *porn* on her phone and, watching a clip, her skin grew hot, and she wondered if she would be expelled. Then she googled: *how to delete google searches.* Charlie was in a different room, wearing headphones at the time, and their parents were talking quietly, and Eleanor deleted her search so Charlie didn't find out.

She heard her father say: *I don't know how they knew.* To which their mother replied: *To me, you getting caught isn't the main issue.*

They fought a lot. Charlie always seemed to have her headphones on.

Eventually, he left, and as soon as their mother was back to normal, Eleanor and Charlie started going to a different school, closer to home, with boys as well as girls.

Charlie often asked Eleanor—especially in her final year, when Eleanor put a post-it note of her dream ATAR above her bed—whether she wished they'd stayed at that other school. Eleanor said of course not, because they both would have gotten eating disorders, and Charlie probably wouldn't have had a boyfriend or a girlfriend 'almost constantly' since she was thirteen.

Meanwhile, their father sought help. Not from his wife, who, for all her faults, spent her whole career helping people, but from God. And not a new-age God either—the Church of England. His was the church of thinking and theologising; he published academic papers and quoted Thomas Aquinas on Radio National.

It wasn't the newfound faith, or even God, that Eleanor found difficult to wrap her head around. Most of her friends were Christian, and she envied their community—Seb's family was Greek Orthodox; Mark had gone to a Catholic school. It was how her father had arrived at it. His humbling was so complete—from disgraced teacher to eager pupil—it looked, to Eleanor, like vanity. Like it wasn't enough to learn from his mistakes: everyone had to see how much he'd improved. The evidence was in his degree, and the Ministerial Development Program, and finally, in ordination.

And so she pitied him for his fragility, and his need to cover it in robes, and she managed his expectations—and although he was clever and insightful and seemed to understand her, she couldn't help but suspect that he might be a bit insane.

—

TODAY, ELEANOR WAS managing her father's expectations of his other daughter.

'Is Charlie on her way?'

Eleanor had not told her father that Charlie wasn't coming. To be fair, Charlie had only texted that afternoon to say she needed more time to work on her big audition. It was one of those rare situations when being proved correct gave Eleanor no satisfaction.

When their father had texted weeks ago to say he'd be in Sydney at the start of January, Charlie had let Eleanor reply on her behalf:

Sounds great. We'd love to see you!

Charlie, meanwhile, had texted Eleanor:

Ugh do we have to?

Yes

Why

He's your father

Yours too

Eleanor had sad-reacted that.

Now, because Eleanor could see her father's reaction, and could see it was sad indeed, she really laid it on thick.

'She's preparing an audition. She only found out about the role today, and she's really stressed. It's the biggest thing she's ever gone for. And she's had such a hard year. Two years. She said to give you her apologies. She was really disappointed she couldn't make it.'

Charlie had expressed no such regret. Instead, she'd said: *So sorry Eleanor! Lollies you!* It was lies like this, Eleanor thought, that enabled Charlie. Her big sister always there to defend her.

'She falls down hard, that girl.'

'Yes.' Eleanor picked up the empty beer jug. 'Same again?'

Her father didn't respond. His hands still clasped in front of him, he stared at them with an inward, unfocused look. 'It just makes it all the more remarkable that she tries again.'

'Shall I order food?'

He looked at Eleanor. 'You're lucky, Eleanor. You're very robust.'

At the bar, Eleanor ordered another jug and two chicken schnitzels, at her father's request. He'd given her his card, but Eleanor used her own. It wasn't generosity that motivated her, but a need to withhold something.

His last comment scratched at her. *Very robust.* With his priestly tones, he implied a moral lesson in every observation. *You're very robust* became: *You ought to be kinder to Charlie.* Or more patient. Or more sympathetic. Or all of the above. He couldn't state how something *was* without suggesting, in that stage-whispered knowing tone, how it *should* be.

Back at the table, Eleanor ripped into the second jug of beer. By the time they'd finished their schnitzels, her father had bought a third. Without either of them really noticing—without the straight angle of his back even slightly relaxing—they were both getting drunk.

'Dad? When you and Mum were married . . .' Eleanor found herself, with a liquid tongue, ready to fill all lulls in conversation.

Her father pushed his clean plate away and made a sound like, 'Hm,' which was reluctant, but only playfully. He flicked at the edge of a cardboard coaster, the corner fraying beneath his touch.

'Did you ever have an affair?'

The hand on the coaster stilled, but he continued to stare at it. After a long pause, he let out a little exhale, which might have been a scoff, or a laugh. It was too quiet to tell.

'I'm going to be honest, Eleanor.' He removed his glasses, and she felt her heart quicken, as if she were waiting at the door to the principal's office. 'I resent the accusation.'

'It wasn't an accusation. I was just asking a question.'

'But the question contains an accusation.' He continued to study the coaster, as if its surface were reflective. 'Not that I did it, necessarily—but that I'm capable of it.'

'I'm sorry. You split up a long time ago. I just thought . . .'

He looked at her now, with a smile that brought relief. 'There are other ways to ruin a marriage, believe me.'

Emboldened by the smile, Eleanor asked, 'Did *she* ever cheat on *you*?'

To her surprise, he laughed, and sat up straighter, as if to inspect her from a greater height. 'What's all this? No. No, for all our faults, I don't think we had it in us. I think it probably requires a certain . . .'

'Selfishness?'

'I was going to say: impulsiveness.'

To her horror, Eleanor felt her throat tighten. It didn't help that her father reached a hand out across the table. Eleanor withdrew hers to her lap.

'Have you been worried about this for a while?'

Eleanor managed a nod.

His hand still on the table, he watched Eleanor as she tossed her drink back, although it was already empty, and swallowed the dregs. When she placed the glass back down, she met his eyes. Hers were glassy and mortified.

'Has your mother said anything to this effect?'

'No.' Eleanor shook her head. 'No. This is all me. All my doing.'

There was a long silence, in which they both stared at the table. Eleanor was about to ask her father a question about his conference. Understanding that small talk was his idea of dignity, she was eager to resume.

Instead, her father broke the silence first. 'People talk about forgiveness, Eleanor,' he said, 'like it's letting someone off the hook. But forgiving yourself is hard. It's a kind of torture, to give up on this idea of yourself . . .'

'What idea?' Eleanor leaned forward. His voice, no longer that professional whisper, was now oddly quiet. She strained for each word.

'To admit that you're flawed. It's very humbling. Forgiving other people is easy. It's playing God. It's very, very hard to forgive yourself. You have to put your hand up and say: *I'm just human. The same as everybody else.* That's very difficult.'

'I'm not sure I deserve forgiveness, Dad.' He started to protest so she sped up, speaking over the top of him. 'I know it's hard work and whatever, and you probably know a lot more about this than I do, but I just can't help but see forgiveness as an indulgence. Surely you don't deserve forgiveness if you know what you're doing is wrong, but you do it anyway?'

She looked up.

His face was slack, his mouth open slightly. He shook his head, very sadly. 'Don't get me wrong, I don't think I *deserve* forgiveness.'

Eleanor noticed, for the first time, how each of his words ran into the next. 'What?'

'I wish very much that we had made it work. Some people do, don't they?' On the question, he banged his fist on the table.

'I meant me, Dad. I . . .' She couldn't look at him. 'I'm lying to Charlie. There's this person she's been seeing—it's not like Charlie *owns* her, I don't think they're technically together or anything—but I think Charlie would be devastated if she knew I was seeing her too. So, I'm just waiting to see where it goes. If it goes nowhere, then no harm done—just awkward for me for thinking we were flirting. But if it . . . I'll look really duplicitous, I think, if it turns out I lied from the start.'

He said nothing.

'I should tell Charlie, shouldn't I? That's the right thing to do?'

Eleanor leaned forward, and tilted her head, so her ear was close to her father. Bent, straining, begging for advice. A prohibition would be ideal. *Don't see that woman.* Then doing the right thing would be as simple as doing what she was told.

Her father didn't reply. He was still staring into his beer. Eleanor waited for several unnatural seconds before she noticed that his eyes were not downcast: they were closed.

She could not pinpoint when, exactly, he had fallen asleep.

—

THE NEXT DAY, Eleanor received a text from her father. As always, it was laid out like a letter. It did not acknowledge that she had ordered an Uber to take him back to his hotel. Or that he had leaned on her arm as he stumbled out of the pub, so much so that she almost fell and bruised her leg as she passed a wooden table. Or that she had ridden to the hotel with him, and walked him into the lobby, and then into the lift.

Of course, even if he could remember any of that, he could not know what it was like to see him slumped on the bed in a dark hotel room—dimly lit and mothball-smelling—and see heavy breaths move his chest. He didn't know, either, that she'd watched him for several minutes, and said for the first time in years, 'I love you.' Because, seeing him so small—his neck sagging and his wrinkled fingers splayed, palms up to the ceiling—it was true. She loved him.

He said:

Hi Girls,

Lovely to see you yesterday, Eleanor. We must go for Round 2 the next time I'm down.

Charlie, that's very exciting about your upcoming audition. Chookas is what they say, I believe.

Love,
Dad X

And Eleanor, the only sister to reply, wrote:

Thanks Dad! Good to see you too!

12

THE WEATHER ON Tuesday morning was, as Helen had predicted, super nice. The sun was generous, and when Eleanor went for a walk in the morning, Rushcutters Bay Park was traffic-light green. There was a storm forecast for the afternoon, but for now the sky was all smiles.

Eleanor took her towel out of her blue, chlorine-smelling pool bag and rolled it up into her *New Yorker* tote. Then, thinking that she did not want to look like the kind of person who carried the tote but didn't read the magazine—or, worse, the kind of person who thought that reading the magazine *was* an accessory, a personal brand—she removed the towel.

Eleanor's phone vibrated. A text from Helen.

Outside!

In a patch of sunlight, Eleanor saw a green reusable bag from the supermarket. She had brought it with her to the New Year's Eve party—full of beers on arrival, and full of discarded hat and tiny sunglasses on departure. It looked nonchalant—not in a studied way; more in a grocery-shopping way. Eleanor crammed her towel into it, and hurried out the door.

—

FOR THE SECOND time in three days, Helen had Charlie's sister in her passenger seat. This time, the car felt even smaller. Eleanor was not leaning against the window in pain. She was sitting upright, her knees neatly together, her head turned to look at Helen.

They quickly resumed the easy, teasing rhythm they'd found that day at the pool.

Eleanor asked Helen how she met Charlie (at drama school) and how she got into drama school (submitted a portfolio). Theatre, Helen said, was something she'd always wanted to do. 'I know it's a cliché,' she added, 'but I quite literally *always* felt that if I wasn't working in theatre, or some kind of creative job, I'd be wasting my time on Earth. That sounds grandiose—'

'No, no.' Eleanor thought it sounded very grandiose.

'—but I didn't think that waste would be particularly important. Like, I didn't think it was morally urgent to do what I was passionate about, or anything. My parents certainly didn't.'

'What do they do?'

Helen waved her hand. 'They have a newsagency in Maitland. Like, they're good people—my father has worked extremely hard for us all—but in a "getting on with things" sort of way. Like, if I told Dad I wasn't "passionate" about my career, he'd tell me to take a hike.'

'I think my mother sometimes feels that way about Charlie.'

'Well, yeah, it's a pretty reasonable take. I mean, I did a law degree—that's how I know *Mark*.' Without intending to, she said his name like a stage name. Or like she had scoured the internet for photos of him and studied them, trying to understand what Eleanor had found so attractive. 'Anyway,' she continued, hoping she didn't sound flustered, 'I only bring that up to say that I dropped out when I got into a proper drama school. Like, I didn't chase my dreams willy-nilly is the moral of this story.'

'How pragmatic.'

'You say that like it's not a compliment.'

'Oh, it is. Actually'—Eleanor paused, 'there's nothing I respect more.'

'Nothing!' Helen laughed. 'What about, like, empathy? Or selflessness?'

'That's a style of pragmatism, surely. Being realistic about the fact that you're not important, in the scheme of things.'

'Right? That's such a good way of putting it.' Helen took her left hand off the steering wheel and reached across the console to touch Eleanor's arm, as if to enact the meeting of their thoughts. 'So, am I allowed to ask what happened with Mark?'

They talked about him for the rest of the drive. Not the break-up, or how it affected Eleanor, but Mark as a character.

As they talked, Helen was struck all over again by how unlike her sister Eleanor was.

Whenever Helen talked to Charlie about other people—like Mandy, or people from the play—she could feel Charlie withdrawing, like Helen's opinions were alienating, or revealed something cruel. It was as if Charlie thought that being a good person meant never saying anything bad about anyone. Or that you couldn't analyse someone without judging them—without assuming a superior position. Helen, who was genuinely interested in other people, certainly didn't consider herself superior to anyone. She just didn't think you could get to the bottom of people without dissecting their flaws. Eleanor seemed to share this curiosity. Yes, she was quick to the point, and unsparing in her view of others, but she could also be eviscerating about herself. Before they'd even reached the beach she interrupted herself (she was describing Mark's habit of mistaking depression for depth) to say: 'God, we're such bitches.'

Helen nodded and took even that statement in the spirit it was offered: not as criticism, but as observation.

As they made their way from the street down to the bay, they both took the sea for granted. Although it glittered and was glorious, neither of them commented. They were too caught up in the pure, dizzying pleasure of good conversation. They both felt that their minds—the places previously impenetrable to other people—were shared and, yet, at the same time, were no less unique for being shared. Instead, each of them only felt more special for having found the other.

When they took off their clothes and arranged their bodies over towels, their conversation lulled. Eleanor was wearing a one-piece swimsuit made from a thick knitted material. Helen took a photo of her on her film camera and said the day was stunning, although it wasn't the day she was thinking about.

Eleanor, conscious that they had spent the car ride discussing her recent relationship drama, brought the conversation back around to Helen's career. 'So what is it about theatre, do you reckon?'

'I don't know,' Helen said. 'It's hard to articulate. I feel like it's an embarrassing thing to be so obsessed with. Like I never grew up, or something. And it can feel almost cultish. Like it's a huge part of some people's lives, but a lot of people just don't like it.'

Eleanor had, of course, already outed herself as one such person the very first time they'd met. Helen seemed to have no recollection of their bathroom bump-in and Eleanor wasn't about to remind her. Instead, she said: 'You're not going to convert anyone with that attitude.'

'I think it's like convincing someone to be attracted to someone they're not. It's beyond argument, you know?'

'For sure. Like how you can objectively see that someone is beautiful without finding them hot?'

'Or the opposite,' Helen said.

'Like, be attracted to someone even though you can rationally acknowledge all their flaws?'

'Exactly.'

Helen's arms were covered in a pleasant, dewy sweat. She was almost at the perfect temperature for a swim—when cool water would hit her skin like it was quenching a thirst. They were both sitting up, facing the ocean. In front of them, a sinewy woman with very short hair laughed as her feet touched the water. Her smile was a string of pearls.

'Now *she's* beautiful,' Eleanor said.

'And hot?'

Helen studied Eleanor's face, looking for a ripple—any proof that her comment had weight; that they weren't talking about this woman, specifically, but all women. Eleanor wouldn't meet her gaze.

'I mean,' she said, 'I wouldn't kick her out of bed.'

They agreed then that it was time to get in.

—

AFTER THEIR SWIM Eleanor lay on her back and tried to look relaxed. To that end, she blocked out the sun by covering her face with her shorts.

She was feeling foolish for spending three hundred dollars on a swimsuit just because she'd seen it on social media. Helen was wearing a black bikini. Rather, she was perfecting a black bikini. It wasn't so much the shape of her body, but the casual ease with which it served her that struck Eleanor. Her legs were long and strong, and she had the kind of stomach—firm but not crunched flat—which suggested a healthy life, independent of a gym.

The clouds assembled as forecast just after twelve. They pushed their sunglasses to the tops of their heads, and tried to ignore the weather. When the first drops fell—heavy and individual—they wiped phones and camera on their towels, and put them in Eleanor's green bag. It was only when thunder interrupted their conversation—shrieks from the surrounding sunbathers—that they finally relented.

'How's this for a plan?' Eleanor said. 'We go get burgers, you drive me home, and we eat them there.'

'At your place?'

Eleanor didn't look at her. There was an allusion in Helen's tone which eye contact could only confirm. Eleanor chose to ignore it. She nodded, and threw her towel over her shoulder.

'Sure.' Helen sounded like a voiceover—jarringly bright amid the greying bay.

Helen was just the type of person who usually rendered Eleanor insecure. Her very existence made Eleanor feel narrow-minded and conformist. Today, for example, she wore purple Crocs without apparent irony. Her ears were pierced in several places, there was a tattoo on her forearm, and clothes hung off her like they were honoured to be there. She played songs in the car that Eleanor didn't recognise, and her back seat was littered with scripts.

Normally, Eleanor would cope with these feelings—the ideological challenge that such people presented—in the same way that most people cope with criticism: by undermining the source. She would dismiss them as 'Charlie's friends' and tell herself that anyone with Marxist leanings was indulgent. They weren't the only ones who had *seen through* capitalism. The rest of us were just trying to make the best of a bad situation.

But listening to Helen, Eleanor felt none of the usual intellectual bristling. Instead of feeling smaller, or attacked by all the ways in which Helen was different, she felt larger, and more important. Helen's charisma—her breezy, brilliant grace—hinged on her authenticity. She had found a way to be kind and curious and interested in all people without giving too much of herself—to be beautiful, always, without sparing a thought for how she looked. In short, she didn't give the impression, which Charlie's friends often gave, that her personality was performance, and that Eleanor wasn't the intended audience.

At the burger shop on Clovelly Road, sun-hungry customers were always lining up around the block. By the time Helen's car pulled up outside, the storm had really let rip. The shop, and the street outside, were deserted.

'I'll get this,' Eleanor said. 'I still owe you for your lifeguard duty the other day.'

'Lifeguards are volunteers.'

'Then I owe you for the driving.'

Helen accepted, with a light touch on Eleanor's upper arm, and asked if she could grab her phone from Eleanor's bag. Eleanor tossed her the bag from the back seat, and went inside to order.

At the beach, Eleanor had felt personally betrayed by the weather. Not angry, just disappointed. A summer's day—she expected better. Now a pimply teenager flipped patties with an air of dignified suffering and Eleanor's chest felt tight, her breathing shallow. It was a lot—too much, perhaps—to invite Helen back to her apartment. Seb might be home. Their fingers would be greasy from the burgers.

Eleanor tried to squint through the rain, to see if she could make out Helen's figure in the car. The water fell in a persistent, impenetrable curtain.

As soon as Eleanor closed the door on the passenger seat, the car smelled of chips: thick and airless. Eleanor offered Helen the warm packet, taking a fistful with her other hand.

Helen, who was staring down at her lap, didn't move.

Eleanor spoke through her food. 'You don't want any?' She nestled the packet between her legs. It was warm like a cat.

'All good.' Helen's voice—uncharacteristically high—had an unfamiliar strain in it. 'I'll wait.' In a poor performance of spontaneity, she added: 'Hey, is this yours?'

In Helen's lap lay a purple fanny pack.

It took Eleanor a few moments to piece it together. The reusable bag she had carried to the party. Picked up off Kevin's floor the next morning. Dumped in her room on her arrival and not opened since—not until this morning, when she'd taken it to the beach.

'Oh, shit. I didn't realise I had that. There's a bunch of stuff in there from New Year's. Kevin must have thrown his stuff in with mine.' Eleanor winced as she said his name. She looked at Helen, anticipating some teasing remark. But she caught no mischief in her face: it was grave.

'Did you open it?'

'No?'

Helen turned the key in the ignition. The engine competed with the rain. In a totally different voice, she said, 'Easy. I'll just take it home and give it to him, yeah?'

'That'd be great, actually. I'm not exactly longing to see him again.'

Helen's laugh was suspiciously generous. 'You're putting on a very brave face. It's admirable.' She reached across Eleanor and plucked a chip from her lap. Then she indicated and pulled away from the kerb.

'Helen?'

'Mmm?'

Already dreading the answer, Eleanor asked: 'What's in it?'

Helen pretended not to hear her. She was head-checking. The street was empty.

'What's in Kevin's bag?'

'Oh that.' Her eyes were fixed ahead. 'Nothing.'

'Helen.'

Eleanor snatched at the fanny pack. Helen swatted Eleanor's hand away. 'I'm driving.'

Eleanor grabbed it by the strap, but Helen was already holding it.

'Eleanor, stop.'

'Let me see.'

'For fuck's sake.' Helen relaxed her grip. Eleanor lurched back. She unzipped it so quickly, its contents poured out—onto the floor and mingling with the chips, soggy and limp in her lap.

'Shit, I'm sorry.'

Helen glanced at the floor. 'Oh god.'

Eleanor stared at the clear capsules, each filled with brown-gold crystals. She recognised them from those that sat in Charlie's open palm on New Year's Eve.

Helen swerved wildly and parked outside a red-bricked house. With the engine off, the rain reached a crescendo. Helen leaned over Eleanor and began to scoop up the capsules, along with fluff, sand, and crumbs that didn't bear thinking about.

Eleanor sat rigid while Helen foraged at her feet. Her throat felt as thin as a straw and her heartbeat was keeping pace with the drumming on the roof of the car.

'I didn't realise Kevin *dealt.*'

'Where did you think we got them from?' Helen was no longer leaning across Eleanor. She had picked up the greasy packet, and was mining the chips for drugs.

'So Kevin's a dealer as well as a DJ?' Eleanor held her hands in her lap. If she moved, she'd shake. 'What a cliché. And eccentricity was the only thing he had going for him.'

'Only to friends,' Helen said. 'It's not on a big scale.'

'Just a criminal scale.'

'You didn't seem to care where they came from the other night.' Helen was brushing capsules from her hands into the open fanny pack. She didn't look at Eleanor. 'Everything we enjoy is the product of someone else's labour.'

The car started again. Eleanor waited until Helen had pulled out before saying: 'I just can't think of a more entitled thing to do. What a way to squander his privilege.'

'Because he went to a private school?'

'Yeah, because he's not dealing out of anything like economic necessity. Just because—I don't know—it looks cool? To some people? Because he can get away with it?' Eleanor found her own outrage soothing. Turning the lights off and wrapping herself in a heavy blanket, she separated herself from the situation even while she lived it. If she weren't so nervous, she might have noticed that Helen was radiating frustration.

'Well, if anyone is likely to get away with it, it's you and me. Or Charlie, for that matter.'

'Charlie deals?'

'Not really.'

At the mention of Charlie's name, the panic that Eleanor had fended off lurched forward—the guilt at being in *this* car, in *this* company, spinning towards her apartment, at her own invitation. The drugs were confetti, a momentary distraction. Eleanor clung to them. With every haughty word, the possibility that Helen might enter through those wooden double doors and then follow Eleanor upstairs grew more and more remote.

'What does *not really* mean? I didn't realise there was such a profitable grey area. I thought being a drug dealer was a question of absolutes.' Eleanor spoke with an artificial authority. She didn't recognise herself.

Although Helen lowered her voice, it was not in a tone of surrender. Her almost-whisper insisted—like a challenge—that Eleanor was overreacting. 'Kevin buys more than he can use personally and sells them to his friends. Sometimes Charlie sells to her friends too.'

'For a profit? God, she'll do anything—*anything*—to make her own life dramatic.'

Helen spoke more quietly still. 'And your job—what you do for profit—is so ethically perfect?'

'I think it's hilarious, frankly, that I'm expressing concern for the criminal quantity of drugs we're driving around with, and *I'm* the crazy one. Well, you're very blasé. Congratulations. It's extremely cool.'

In Helen's accusatory silence, Eleanor felt shocked—even a bit embarrassed—by how much contempt she'd managed to muster. She contemplated apologising. Or demanding that Helen stop the car, so Eleanor could get out and trudge the final few kilometres home in the wet. The latter would be easier. Then the day would be an unmitigated mess. Helen wouldn't contact her again.

It was then, just as the rain was easing and Eleanor was settling on this new plan, that they saw at a short distance the blue and red dance of sirens. They refracted off the wet windscreen.

Just before the turn-off to Eleanor's apartment was an RBT. Helen indicated, and steered the car where the police beckoned.

A female police officer, her hair pulled back with balletic severity, poked her head through the driver window and told Helen to place her mouth near the device and count to nine.

In Helen's lap were the remainder of the chips and Kevin's fanny pack, its zipper still open.

Helen counted so slowly that she was stopped after *three*.

While they waited for the outcome the officer's eyes roved around the car. She nodded towards Eleanor. 'She alright?'

Eleanor was imagining how she might explain to her hardworking mother that her good child—the uncreative, well-adjusted one; the one she never had to worry about—had been caught in a drug bust. Helen was right. Nice, white, young professional—to a court, these attributes would make her seem full of potential: someone who might do good in society, even though what she'd done to date was earn a lot of money and spend her free time ferrying drugs around. She disgusted herself. Still, she wasn't about to go to prison to prove a social point. Although Charlie wouldn't have legitimate grounds to be upset if Helen and Eleanor were fellow inmates. Co-incarceration would be very bonding. Charlie couldn't begrudge them that . . .

'She's having a migraine,' Helen said.

'They're the worst. I get them all the time.'

The machine beeped.

'All good,' the officer said to Helen, and then she called across the front seat to Eleanor: 'Feel better!'

When Eleanor finally removed her temple from the windowpane, she turned and saw that Helen was making no effort to fight a smile. It romped across her face.

'I don't know what you're so pleased about,' Eleanor said. 'To your earlier point, they didn't search the car because we're white.'

'Looking at it another way,' Helen said, '*I'm* ferrying the drugs that *you* stole.'

'Inadvertently!'

'*I'm* the Schapelle Corby in this situation.'

Eleanor didn't laugh. Her jaw was locked and painful.

Helen pulled up a few metres from Eleanor's apartment. She moved the gearstick to park, then placed her hand just above

Eleanor's knee, her torso turned towards her. 'I would've freaked out too.'

Eleanor looked at the hand on her thigh and willed her mouth to words. 'You were very level-headed.'

'Is that another of your favourite qualities?'

Eleanor's grip on her righteousness was weakening—it bled out beneath Helen's warm hand. They were outside her apartment, Helen was leaning in, a personal joke—like an offer—vulnerable between them.

Eleanor swallowed. It had the aftertaste of a sob. 'I'm not really hungry . . . you can just have the burgers. Give them to Kevin along with his wares.'

Helen nodded once. There was pity in it. 'Sure.' She removed her hand from Eleanor's leg and placed it on the wheel. 'Maybe we should hang out before you go back to work?'

Then, Eleanor admitted a laugh. 'Yeah, maybe. Call me if you've got some cocaine or firearms and need someone to freak out about them.'

Helen didn't look at her as she got out of the car. Eleanor tried to close the door gently, while mumbling inanities like *thanks* and *that was fun*.

Outside, the rain had stopped. Light protruded through thinning clouds. The city skyline was gold-plated against the afternoon sun. But the streets—trees and wet leaves—still wept. It was hard, when it rained in Sydney, not to feel cheated. The city didn't suit the grey. It looked abandoned: like a failed project.

Eleanor climbed the stairs to her apartment, the tiles slick and muddied underfoot. With every step, she replayed her exit from the car. By the time she reached her floor, a little breathless from the climb, Eleanor was confident that Helen would not want to see her again.

Yet she registered none of the self-satisfaction that is the usual reward for self-sacrifice. She felt, instead, a panicked dread, as if she'd broken something but was too scared to look at it and assess the damage.

13

POROUS WAS A Sydney-based musical collective which continued to identify as 'underground' despite operating for several months (and to great success) at sea level. They had approached Kevin—a frequent collaborator—to play a set in their upcoming (unambitiously titled) 'Evening of Sound'.

After the success of their New Year's Eve party, Charlie asked Eleanor if she'd like to attend.

'Absolutely not,' her sister said, and then listed several reasons:

'I'll be exhausted from my first week back at work.'

'It's not really my scene.'

'I'm doing literally anything else.'

Because they considered themselves countercultural, Porous had an anarchist's passion for rules.

During lockdown, Kevin had observed social distancing with Stasi-like zeal. As with almost everything else, Helen had a theory about this. Because he was Singaporean, Kevin had served two years' compulsory national service after he graduated from boarding school. The army, Helen said, gave him an instinct for order which he spent the rest of his self-proclaimed 'poetic' life trying to repress.

Whatever the reason, the residents of 93 Bethel Street had come to understand that, in a crisis, Kevin fell back on rules. During pandemic-induced lockdowns, when movement was restricted to five kilometres from home, he spent up to an hour each day watching his friends on social media, discovering their location, and checking on an online map whether they'd ventured too far from their place of residence. He made every member of the house download Find My Friends, so he could conduct these investigations more efficiently.

Once restrictions eased, rules were no longer a stick with which to beat his friends, but a measure of his work's importance. Restrictions on the number of people allowed indoors and the noise you could make outdoors proved that the government hated fun and wanted to oppress Kevin. This only made Porous events more essential. After all, a rave is just a party, unless there's a threat of it being shut down.

'If we can't find a venue big enough to obey the two-square-metre rule, we're cancelling,' Kevin said, imbuing 'we're cancelling' with the same sense of resolution and authority that a primary school teacher uses when they 'count to three'.

Mandy had suggested a bunker on the coast near Manly. It had been built when the Japanese bombed Darwin. Helen said that was an interesting slice of history. Kevin said that was a contemptible suggestion, because if she had ever been to Berlin, let alone a 'proper rave', she would know that bunkers are not renowned for their square metreage.

A week later, Kevin 'discovered' the Malabar Battery. It was perfect, he said. A World War II-era bunker on the coast, with plenty of shrubbery on all sides. When Charlie asked what purpose the shrubbery served, Kevin told her it was 'nature's portaloo' and, to everyone's mortification, he winked. Helen said if he was looking for 'equivalently rapey' settings, then a dark, sparse coastal cliff was a fitting substitute for a portaloo. If a wink could curdle, that was what occurred on Kevin's thick-lashed face.

The only person more anxious about the event than Kevin was Charlie. She saw it as the perfect setting for a reunion with Helen. To date, parties had always led to sex. Opening night, closing night, New Year's Eve—it seemed they played best to a crowd.

The Evening of Sound was scheduled for the second weekend in January. Helen had spent the year so far maintaining a slippery presence. All she said to her housemates was *Hi, how are you* (said as a single word, not like a sentence), and the only time they spent together was while Helen made her way towards a door. In the interminable stretches between Helen-sightings, Charlie worried about what she might wear, what she might say, and what combination of drugs might induce the mental state required to look effortless and say whatever it was truthfully.

When the day finally arrived, Charlie felt less rather than more prepared for all that worrying. The only thing she knew for certain was what she would tell Helen.

—

SEVERAL MONTHS AFTER lockdowns had lifted, dance floors still felt like blessings. Proximity was promiscuity. Standing so close, skin on skin, Charlie gave some of herself to the people around her. Sweat mingled, people kissed, foreign hands massaged her neck.

Mandy had posted an Instagram of the four of them before they left Bethel Street. She took it on self-timer, propping her phone up against the fruitbowl on the kitchen table. She captioned it: *Ours is a godless age.*

They'd taken another photo when they got to the bunker, this one on Helen's film camera. Charlie stood as close to Helen as possible. Against the shrubs, the shape of their shadows formed a single figure.

Now Charlie, Helen and Mandy were right at the front, dancing just beneath Kevin's decks.

Although she didn't know it—in fact, *because* she didn't know it—Helen was an irresistible dancer. People crowded her. She smiled at them, included them in her orbit, and, through sheer joy, turned a crowd into a community. At the perimeter of their little circle, people competed to dance closest to her and, by competing, lost before they had begun. To get to Helen's level, you had to have nothing to prove. You had to let the music move through you like you didn't exist at all.

Charlie, who had taken two pingers and several bumps of ketamine, was getting close to Helen's level. She held Helen's waist in both hands and slid behind her, so they moved as one. It wasn't enough to move—Charlie felt empty and restless unless there was someone else's skin on hers. A point of contact, to confirm that other people were real.

Helen was wearing a backless leotard. When she'd put it on at home and they'd posed for photos together, Charlie hadn't noticed that the leotard was made of leather. Now it was slick and slippery beneath her sweat. Like skin, but smoother.

Charlie leaned in and whispered in her ear: 'Breather?'

Now, Charlie was thinking. *Now* was the time to talk. They could go outside among the shrubs and let the cool wind melt from their heads down their spines, and Charlie would tell Helen, in this open, unpeeled state, how she really felt.

Charlie removed her hands from the waist in front of her. The face that turned around, when Charlie whispered in her ear, was not Helen's.

The hair, Charlie now saw as she took two steps away, was not Helen's either. This girl was almost the same height as Charlie. A different person altogether.

Charlie fumbled, as she tried to resume her dance. She lifted her face, and found a very low ceiling. Where was Helen?

—

ON THE THIRD ring, Eleanor knew that she was dreaming and that the ringing was happening in two places at once. On the desk in her dream, her phone vibrated while she tried to maintain polite eye contact with her manager. On her bedside table, in reality, her phone demanded she wake up. On the fourth ring, Eleanor picked it up, saw the time and the name, and put it down. Kevin must have truly lost his mind.

The fifth time her phone rang, she picked up, because she was awake now at three thirty on a Sunday morning, and the only thing that would make her feel better—apart from sleep—would be to reject Kevin's advances.

'Hello?' Eleanor was whispering, but still—with a single word—she managed to sound furious.

'Eleanor, it's Kevin.'

Eleanor could hear the wind, fuzzy against her ear.

'Kevin, it's so late.'

'It's about Charlie. She's a bit cooked.'

Eleanor was sitting upright, although she wasn't conscious of having moved. She forgot to whisper. 'What's happened?'

'She's fine. She's stopped throwing up.'

'Throwing up? Is she okay? Should you call an ambulance?'

'No, she's fine. But I think she probably needs to go home. And it's just'—Eleanor had to press the phone very close to her ear to hear the end of his sentence—'we're in a bit of a remote place.'

Eleanor switched to speaker, so she could type the address while Kevin spoke. When she saw the pin—a red dot in an expanse of green, right at the edge, the pin almost pricking blue—she gasped. 'Okay, I'll leave right now. I'm coming.'

—

TURNING OFF THE main road, Eleanor slowed the car. She'd taken Seb's keys from the kitchen bench, and during the half-hour drive hadn't recovered from the sense that she had stolen something. If everything went wrong, she thought, it would be because she was a chaos-tempting thief.

With her foot on the brake, she crawled forward, unable to see past the ominous ring of headlights. Outside, the gravel crunched loud and eerie.

She found them at the end of the road, in a car park ringed by a wire fence. Two figures stood at the corner closest to the sea. A hole in the fence at their feet, big enough to crawl—or drag a body—through.

Eleanor couldn't identify the figures until she got out of the car.

Her hair was out, all dramatic in the wind. Charlie was on the ground at her feet, seemingly unconscious.

Eleanor ran towards them and crouched so she could better see Charlie's face. She shone her phone torch at it and saw her sister's eyes were closed, but she appeared to be breathing normally.

'What happened?' Eleanor's tone turned her question into a demand—all conviction and no curiosity.

Helen crouched, so she and Eleanor were eye level. 'You should have seen her before.'

'Throwing up?'

'No, after that. She wasn't moving but her eyes were everywhere.'

'How did you get her out here?'

'Kevin helped.'

Eleanor looked past Helen's shoulder, then stood to scan the scene. By way of explanation, Helen added: 'He was anxious to get back to his set.'

Eleanor said something under her breath about priorities.

'You know,' said Helen, 'if you leave the decks unattended, people start claiming squatters' rights.'

Eleanor's hands were on her hips and she was looking down at Helen, but her laugh—quick as a breath—betrayed her.

Helen sprung up: a fluid movement. Eleanor realised then that Helen was wearing extremely short shorts. Next to Charlie, crumpled in the dirt, Helen looked vital: muscly, in her shorts and backless top. This was how any woman would look, Eleanor thought, if she didn't own a mirror and just happened to be perfect.

It was with deliberate will that Eleanor looked away, and only then, when she looked at her own Birkenstock-and-socked feet, did she realise she was wearing pyjama shorts and a hoodie. 'Well,' she said, 'I guess I'll just take it from here.'

Eleanor brushed her thighs down, although they weren't dirty, and thanked Helen for her time.

Helen motioned over her shoulder. 'Oh, I wasn't planning on going back.'

'Did you want a ride somewhere?'

Helen's face, even in the dark, was visibly contemptuous. She leaned down and took Charlie's arms. Charlie was limp. Eleanor took Helen's point. This was a two-person job.

—

A THIRD CAR journey, Helen reflected. Only now, Eleanor was driving.

Helen was finding it difficult to reconcile this Eleanor with the woman she left in the rain-drenched streets more than a week ago. Then, Eleanor had been appalled by the sight of drugs—so appalled, in fact, that Helen had told Kevin not to call her. *It's not worth it,* she'd said.

But now that Charlie needed her—now that Eleanor was actually in a position of power, and not trying to manufacture superiority—she could not have been more generous. She came as soon as she was called and did not stop to judge.

In the car, she kept glancing in the rear-view mirror, or, if Charlie stirred or murmured, slowing down so she could look over her shoulder. And when they'd lain her down in the back seat, Eleanor had extended two fingers and smoothed the soft sweep of Charlie's fringe across her forehead—not tidying it, but just for the sake of touching.

Now silence stretched across the front seat, the memory of their last encounter holding its breath.

Because the cap she'd taken several hours ago was making her feel both sickly and stimulated, like her blood was a soft drink, Helen couldn't bear the quiet. She said, with a nod to Charlie, 'Will she get a lecture on drug abuse when she's awake?'

Eleanor's smile was pained. 'I reserve the harshest judgements for myself.'

'Is that so? What kind of judgements?'

'Oh,' Eleanor said, 'that I'm too old to be taking drugs to impress the cool kids.' She kept her gaze resolutely forward. 'And that I shouldn't have taken it out on you the other day.'

'It's fine. It was a stressful situation.'

'So did you manage to get rid of them?'

'Charlie's been very helpful, gobbling them all up.'

Eleanor laughed then, and turned to face her. Helen hoped her smile didn't look too triumphant.

'Do you have siblings?' Eleanor asked.

'Yes, two brothers.'

'Older or younger?' They'd stopped at a red light, and Eleanor turned to look back at Charlie again. She was speaking softly, so as not to wake her, and their conversation had none of its usual rhythm: it wasn't pacey or performed. The silence before Helen spoke again was tranquil.

'Three, actually.'

'What?'

'I had another brother, but he died when I was young.'

'Oh, I'm so sorry.' Eleanor was still speaking quietly. What she said next was barely audible: 'That's horrible.'

'It's okay.'

'How did he die?'

'He drowned.'

'How horrible,' Eleanor said again, like it was such an inarticulable tragedy, it was better to repeat the same hollow word than to throw synonyms at it. 'Your poor parents.'

'Yeah, I was only seven at the time, so I don't really remember what my parents were like before. And they're great parents, but I . . . I don't think it's the sort of thing you can ever get over.'

'Of course.'

Eleanor turned and met Helen's gaze. The same gentle eyes that, moments ago, were watching over Charlie. She didn't say anything else. She seemed to be waiting for Helen to speak.

Helen didn't know what she'd expected. This silence was probably the best approximation of an adequate response. But the longer it went on, the more sympathy it gave. And Helen, as she always did when receiving sympathy, felt ashamed, like she'd asked for it.

'Anyway,' she said, 'my brothers are great. It's quite motivating, actually, having a dead sibling. We're all obsessed with making our parents proud. Like, we're the consolation children, so we'd better be good.'

'I'm sure they're very proud.'

Helen didn't recognise that voice. It was timid, and it cracked with emotion. She turned to the window so Eleanor wouldn't see how wet her eyes were. The streetlamps were bright, they hovered behind her eyelids. It all seemed unreal: the empty road, the green traffic lights, the night-quiet trees—all of it, except for Eleanor, silent at the wheel.

—

ELEANOR LAY VERY still for several minutes. When she did get out of bed, her movements were cautious, so as not to wake her sister.

They had slept in Eleanor's double bed. At first, Eleanor was watchful, but then Charlie started moving in her sleep—fitful tossing, like she was trying to wring the sheets with her feet. Eleanor, knowing that was how she always slept—not lightly but furiously—was relieved. Surely, she thought, her sister wasn't going to die from having had too much fun.

Helen, meanwhile, slept on the couch. Eleanor saw something funny in the situation: the opening for a joke. Only a few days ago, when they'd gone to the beach and Eleanor had invited her up, the implied destination was clear. Now, bed was out of the question and the couch was the extent of the offer.

But Eleanor was tired—too tired to join the dots, or formulate her thoughts, or make it to the punchline. So she'd just said, 'Goodnight, sleep well,' and climbed in next to her sister.

Now, at ten o'clock, from the sounds in the kitchen, Eleanor could tell that she wasn't the first one awake. The voices, as well as the smell and pop of bacon, clarified as she opened her bedroom door.

At the stove, Seb was wearing an obnoxiously endearing apron and using a spatula for emphasis. 'I try not to think about it too much,' he was saying. 'But since I started full-time work, I go out every weekend and feel hungover until Wednesday, and I'm confronted by the idiocy of my colleagues on Thursday, and then on Friday I go to the pub and try to forget. So, there's about a five-hour window on a Friday night, and that's when I'm happy.'

Helen laughed. She was sitting on a stool, her elbows on the counter, wearing one of Seb's shirts: white, barely buttoned. Last night's make-up had made a wreckage of her face.

'Helen,' Eleanor said, and slid onto the stool next to her. 'You've obviously met Seb.'

'We're having a great yarn.' Seb motioned to Helen, oil flicking from his spatula. 'Helen's just giving me her life story. She said she likes her job, among other things.'

'And what about you?' Helen said.

Eleanor looked at her without making eye contact. 'What about me?'

'Do you hate your job?'

'Oh yeah, why not.'

'The money must be nice though.'

'It is, I guess.'

Seb looked over his shoulder as he piled bacon on top of a paper towel. 'You guess?'

'That makes me sound like such an ingrate, doesn't it? Of course it's nice. I do like the idea that I might be able to help my mother out with her mortgage one day or give her somewhere to live. That makes me feel, I don't know, like my life is for something—other than myself.'

In the silence that followed, Seb cracked two eggs into the pan. They listened to the oil spit.

As if she had been hovering at the door, waiting for a lull, Charlie emerged. She was wearing last night's top: black, fastened by a crisscrossing ribbon that ran from the neck to the waist. Except last night, she'd worn it with the ribbon at the front. Now the skin-revealing part was discrete at her back. She'd also taken one of Eleanor's skirts. It was a loose midi skirt with a floral pattern that managed—like all expensive clothes—to look fussy, despite how hard it tried to appear bohemian. It was probably the buttons, Charlie thought, sewn right next to the zip.

'Morning!' Helen said. 'You're just in time.'

Seb was distributing the eggs and bacon between two plates, readied with toast. 'Do you want some?'

'I want to throw up,' Charlie said, which Eleanor found a bit ungracious.

Helen stood and placed a gentle hand on Charlie's arm. 'Let's get you home.' Her small, tired smile still had the impression of giving all it could.

Charlie shook her head—shaking herself awake. *See?* she told herself, finding something maternal in that smile. In her exhaustion, she was capable only of simple, wading thoughts. In this case: *I'm not hungry, I've been a fool*, and, when she looked at that smile, *Helen does care.*

Eleanor saw it too. The apartment seemed, to her, very small and very silent when she'd closed the door behind Charlie and Helen.

Ever since she'd met Helen, Eleanor had been trying to hate her. In the car after the beach, she'd almost succeeded (although not without hating herself too) when she'd decided that Helen couldn't come upstairs and, instead of leaning in for a kiss, she'd got out and slammed the door. She had told herself then that Helen was an unserious person: cavalier with her privileges and lazy with her intellect—doing whatever she wanted and justifying it later.

It was difficult, after last night's revelations, to maintain that position. That tragic family. Helen's stoicism. Eleanor wasn't sure she would have even mentioned it if she hadn't still been high. How faint Eleanor's picture of Helen was—how easily replaced. She must try harder, she thought. No use romanticising her.

'Helen's great, isn't she?'

Eleanor jumped. Seb, still wearing his apron, was sitting at the table with two plates—one originally intended for Helen—in front of him, a soggy piece of toast dripping from his fork.

'I don't think she likes me much.'

Seb popped the toast into his mouth, and talked through it. 'Why'd you say that?'

'We're just . . . she probably thinks I'm uptight.'

'I think you're uptight and I like you.'

'You're too kind.'

'Actually, she was singing your praises this morning.'

'Really?' Eleanor pulled out the chair opposite Seb and sat down.

Her desperation must have been audible, because Seb's smile was all-knowing. He took a large bite, emptying his plate, and chewed slowly, savouring it, before responding. 'She said she thinks you're one of the smartest people she's ever met. And she can't believe how devoted you are to Charlie.'

Eleanor's mouth writhed as she fended off a smile. 'And what did you say?'

'I reminded her whose car you were driving—'

'Sorry—'

'—because I figured, if she was handing out medals . . .'

'—I should've asked.'

'Nah, I'm kidding. It's not like I was using it.'

'Thank you.'

Seb's plate was clean now, and he pulled the second one towards him. Before he ripped in, he looked at Eleanor, his perfect teeth no longer on display, his mouth firm in thought. 'You know, you are very good to your sister.'

Seb was right, of course. She was—she had been—very good. Last night was typical: Eleanor rushing in to save her, as comfortable being helpful and self-satisfied as Charlie was being helpless and self-pitying.

And if Charlie hadn't been so surly that morning, or if she'd texted Eleanor to say thank you or even to imply it—just one video of their favourite Russian dwarf would've done the trick—Eleanor might not have felt so emboldened. But, as people tend to do—especially with those they care about the most, who've known them the longest—Eleanor threaded the past into the present, and acted with righteousness.

It was because she was such a good sister, because Charlie now owed her one, that it didn't feel like treachery when later that day, under the guise of thanking her for all her help, Eleanor messaged Helen.

14

AN OUTLOOK NOTIFICATION from Seb was always met with relief. It didn't matter whether she was having a full, flailing day, where every pause for breath invited a new wave of work to smack her in the mouth. And it especially didn't matter if her workflow was stagnant and existential dread, like algae, had started to bloom. She always had time for Seb.

They worked in adjacent buildings. Although they lived together, they commuted separately by a matter of hours. Seb liked to run to work (he would rather people admire his fitness than enjoy his company) and Eleanor liked to leave the house fifteen minutes after she woke up. She ate breakfast at work, and hadn't worn make-up since the first day of her internship, on the principle that to lower expectations was to lower the risk of disappointment. Also, as the only woman in her team, she realised that people would be too busy noticing the fact of her existence to observe whether her eyelashes were long, thick and natural brown, or longer, thicker, and mascara-black.

Despite arriving separately, Eleanor and Seb usually found a way to spend some of their working day together: a 'networking lunch' (stir-fry in Tupperware at the Eye Hospital fountain), a 'corporate fundraiser marathon' (a walk around the Botanic Garden), or a 'mental health seminar' (coffee in the lobby of Seb's building).

In the middle of her second week back, still tanned from her summer leave, and still on that thin stretch of January time when she could squeeze in a swim after work, Eleanor received an Outlook invite from Seb. It read: *Actual Networking Actual Event.* He'd put it in her calendar for that Friday, six to nine pm. The event was titled: *Pride in the Law.*

She texted Seb.

I'm not a lawyer

It's free alcohol

But the company . . .

I'm the company! Plus one me

An incoming email distracted her. When she didn't reply for three minutes, he sent a text with animation, so fireworks exploded across her screen.

Canapes!

Eleanor clicked *Accept.* Only then did she open Seb's email, revealing a rainbow header. She now read *Pride* as intended. *LGBTQIA+* appeared several times in the body of the email, in bold and in pink.

Eleanor rolled her seat away from her desk, and craned her neck so she could look out the window. At this height—the thirty-third floor—the city acquired toybox proportions. Only the harbour, all blue and glittering, retained some majesty.

She picked at the pink letters, like chewing gum dried inside her head.

At the building opposite: a window cleaner suspended and precarious.

As a matter of definition, Eleanor and Helen were friends. This was the only logical interpretation of the relevant facts. Eleanor was a good person, and good people did not hurt the ones they loved, if they could help it. They did not, for example, sexually pursue their sibling's love interests. And her text chain with Helen—unbroken across the three days since Helen and Charlie slept over—was hardly evidence to the contrary. After all, Eleanor told herself, what was female friendship for, if not constant conversation?

Still, the pink-lettered, rainbow-headed email scratched at the scab of Eleanor's conscience. As if Seb knew not what Eleanor had *done*, but what she thought and felt; what she might do yet.

—

ON FRIDAY EVENING, Eleanor extracted herself from the desk at which she'd spent over thirty hours in the last forty-eight alone, and set off towards an unfamiliar building.

At the entrance to the thirty-seventh floor, the receptionist was obscured by a sculptural floral arrangement. What looked like tree branches arose out of a translucent pink vase. The effect was chaotic: the whole thing looked ready to topple at any moment. Beneath its vast arms, nametags covered the marble-topped desk. Eleanor took hers and put it in her pocket. She would wait and see whether others wore theirs.

Entering the room, it became apparent that no-nametag was the consensus. They would have helped. While on closer inspection the assembled crowd was made up of individuals—each as unique as the last—at first glance, all Eleanor could see was their similarities. Homogenous features included: clothing (suits: navy, shoes: black), haircut (no hair on the face, and whatever was on the head was short, faded at the sides), glasses (if they had them, the frames were statement tortoiseshell or understatement wire). Also, a quick scan revealed Eleanor to be the only woman in the room.

At the podium, a navy-suited, clean-shaven man was making a speech about diversity.

Eleanor took a glass of champagne from a smiling waiter and searched the room for Seb. She spotted him waving at her from the bar.

'Do you want anything?' he asked as she joined him.

She shook her head, and he took two red wines and a champagne. He gave the champagne to her. 'Double parked.'

Eleanor took her second champagne without thanks, and drew him to one side. 'I'm the only woman here.'

He refused to match her whisper. 'So?' he said lightly.

'It's a gay networking event.'

'Gays, the law, rich straight woman'—he motioned to her with his glass—'it's all gay culture.'

Eleanor gave an extra loud laugh—not just of amusement, but of identification. Like the joke included her. At the same time, she shoved her phone in her bag, with an unopened message from Helen still flirting on the screen.

Wyd tonight?

Encouraged, Seb dropped his voice to a gossipy whisper. 'Seriously, I want you to name one gay icon who's not a rich straight woman.' With a red in each hand, he couldn't count on his fingers. 'Madonna, Judy Garland, Janet Jackson, Princess Diana . . .' On each name, he made a rolling motion with his head.

In spite of herself, Eleanor laughed. 'I'm not seeing the parallels.'

'You're not out of place is all I'm saying.'

'Am I Madonna in this example?'

Seb's eyes—formerly crinkled around a cheeky smile—were suddenly wide. 'Oh fuck.'

'What's wrong?'

Seb was looking past Eleanor's shoulder. He turned so his back was towards her, and she had to shuffle around him to regain eye contact. 'See that man with the glasses?'

Eleanor looked over his shoulder. 'The tortoiseshell ones?'

'Yep. I ghosted him pretty badly a few months ago.'

'How bad?'

Seb put a wineglass to her shoulder, steering her backwards. 'Let's just stand over here.'

They were in the corner of the room now, under the generous beams of another ambitious floral arrangement—arboreal arrangement, really, given the absence of blooms.

Normally, Eleanor would have asked to see screenshots: the ghosting storyboard. Today, however, she felt no interest. Standing under the branches, watching identical people alternately flirt and flee, talking themselves in circles, she felt too anxious to leave and too depressed to like herself if she stayed. The whole event—the pink letters; the speeches; the assembled crowd—*offended* her. Because she was someone who thought *offence* was taken too readily, when sharper tools (reason, common sense) weren't at hand, offence did not express itself in her thoughts. But she felt it as a tightness in her throat and a skin-prickling irritation. In light of what she newly felt for Helen—the gut-wrenching complexity of it—this event seemed a kind of treason. To take something as complex as attraction—let alone *love*—and reduce it to a label before sticking it on a company so it might increase in value . . . nothing, it seemed to Eleanor, was sacred.

During this reverie, she had accepted a duck pancake from a passing tray. Hoisin sauce blossomed in her mouth.

'So, having fun?' Seb bit delicately on the end of a spring roll. Deep fried flecks flew onto his lapel.

'I guess?' Eleanor could only articulate herself by anecdote and analogy. 'When they have these women's events at work, I always find them vaguely patronising. I can't put my finger on it. It's just like, they'll buy me a consolation cupcake at an annual morning tea, but every time I go to a client lunch I have to either sit in silence or talk about sport. So I sit in silence because I obviously know fuck all about sport.'

'Yeah. I know.' Seb sighed, but continued with the enthusiasm of a gossip, 'My partner told me the other day—like, actually told me, to my actual face—that it'll be good when I'm a senior associate and more client-facing because I'll be able to attract the gay clients.'

Eleanor wasn't sure that Seb's story was illustrative of the point she was trying to make. So she said a bland: 'Fucking hell.'

'I don't know, though . . . We spend all our time at work; surely it's better that it's not totally morally neutral. It's kind of a huge part of our lives.'

'But making money *is* morally neutral. I think that's what's grating. It's disingenuous to act like diversity is the end goal, when the goal is and always will be profit. Like, you can work on a billion-dollar deal to refinance a fossil fuel company, but as long as there's a lunchtime seminar about mental health or minorities in the workplace you can pat yourself on the back for achieving value alignment.'

'Still, I'd rather live in a world where I'm encouraged to bring my whole self to work than one where I'm made to feel ashamed.'

'I don't think the opposite of shame is a *whole self*.' Eleanor handed the phrase back to him with disgust. 'You can't bring your whole self anywhere. It doesn't exist.'

'Not if you insist on leaving your soul in the lobby every morning.'

'But the self is relational. It depends what other people want from us.'

Feeling at last like their conversation was working towards a point, Eleanor felt a stab of disappointment to see Seb look through her, his eyes darting across the room. 'Oh my god, what is *he* doing here?' he said. 'Fuck, he's seen me.' Then, he took Eleanor's shoulder, yanking her attention. 'Sorry, I've made eye contact now. He's coming over.'

'Who is it?'

'I'm so sorry.'

Another hand at her shoulder, this time on the other side. It was more tentative than Seb's. Eleanor turned around.

He was taller than her, and his face was as pretty as ever—the blue eyes, the straight nose. But all Eleanor took in, as she turned and her jaw dropped, was the ridiculous swish of his hair.

'Mark! What are you doing here?' Eleanor turned to Seb, only to discover he had made himself scarce. 'Sorry,' she said. 'Of course you have as much right to be here as anyone. I didn't know you were . . .'

Mark's hands were in his pockets and he was shuffling his feet, not looking at Eleanor while she spoke.

'Well, that's great,' she concluded weakly.

Mark met her gaze now with open-eyed surprise. His face was tense, pulled apart by instinct and theory: wanting to assert how straight he was; knowing it was offensive to be so offended. This dance—between the heteronormativity he so valued, and the fluidity he knew he ought to value—played out across his mouth, which wobbled and tripped through several false starts.

Eleanor, who was beginning to have fun, said: 'The lady doth protest too much!'

Mark at last formed words, although they were mumbled almost to incoherence. 'I'm just here with a friend. I thought there'd be some women, actually. Plus ones, you know. So, egg on my face, I suppose.'

Thinking back to Seb's comments about rich women and gay culture, Eleanor had to concede that there was logic to Mark's reasoning.

Motioning to herself with both glasses of champagne, she said, 'And all you got was me.'

Mark laughed then. They had to laugh.

With the laughter, the interaction grew less tortuous, and Eleanor's enjoyment plummeted accordingly. She told Mark to have a nice night, and hunted the room for a good time with the same determination as if she were proving a point.

—

SEVERAL HOURS, FIVE glasses of champagne, and two Helen-dense texting trips to the bathroom later, Seb invited Eleanor to Oxford Street for kick-ons. Already bubble-headed, she declined. She had to work on the weekend.

Before the lift doors closed, Mark, with a foot extended to block their path, slipped in. Eleanor exhaled. 'Watch this lift break down,' she said.

Mark laughed and said, 'That *would* happen to us,' as if whatever they shared was iconic enough to be reducible to tropes. Eleanor watched the floor numbers count backwards on the little screen.

When the doors opened, Mark followed her across the deserted lobby. 'How are you getting home?'

If the lift was too confined, and the seconds-long descent to the ground floor unbearably long, then there was no way she was getting in a taxi with him. 'I'll walk.'

'Can I walk with you for a bit?'

Eleanor didn't respond. She looked from Mark to the revolving door. It had been switched off for the night.

'It's very late,' he said.

Eleanor contemplated a quip about frying pans and fires, but said instead, with sarcasm so dry it aged her to a matron: 'How chivalrous.'

They set out through the only open door—the fire escape—and into the night. The city was in its Friday mood: men with their ties in their pockets and women insecure in heels.

Mark started. 'How are you?'

'Well. Work's busy. You know how it is. Not much to report.'

'Sure.'

There was a silence, which Eleanor refused to break. St Mary's Cathedral rose up on their left, the floodlights casting the sandstone in a soft, fireside glow.

'My parents will be glad I saw you. They were devastated, actually.'

Given that his comments were eliciting no answers, Mark gave up on the pretence of conversation and launched, instead, into his preferred form. Tonight's soliloquy displayed his full range: from self-deprecation to self-pity. 'Of course, I haven't told them what happened—I never really got round to telling you, either. If I did, I suppose I'd just wither away and die. And then where would you be? Walking home all alone, without Mr Muscles over here as your protector. But yeah, Mum keeps asking whether I think I should apologise or something. She's got this real thing about not taking sides. Although, not taking your child's side is probably the same as taking a side. It's not like impartiality is the cornerstone of maternal love. Not that I deserve to have anyone on my side—it's appropriately desolate over here.'

He said the last part in that infuriating way he had, like he was reciting a line from a play. Mark often gave Eleanor the impression that their conversations were just drafts. It was, therefore, years of irritation that fuelled her reply. 'To be honest, that's what happens when you fuck a strip—

'I didn't—'

'—Sorry, *almost* fuck.'

'I wanted to talk about that, actually.'

'Mark—'

'I just feel like I handled it really badly and gave you the wrong impression. I'm not sure I explained the situation well, and I think we need another conversation before either of us can have any closure.'

'I feel very closed about the whole thing.'

Mark spoke louder. Their strides were matching, and their conversation slipped into the combatant rhythm of two people who have fought many times before. 'But that's just it! You're so *closed*, Eleanor. About everything.'

'I really don't think *my* behaviour is at issue here.'

'I know Eleanor. I know. I fucked up. Do you know how I know? Because I *wanted* to fuck up.'

'Okay, well. Thank you for twisting the knife.' Eleanor was almost enjoying herself. She had forgotten, in the time since she last spoke to Mark, what a gift he'd given her—what freedom—when he vacated the moral high ground.

They were halfway down William Street. Several hundred metres away, a red neon Coca-Cola marked the finish line. Eleanor's apartment was only a short walk away, so she'd part with Mark there.

'I don't mean I wanted to do . . . that specifically.'

She wasn't looking at him, but from the way he said *that*, it sounded like he was wincing.

'In hindsight, I think I must have known it wasn't working. But instead of addressing it I just did something drastic to make you break up with me. Like, I must have known on some instinctive level that it needed to end.'

The Coca-Cola sign, flicking on and off in vertical bars, suddenly infuriated her. There were whole strips of red lights that had been blown for months. She looked away, down at her feet, and then at Mark. 'What are you talking about?'

'You're too nice, Eleanor. You never do things for yourself. It's so dispassionate. You obviously weren't in love with me.'

She started to protest—not in words, but with vowels.

'No, it's okay. This isn't a pity party.'

'Could've fooled me.'

'It's just—' he sighed, 'it would never occur to you to break someone's heart. You thought you *owed* it to me, to us, to keep at it. We weren't married. You don't owe people anything.'

'So it's *my* fault you cheated on me?'

It was Mark's turn to look at his feet. His hands were in his pockets. 'That's reductive.'

'Well *I'm* sorry for *your* behaviour. Is that the point of this?'

'That's not—'

One large intersection separated Eleanor from the red sign. Beneath it, the pavement flashed neon.

As they waited for the lights to change, Eleanor turned to Mark. 'Look, you've obviously gone to a therapist and outsourced some insight. And I'm happy for you.' Her anger was clarifying—her thoughts became known to her even as she spoke them. It was the anger of someone with something at stake: anger that admitted, at least in part, that Mark was right. 'But that doesn't make me the villain, or make me feel like I need to apologise to you. And what for? *Sorry I let my concern for your feelings guide my behaviour?* Sorry I didn't just do what you do—take whatever I want when I want it, and then worry about who I've hurt later?'

'I just . . .' Mark looked at Eleanor, checking that she didn't have more to say. 'Happiness is important, Eleanor. I worry about you. When will you be *happy*? I just feel like, if you never do anything for yourself, it's . . . it's toxic!'

'Believe me, Mark, I've done some very selfish things.'

'I don't . . . I didn't . . . you don't understand what happened. I just want you to be—'

The light changed to green, beeping an urgent, merciful pace. Eleanor took her cue and held out her hand, commanding Mark to stay. 'Goodnight, Mark. Say hi to your parents for me.'

He watched her walk away, pulling out her phone as she went. Neck-bent, she charged down the street: heels clacking and fingers tapping, determined to do something selfish.

—

THE TRAIN WAS slowing into Newtown station when Helen's phone vibrated with a text.

You still out?

Even though this was her stop, and Helen was only ten minutes from home, when she alighted she did not exit the station. Instead, she crossed the platform and waited for a train that would take her back the way she'd just come. She was at Eleanor's door in under half an hour.

'Is this a bad idea?' she said, when Eleanor met her in the lobby.

From Eleanor's choice of words—their crude precision—Helen could tell that she had been drinking. 'Sexually speaking,' Eleanor said, 'there's nothing better than a bad idea.'

They kissed then, with hair-clutching, tongue-touching ferocity that acknowledged the act's significance.

When they took the stairs together, Helen felt simultaneously that her legs didn't work and that she didn't need them, because she had learned how to float.

Eleanor's apartment was small, the journey from the front door to the bedroom only a few steps. There was an intrinsic order in Eleanor's room, which suggested she hadn't just cleaned it for the occasion. A framed print in block colours. A ceramic dish on her bedside table, in which gold jewellery was neatly piled. A throw rug folded at the base of the bed, even though it was the height of summer. Helen took all this in as Eleanor turned on the lamp at her bedside table then rushed back to flick the light switch off at the wall.

They kissed again. Eleanor lay back on the bed, and Helen straddled her. They were both still clothed: Helen in jeans, and Eleanor in smooth pants and a crisp white top. Helen looked down at her face, nose soft and eyes dark in this light. Eleanor looked chaste, with her collar up around her jaw, her lips slightly parted.

'I really like you.' Helen had not planned to say it. She just heard the words, and saw them tremble in Eleanor's perfect face.

At the best of times, Eleanor thought humans were nasty and selfish, and true connection improbable. That evening, when the improbable occurred, and she whispered, 'I like you too,' it was as if probability itself trembled. Everything, it seemed, was possible. *Really like* might turn to *love.* Charlie might understand.

The first time Helen touched her, Eleanor thought she might cry. She put a pillow over her face, as if to smother it. Helen removed it, and held her wrists above her head with her free hand. Her gaze was penetrating: Eleanor had never known sex to communicate so much.

Helen drew circles in Eleanor's most private self, adding one finger at a time, then her tongue—wet and eloquent—until Eleanor felt as if her soul—once solid and housed in her brain—was now liquid that trickled beneath her skin, everywhere at once.

Then, when she had caught her breath, Eleanor traced kisses down Helen's body, each one a poem—not links in a chain, not leading anywhere. Every kiss, every tonguing stroke had its own point. Everything she couldn't put in words, she put to Helen's skin. Helen didn't look at her, but scrunched up her eyes, as if against pain. Eleanor touched Helen and herself at the same time—one hand each—and contemplated the long arc of Helen's neck where she threw her head back. It looked taut enough to snap.

Whenever Eleanor had slept with men—especially with Mark—she couldn't say she was ever entirely *present.* She only knew what that meant by contrast. Mark's face, slack and absurd, looked very present. Somewhere between the foreplay and the climactic final thrusts, Eleanor's mind would drift towards the finish line. *When will it end?* she'd wonder. Not so much that she wished for it to end—or that she suffered in the present—but the end was where her mind rested, while her body bumped behind.

With Helen, Eleanor's orgasms overtook her. They were a natural force—inevitable and unpredictable—like rain that has threatened all day and finally, seemingly suddenly, bursts. The present stretched until it snapped. It was all Eleanor's thoughts could do to chase it.

Afterwards, they held each other, and Eleanor talked about the first time they'd met in the bathroom at the theatre. 'I knew we'd met before,' Helen said, while Eleanor reminded her just how embarrassing that encounter was; how relieved she'd been when Helen couldn't remember it.

Helen then said that, after Gordons Bay, she'd assumed that Eleanor hated her. They laughed, and Eleanor said she'd tried.

'I obviously feel very strongly about you.' Her fingers were light on Helen's back, and her voice shook on *strongly*. 'I think I knew that then, so I thought hating you would be easier. I tried to tell myself I was better than you.'

'A difficult case to prosecute.'

'Well, evidently.'

It was such an intimate thing, to reflect on the way they perceived things before they had the opportunity to perceive them together. The miscommunications that only a few hours ago were agonising now seemed hilarious. Better than funny, they were profound, insofar as they created a shared history. In this mode, with bare skin on warm sheets, Helen and Eleanor could collaborate: they told their story together, their echoing voices amounting to truth.

From her vantage on the bed, Eleanor could see the night sky: office navy, with black powerline stripes. She saw the scene through the window as an illusion. This room—this bed—was all the world.

At the time, she'd said it to sound sophisticated, but she really did feel it when she told Helen that nothing was more erotic than a bad idea. It was only now, empty and entangled, that it dawned on them: the nuclear power of a secret.

15

ELEANOR WAS FULLY aware that, if she were presented with her own biography, or at least its most recent chapter (*hardworking corporate consultant secretly sleeps with her sister's on-and-off-again fling*) she would conclude, with maximum glibness: 'sounds like she needs therapy'. Objectively, then, she probably did.

It was self-abnegation that pulled her back. She didn't deserve the attention, she thought. To have her version of events heard, and a therapist help her work through her guilt, as if it could be worked through when it was unabsolved, seemed indulgent. Her unhappiness—although, infuriatingly, she was happy—her *unease*, then, was a price she wanted to pay. It was her only evidence of a conscience. If she did terrible things, at least she felt bad about them.

And she was happy. Hers was not a bouncing, laughing happiness—no drugged-up flights of delirium—but an existential settling she had never felt before. There was not a care of hers that she couldn't laugh at—her very pettiness and self-obsession were hilarious to her now that the world had opened up, and included Helen. All the things she used to care about—career, money, being asked to speak at her old high school—all these narcissistic little goals remained, but they were, for the first time, little. Because if she achieved none of them at all, she would have at least achieved this: this intimacy with Helen.

It had been two and a half weeks since Eleanor and Helen first had sex. In that time, they'd been messaging each other constantly—all day at work, and then as soon as she left, so Helen could head to Eleanor's apartment.

Now the privacy they'd enjoyed—the secret world of their own making—was under threat. Up until this point, the lying and sneaking had been hypothetical. But tonight, for the first time in several weeks, Eleanor could no longer avoid her sister. It was Charlie's birthday, and Eleanor was taking her out to dinner.

Seeing Charlie in person meant Eleanor must confront her own duplicity: wearing each of her two faces. Even if Eleanor told Charlie nothing. After all, a story only becomes a secret when there's someone to keep it from.

—

CHARLIE WAS TEMPTED to cancel dinner. For weeks, she had been dreading her birthday. Although she was only turning twenty-three, she had a much older person's sense that doors had closed behind her. All the actresses she most admired had been in major Hollywood films by her age. Charlie, meanwhile, had performed in a few television commercials, her drama school theatre, and in that one show with Helen. This last was reviewed with a modest four stars and a reference to an 'engaging'—but sadly collective—cast.

In the weeks since sending off her audition tape, Charlie had become an impossibly delicate instrument—producing wild moods at the slightest pressure. She was intimately attuned to the rhythms of her phone. Different notifications—the short vibration for an email; the longer hum of a text—resounded in different parts of her body. Emails shook right in her chest.

Helen, however, was still a tortured source of hope. Lying on her bed, putting off getting ready for dinner, Charlie grabbed her headphones and selected The Smiths as the soundtrack for her scroll through Helen's Instagram. She moved from her posts to her tagged photos, careful not to like anything from years ago. She also listened for a key in the door, a creak on the stairs, which might indicate that Helen had come home.

Helen was using the house like a transit lounge. She was often out: work during the day, or 'seeing a friend' at night, which always seemed to involve sleeping somewhere else. Charlie, not wanting to seem jealous, and because it was what she most ravenously wanted to know, didn't ask who these lucky friends were.

Charlie put her phone away. She had taken a cold shower and was lying un-towelled on her bed, the sheets and doona discarded at her feet. Water had mixed with sweat. She felt damp, and sensuously sorry for herself. She traced her body with her hands.

A string of fucks didn't constitute a summer fling. But they amounted to more than a one-night stand. And, whatever it was, Charlie *missed* it. If they could only work together on another play, Charlie thought, they might re-entangle.

Charlie touched herself and registered desire, but it was distant. Her fantasies distracted her. She imagined how she and Helen would look turning up to rehearsals together, Charlie with her open face for screen and Helen with her clean, analytical lines. They would be strictly professional and then, after weeks of rehearsal, the rest of the cast would discover, with delight, the private relationship they shared. *You're, like, together?*

She scripted fights that they might have: silly bickerings, which would prompt everybody else to say, *You're just like an old married couple.*

When Charlie came, it was quick and thoughtless. A far-off clench of muscles. Her imagined scenes persisted, sweating out into the afternoon heat.

—

IN THE LIFT on her way out of work, her manager asked her where she was headed. Eleanor wasn't sure which surprised him more: that they were both leaving before seven, or that there was a restaurant he hadn't heard of.

'*Where?*'

'In Haymarket.'

'And it's Chinese?'

'Yeah.'

'Which one? I feel like I might have been there.'

'It's got grapes on the roof.'

'Like a vineyard?'

'They're made of plastic.'

'Quirky.' He looked revolted.

In her office, eating at fancy restaurants had assumed the status of a hobby. A response to the obligatory *What's on for the weekend?* was often a list: Fred's, Mimi's, Will's, Charlie Parker's. These were the names of restaurants, not friends. At such venues, Eleanor and her colleagues could dispose of the income that they lost so much sleep amassing. There, they could continue the slow existential leaching—the gastronomic lobotomy—that was 'living for the weekend'. As if, in the reliable procession from entrée to mains (peppered with frequent trips to and from the bathroom) there might be found a sense of direction: of purpose.

For all Eleanor's smugness about the venue, she approached the dinner with a healthy sense of dread. Affordability, authenticity, and general lack of fuss are all ingredients in a great meal. What Eleanor was lacking, on this occasion, was the ability to look her companion in the eye.

—

WHETHER IT WAS the special braised eggplant, the burst of flavour in the soupy pork dumplings, the severity of the matriarch who served them (and gasped when they said, 'Could we have five more minutes, please?' like their indecision was a hate crime), or the fact that the heat had finally relented and a breeze relieved the sidewalk diners—for whatever reason, the Hamor sisters were having fun.

Charlie found Eleanor somehow changed. She had brought two cheap rosés with her, but had none of that BYO-fun, forced chirpiness. She seemed—Charlie could think of no other word for it—*happy*. And not deliberately so, for Charlie's benefit. Happiness was a force she had absorbed, and reaching surfeit, now radiated outwards. Her face was tanned, which made her eyes look copper-coloured in the evening light. She still made bitchy comments about people at the other tables (on the white man at her elbow, trying to define 'real' grime: 'That could only be a first date'). But there was nothing routine about her laughter: it was alive to possibilities; loud and shameless when it rocked her back in her chair and made her shoulders shake.

In the glow of Eleanor's light, infectious mood, Charlie felt her troubles were small enough to be discussed.

When their second serve of shallot pancakes arrived, Charlie said, 'I've been thinking about it a lot lately, and I think I need to quit.'

Eleanor was concentrating on dipping but not soaking her pancake in vinegar and soy sauce. 'Quit what?'

'Acting.'

Eleanor lifted her chopsticks. The pancake fell into the porcelain bowl. 'Why?'

'I'm just not getting enough work.'

'What about that big play you auditioned for in January?'

'I haven't heard.'

'No news isn't bad news.'

'It's not good either. I don't know. Even if I get it, that's what? A couple of weeks' work? And I could continue like this—get another shitty job so I have the time and emotional energy to keep acting—but it's exhausting. Like, I only do the unfulfilling jobs on the side so I *can* do the thing that fulfils me. Except I never get the opportunity to do the thing that supposedly fulfils me, so I'm just resigning myself to being—'

'—unfulfilled.'

Charlie nodded but said, 'Whatever that means.'

Eleanor picked up her pancake, sodden and stained brown, and chewed thoughtfully. Charlie looked at her food. She braced herself for Eleanor's comments, playing her sister's lines in her head so they'd sound less harsh in person: *You can just work to live, not live to work, like most people do . . . a job is just a means to an end, there's no shame in that . . . it's very middle class to perceive your work as a reflection of your personhood . . .*

'I don't think you should quit.'

Charlie looked up. Eleanor's eyes were on Charlie's, her mouth downturned with concern.

'It would be so *easy*, though,' Charlie said. 'I could go back to uni, get a proper job in, like, I don't know, marketing or something.'

'I'd rather have this conversation on your thirtieth birthday.'

'Thirty!' Charlie put her chopsticks down, so she could put her head in her hands.

Eleanor laughed at the melodrama. 'It's not that old, Charlie. Humans have been known to live well into their thirties.'

'I can't still be a broke failed actor at thirty. What if I want to have children?'

Eleanor nodded, and it struck Charlie as a strange reversal: her sister the one conceding principle to practicalities. 'Okay, twenty-five, then. Give yourself a two-year extension. For the pandemic.'

'I can't keep blaming the pandemic.'

'I think it's a salient factor, Charlie. The whole industry shut down. For the first time since, like'—she paused to swallow—'Ancient Greece.'

'That's a very Eurocentric view of theatre.'

Charlie had hoped to elicit at least an eyeroll, but Eleanor, usually so ripe for goading, remained silent. She pushed her bowl away from her, chopsticks balanced on top, and held her wineglass by its stem, rotating it between her thumb and forefinger. She didn't look at Charlie as she spoke. 'I just think that loving something is really important. You're good at acting, obviously. You know that. And you could be good at other things too. You *love* this, though. You've always loved this.'

'Well, maybe I'll love something else. I'll love being good at something else.'

'I don't think it works like that. I just think that loving something—for its own sake—is so important. It's all we've got, really. The only worthwhile thing. To love something outside of yourself, and *work* for it.' Eleanor took a sip of wine. 'And, you know, we can't help what we love. It's irrational. You happen to love theatre, which sucks, because, yeah it's brutal and probably not super lucrative—'

'*Probably* not? Thanks for the vote of confidence.'

Eleanor shook her head. She didn't pause—not even to indulge Charlie's insecurity. She needed to finish her point. 'To know what you love and give it up'—she looked at Charlie, right in the eyes—'that just seems such a waste.'

As if to lighten the mood, and because Charlie wasn't responding, Eleanor added: 'You'll be dead one day is basically what I'm saying.'

Charlie laughed. 'No pressure.'

'I understand the financial strain is real. But what's the point of me working in a—let's say, generously, "ethically neutral" industry, if I can't help the people I love? If you need help with rent, if you'd rather I just give you money for your birthday . . .'

Charlie's skin was stinging. Not with heat or sweat, but with that intense, body-defining self-consciousness—that sense of being watched. She lowered her eyes from Eleanor's loving gaze. Her throat taut with tears, she swallowed. 'You're a good sister, Eleanor.'

'Don't say that.'

At the time, Charlie didn't pay enough attention. She didn't even look up to see that Eleanor was almost in tears too. Not seeing that, Charlie didn't see the shame that wet her sister's eyes. Nor did she see that Eleanor rejected the compliment not to be polite, but because guilt, with a serrated edge, twisted, and told her she didn't deserve it.

16

THE ONLY THING that could make Charlie happier was sharing the news with Helen.

'Helen!' Charlie stood in the corridor, one hand knocking on Helen's bedroom door, the other at the doorhandle.

'She's outside.' Mandy stepped out of the bathroom, towel precarious and skin steaming. 'What's up?'

Charlie pushed past her. 'It's a very, very good day.'

She found Helen under the Hills hoist, a basket of laundry at her feet.

Charlie charged towards her and hugged her from behind. Helen cried out, and put a hand on Charlie's arm to remove it.

'You scared me.'

'Guess what?'

Helen shielded her eyes with her hand. It was a heady, grass-smelling day. 'What?'

'I got a callback.'

And Helen's arms were around her, and her laugh was genuine in Charlie's ear, and Charlie thought, *This can't be normal, to feel such uncomplicated joy on someone else's behalf.* Emboldened, she grasped the Hills hoist with both hands, and flung herself around it. Helen smiled, and added her hands right next to Charlie's. Above their heads, Helen's fresh laundry danced in the breeze. Her undies, like little faces, smiled down on them.

Mandy had changed, although her hair was still dripping. She stood in the laundry, one hand on the doorframe, her bare toes curling over the step. 'What's happened?'

Helen called out across the yard, her voice louder than the space required, 'Charlie got a callback. For that big play at the Opera House. It's for the main character. She'd be on stage the whole time.'

Mandy's response confirmed Charlie's intuition: that Helen must be at least a little bit in love with her. Because when Mandy heard the news, there was a pause—a yawning gap, wide enough for self-interest—then she hugged Charlie too, and there was some jumping, and Mandy smelled of shampoo.

'This is the best news I've ever heard,' Mandy said. Whatever piece of her had died upon hearing her friend's good news, she was now burying it under her more routine, more manic style of support. 'You're one hundred and ten per cent going to get it. You're going to be so famous you won't be able to leave the house. Will *we* be able to leave the house? We should celebrate tonight, while we still can.'

'Oh, it's just a callba—'

Mandy had her phone out, and was already texting the group chat. 'Kevin's in,' she said. 'We've got to celebrate every win along the way.'

Charlie's stomach filled with wet cement at the implication that this—this very preliminary step—might be as far as she would go. She tried to meet Helen's eye, but found her with the plastic laundry basket paper-white at her hip, and squinting. 'I have plans tonight,' she said.

'Oh, nice.' Charlie's voice didn't sound like her own.

'Nothing I can't cancel.'

Mandy looked from Charlie to Helen, as if there were a thread linking them—a thread which, if followed, would make their relation clear. 'A date?' she asked, not as facetiously as Charlie would have liked.

Helen said no.

Charlie wished that there were such a thread, so that she too might see it.

—

KEVIN INSISTED ON cooking. He cooked pork chops with an orange and ginger sauce, except when he sliced the oranges it turned out they were grapefruits. Helen suggested he serve the bitter-smelling sauce on the side. He said the kitchen was no longer a safe space in which to experiment and that if she really wanted to help with dinner she could commit to doing the dishes.

They ate outside, using a sheet as a tablecloth, and lit some expensive candles. Mandy made them wait until she had uploaded her Instagram before they were allowed to lay out the mosquito ring, or the tomato sauce, which sat next to the bowl of untouched grapefruit sauce.

Overhead, the planes flew low and loud. After they'd finished a bottle of red, Helen felt that if she stood on the table and raised her arms, she might scratch one of their tin bellies.

In recent weeks, Charlie had been quiet and dismissive around the house, and Helen had been avoiding her, thinking that her mood could only worsen if she knew that Helen was sleeping with her older sister. Tonight, however, Helen felt they were regaining some of their old rapport. Charlie's lips remained curved into that smiling bow shape and she talked as loudly as Mandy, and did impressions of Kevin that were so accurate, everyone—especially Kevin—demanded more.

Kevin insisted on a toast. 'To Charlie,' he said. 'The Meryl Streep of Bethel Street.'

Charlie told them that the next audition would be in person.

'It's a fun role,' Charlie said, 'because it's playing against type.'

Helen had been drawing shapes on her plate using a knife and the remaining tomato sauce. Now, she looked up. 'How do you mean?'

'I mean, it's not *me*. Which is, like, why I love acting. I find it depressing when they just want me to be myself.'

Kevin nodded. 'No craft.'

'I'm just not mad about being me.'

Helen laughed, but Kevin and Mandy were both nodding.

'I feel that way about standup,' Mandy said. 'It's exhausting after a while to turn your actual personality into a product. You'd much rather sell a character.'

Helen made a leap for her preferred territory, and tried to turn the conversation to theory. In her experience, she said, actors embraced the 'inescapable ego'.

'At drama school,' she said, 'they're always encouraging people to emote via analogy: to think about situations they've experienced and how they felt at the time. So even these fictional characters are always tied to you. In fact, it's encouraged.'

'Isn't that what empathy is?' Kevin said. 'Emoting via analogy.'

A moment of silence, before Helen laughed, and admitted he had a point. She stood then to fetch her camera from her room. When she returned, she arranged her housemates around the table—Charlie at the head, Kevin on her left and Mandy on her right. With that photo, she finished her roll of film. The camera whirred for several seconds. Helen hoped the outdoor lights were bright enough to capture the scene: those wide, genuine smiles.

It wasn't something she had considered before, but that night, taking that photo—the three housemates all together, the picture looking perfect without Helen—it seemed obvious what she should do next.

When they fell to their next satiated silence, Helen announced to the table that she intended to move out.

Kevin said, with great solemnity, that her spirit would remain there always. Mandy said that the happiest days of her life were surely behind her.

Charlie just smiled and said nothing.

—

THERE WAS NO dishwasher at 93 Bethel Street. Helen was scraping the plates when Charlie entered.

'Can I—'

Helen kept her eyes on the sink. 'Why don't you dry?'

Charlie hovered, watching as Helen squirted detergent on the pile of dirty dishes and filled the sink with hot water. On the other side of the kitchen, the laundry door was open to the backyard. The fairy lights on the Hills hoist were emitting a tired light, like a pub after closing.

Helen opened in a light, remote voice she used when she wanted to keep an exchange short. Conversation, at these times, was not her usual act of discovery or invention: her questions came from a script, and the answers didn't matter. 'I really hope you get it, Charlie.'

'Me too.'

'How are you feeling about it?'

Charlie picked up a tea towel and Helen passed her a wet plate.

At dinner, when Helen said she was going to move out, and Mandy and Kevin started to protest, Charlie had sat in silence.

She'd stretched her lips and locked her teeth, biting down until her jaw felt sore, and tried very hard not to cry. Now, in the kitchen, Helen's voice was just ambient noise—distraction from the single thought that had been recurring since Helen raised it. *She's leaving.*

Helen was so rich in beauty and charm that her attention felt like charity. It didn't seem possible that she could dole it out—smiles, conversation, personal questions—without some sense of her own worth. And to withdraw it so quickly—to leave without explanation—seemed to Charlie not a retreat but a rejection.

'There were so many times in the last few years, even in the last few weeks, where being an actor just felt impossible,' she said. 'I know that's dramatic and, like, in the scheme of things, what's theatre? But I can't really make anything on my own. I'm not an artist in that sense, like Mandy. Anyway, it was . . . I was very lonely and, like, hopeless.'

Helen was nodding, but her focus was still on the dishes. When she handed Charlie another plate, she immediately withdrew her hand and plunged it back into the sink, as if to prevent any contact. 'I think a lot of people found that,' she said. 'I just hope we're heading into a better time.'

'But, you know, it's not just about theatre coming back or whatever. Moving in here'—Helen was holding out a wineglass, but Charlie didn't take it; she looked at Helen's profile, willing her to meet her gaze—'moving in with you guys has really changed me.'

Helen reached across Charlie to put the glass down. It made a fragile sound where it struck the wire rack.

It wasn't until Helen responded—spinning around, reaching out, spraying the sink with foam—that Charlie realised she'd said it out loud.

Are you leaving because of me?

'Oh, Charlie. No. No, please don't think that. It's not your fault. You haven't done anything. I just . . .'

'I know it was always very casual. I know that's what we said. But I'm just a bit shocked to hear that you want to leave. I wondered if it's maybe awkward with me now, or something?'

'No. That's not the reason.'

Helen's reassurance only made her feel worse. She sounded so firm—like there was a reason, a very specific reason, that didn't involve Charlie. Helen's cadence reminded Charlie of her sister: the quick, assertive sentences. Charlie felt a familiar constriction in her stomach—the sense that words were the world, and anything that could not be articulated was not worthy of being seen; did not—in a tangible, real, useful way—exist.

So she inhaled deeply, through her mouth, and tried to articulate her fear. 'So it was just casual sex?'

Helen had both hands on the edge of the sink. She was looking at them, her arms straight. They were metallic in the dull kitchen light: two poles in a fence.

'Helen?'

When Helen met Charlie's gaze, her eyes were glistening. Charlie pursed her lips so as not to smile. Tears! Moonlight! Her words must have penetrated.

'I'm really sorry.' Helen looked back at her hands, at the bubbles fading on her fingertips. 'You're a great friend, Charlie. And you know I admire you a lot—I think you're very talented. This is my fault. You see, I've been . . . I am . . .'

Helen looked at her: the inquisitive gaze—darting from one eye to the other, as if Charlie's face were a sentence—that usually preceded a question. This absorbed, curious look was the heart of Helen's charm. *We're the only people in the world.* Helen took a sharp, preparatory breath.

Charlie had been so focused on Helen that she hadn't noticed the silence that fell outside, or noticed the pad of shoes on tiles, and the clanking of empty bottles, as Kevin and Mandy came in from the garden.

Now they were in the kitchen, which was too small for four, and Mandy's hands were on Kevin's shoulders, and she was saying that he was the best cook in the world.

Charlie nodded her agreement.

Then she listened to their footfall as they ascended the stairs. The gap between each tread was excruciating.

'You were saying?' she prompted.

Helen shook her head. 'I don't know what I was saying.'

'You know, I'm—' Charlie swallowed, and rehearsed the words first in her head.

In drama school they'd learned about performative utterances. Actors, they were taught, shouldn't think about words and actions as distinct—a character saying a line isn't just describing, sometimes they're *doing*. Some words *were* action. *I promise. I apologise. I forgive.* By saying it, you *did* it—things shifted, consequences cascaded. In that lecture, Charlie had put her hand up.

What about love? 'Saying: *I love you.* Doesn't that change things?'

The teacher had said yes, if the statement were true.

It was this Charlie thought of before she spoke. What she really wanted, more than to change things, was for things to be accepted as they already were. For Helen to realise that she held Charlie in her hands: that Charlie was *hers* to be directed. *I'll do whatever you want,* might have been one such utterance. Except Charlie had already said that, when she said that it was 'casual'. Then, what she'd meant was: *Do with me what you will.*

'Helen.'

Still, Helen didn't look at her.

'Helen,' Charlie said again, and put her hand on Helen's. It was slippery with detergent.

'I think I'm in love with you.'

As soon as she'd said it—the most significant thing she'd ever said—it suddenly lost all meaning. Like a word from another language, or a dance without a partner, it moved through the air and expressed nothing.

—

'DO YOU THINK I'm a bad person?'

Helen was sitting on Eleanor's bed, and Eleanor was standing by the window. It was open just a crack, the night air seeping in.

Eleanor crossed her arms and leaned back against the glass. 'Of course not.'

'She was so upset.' Helen's face—that neat and tidy face, every feature in its place—had collapsed. 'Like, she was brave about it, and whatever. And I felt awful seeing her cry. I could tell that me seeing it was making it all so much worse.'

'Well, it would,' Eleanor said. 'I struggle to imagine anything worse, actually.'

'Thanks.'

'No, it's just—I don't know what I would do, if I put myself so totally in someone else's hands. It's such a powerless position.'

'I just think . . .' Helen passed a hand over her face. She rubbed her eyes with two fingers each—almost like she was gouging them. 'When we slept together the most recent time . . . sorry.' (Eleanor had tried not to wince, and failed.) 'Charlie seemed genuinely quite chill about it. From everything we said, and how—I don't know . . . how remote and professional she'd seemed around me, I really had no idea she was in love with me. I thought it would be chill if I saw other people.'

'I'm not other people.'

'It's not about you, though. I mean, it is. And we need to tell her. But I just felt so guilty when she said she loved me. Like I haven't paid enough attention, or something.'

Eleanor, who cared so much for Helen, and who had paid attention to Charlie her whole life, was not surprised at all. Did that make her worse than Helen, she asked herself, or better? Was she worse for seeing, from the outset, the consequences of her actions? For acting anyway, but always with a rich responsibility? Was it not better to look back in horror and plead carelessness?

Eleanor wondered, for a moment, whether she believed Helen. Perhaps, owing to Helen's endless interest in other people, she was never at the centre of the picture—not even in her own mind. It occurred to Eleanor that this might be its own kind of vanity: to insist, always, on your own irrelevance.

'We need to tell her, Eleanor. I almost told her tonight. But I couldn't—she was so upset. We've done that to her.'

'She'll be crushed when we tell her,' Eleanor said.

'She's pretty crushed now.'

'Let's wait until after her callback.'

Helen frowned, like she was looking for a rebuttal.

Eleanor sat on the bed, her leg pressed up against Helen's. She took Helen's hand, turned it so her palm was exposed and asked her what, exactly, she and Charlie had said. Eleanor then made her repeat the word several times, with lawyerly exactitude. As if conversations were contracts. *Casual* was the word at issue. Eleanor cited its objective meaning, and asked Helen to agree. Even though she'd known all along it meant something very different to her sister.

Her face a little less desolate, Helen sighed and flopped back on the bed. Eleanor lay down too, over the doona, on her side, so she could prop up her head with one arm and look down on Helen.

'This whole thing'—Helen spoke to the ceiling—'Charlie really liking me and whatever, it just shows: you can never really get inside someone's head.'

Eleanor wasn't sure that was the case. She felt she knew her sister intimately. What it showed, Eleanor thought, was how much suffering you might be prepared to cause, if you wanted something enough.

'Of course,' she said, her voice just a murmur.

Helen lifted her head and rested it on her hand. 'It's not *of course,* though. Because we think we can. That's pretty much the whole point of art: thinking that we can tell stories and help people empathise, as if there's any way in the world to *actually* reveal what it's like to be someone else.'

'Surely there is, though. Isn't that why people like art?'

'I disagree.' Helen lay back again. 'I think the best art knows it's not possible. Like, when you're in a live theatre, this fictional world exists in the same space as you. And there are people right there—people so close you can smell their sweat, so close you could reach out and touch them, but you can't. They're in the same literal space as you, but they exist in a different world. And you can feel their pain—sometimes you feel it so much it makes you cry—but no matter how much you empathise, you can't alleviate it. You can't exist in their world. That's why it's so powerful. Because that's what life's like. So close to other people, but always apart from them.'

Turning back to Eleanor, Helen found her eyes closed and her lips parted just a touch.

'Are you asleep?'

Eleanor opened her eyes. 'No. Just digesting.' She toyed with a smile. 'How very profound.'

Helen sat up and put one leg on either side of Eleanor so she was straddling her. 'I could strangle you.'

Eleanor's laugh was wide awake. 'This is some pillow talk.'

With one hand around each wrist, Helen pinned Eleanor by her arms. 'I've never told anyone that. I thought it was too wanky.'

'I can only encourage you to use me as a sounding board.'

'Fuck off.'

They were both laughing now, and when they looked at each other, it felt so private and so perfect—that they should see each other so clearly: Helen's brief flash of self-importance; Eleanor's disdain for anything like sincerity, which, she saw in Helen's gentle smile, was also self-importance. That they could see all that—in themselves and in each other—and laugh was such a clarifying pleasure that there was only one possible thing to do next.

When they kissed, it was with urgency. And when Helen released Eleanor's wrist so she could move her hand across her stomach and down beneath her underwear—still holding her, willingly trapped with the other hand—Eleanor made a sound she didn't recognise. It didn't communicate anything; it wasn't intended to encourage Helen, or make her feel a particular way about herself. It wasn't intended at all: it just emerged, and it was only when they were finished, feeling liquid and weepy, that Eleanor reflected that the sound had come from her.

Afterwards, Eleanor told Helen that she loved her, and Helen said she loved her too.

Then, in a voice Eleanor hadn't heard before, Helen said: 'Come here, beautiful girl.' Her voice was high-pitched and cooing, but it brought Eleanor no shame to hear it. She lay her head on Helen's chest.

Something in them—between them—had changed. It was as if, having exposed themselves this way—talking to each other like dogs or children—they could never again be real, proper people. They could only pretend: to be adults; to be two people who conducted sovereign lives, and needed each other a normal amount.

17

THE NEXT MORNING, Charlie tried to pull the threads together.

She replayed those last moments together when she had started to cry, but Helen hadn't yet left the kitchen. Before Helen flicked her hands into the sink, wiped them on her jeans and turned to leave, she looked at Charlie—down at her, because Charlie was sitting on a kitchen chair, her face turned towards the table, as if it would be less mortifying if Helen didn't see her tears. Even though Helen was in the room, and Charlie's shoulders were shaking, and she'd made a sound that was so much like a sob she heard it at the time and thought: *I should remember that, in case I ever need to play a broken person in a scene.*

Now, Charlie's stomach writhed beneath that recollected gaze—Helen's face before she left. Pity, Charlie thought. Or guilt.

Charlie tried to convince herself that it wasn't embarrassing. Or, at the very least, that it was embarrassing for Helen, too—to be so ferociously scared of vulnerability that she ran, literally, into the night.

What Charlie couldn't understand was where Helen had gone. Because it was her worst fear—the most embarrassing possible explanation—it also seemed the most likely: Helen was seeing someone else.

She considered it a lie by omission that Helen hadn't said as much. It made Charlie feel small and weak and stupid, like she wasn't worthy of the truth. And more maddening than the lie—or concealment—was that it was so clumsy. *If I'm going to be manipulated,* Charlie thought, *I'd like it to be done with care.*

—

WHEN HELEN MOVED out of Bethel Street the following Sunday, she packed one bag and several boxes. The furniture was mostly Kevin's and Mandy's—she even slept in Kevin's old bed, which he'd passed on to her around the time he started collecting milk crates.

Her boxes were full of books, clothes, vinyls, tinklings of cutlery and the odd pot and pan. Plants were arranged on the floor of the back of her car. The suitcase on the passenger seat had all the clothes she needed for the next couple of weeks.

In her exit, Helen was as breezy and self-sufficient as always. She told Mandy not to worry about her—she could crash at a friend's place until she found another sharehouse.

She offered to pay rent for a month, so they had plenty of time to find someone else for Bethel Street. Kevin and Mandy took this as a gesture of goodwill. Charlie thought it smacked of bad conscience.

Despite moving out so quickly, Helen left little behind. There was the odd spatula, which everybody swore wasn't theirs. On the clothes rack in the living room was a hat everyone assumed was Helen's, until they messaged her about it, and she replied, somewhat cryptically, *Is that really what you think of me?* When Mandy sent her a photo of a shoebox in the bottom kitchen cupboard, where they kept the Tupperware, Helen responded: *Oh yes! My Stuff Box!*

The 'stuff box' contained an old disposable camera, a Nokia brick phone, a spaghetti-quantity of obsolete phone chargers, and a wand for blowing bubbles. Kevin smiled at it fondly and said that Helen had a system for everything. 'Even chaos.'

The bubble wand had been handed out by the crew on their last show before Christmas. Charlie wondered whether its inclusion in the box was sentimental or dismissive. Her throat constricted at the thought. She couldn't decide which would upset her more.

In the wake of Helen's absence, Charlie's only consolation was that her room was now unoccupied and therefore perfect for learning lines in.

—

AT ELEANOR AND Seb's apartment, Helen's boxes stayed in the living room. After two days of grazing them when he tried to salute the sun, Seb moved them so they were flush against the kitchen wall.

Eleanor and Seb worked late, so Helen usually had the apartment to herself, even if she was working until seven pm at the box office. On her days off, she sat at the kitchen table on her laptop, looking for jobs.

She would sit with her back towards the stove, facing the living area, and try to distinguish Eleanor's things from Seb's. The apartment was as tasteful as possible, given that it was inhabited by two people without discernible tastes. There was a full drinks trolley shoved in one corner and a house plant in the other. The furniture was all white, and matched so perfectly it never quite shook off its flatpack, showroom sheen.

Eleanor's bedroom was similar: all right angles and everything in its assigned place. Even the sun was organised, cutting through the east-facing window in harsh, investigative shards. The suburb, too, Helen found boxy and conformist. The homeless congregated neatly at a designated shelter. The sex workers who walked from the station to the brothels trod the same reliable route, never loitering to solicit. Diversity was orderly in Potts Point: not a cacophony, but a careful composition of people. However, the thought that her stay was only temporary—that she was a visitor not a resident—made it easy for Helen to dismiss any concerns she might have had about gentrification. She was just passing through.

And Eleanor, perhaps for the same reason (because the stay was temporary) felt no awkwardness about Helen's presence. Staying over was not the same as moving in. Helen's stay—for the moment—made sense.

—

CHARLIE LAY ON Helen's bare mattress. The sunlight was striped through the blinds, and sliced across Charlie's bare legs. She looked around and marvelled that the room bore no traces of Helen—not even her smell.

She had been rehearsing in there with the door closed for three hours. Just when she thought she might go mad, or slip into a nap, her phone buzzed with a call.

She picked up so quickly, she didn't even see the caller ID.

'Hello?'

'Hey! I've been meaning to call you all day. I just wanted to say congratulations.'

'What?'

'About the callback.'

Charlie sat up. She'd mentioned the callback to Mark in an email. But she'd also mentioned Helen moving out—that, in fact, had been the whole point. It seemed deliberate: Mark's focus on that one positive detail and his cheery tone.

'It pales in comparison with my housemate's news,' she said. 'She's just booked some big comedy festival gig.'

'Mandy? Yeah, I saw she posted about that.'

'You saw it?'

'What can I say? I'm a fan. But I'm a bigger fan of yours. Tell me about this audition.'

Charlie was standing now, pacing the room, no longer on the verge of sleep. She felt electric.

When Mark's words were on a screen, Charlie read them like she read anything: in her own voice. Now *his* voice was in her ear and he was suddenly not just an idea but a real physical person. 'Thinking about it actually makes me sick,' she said.

'Okay, tell me about anything else.'

Charlie paused and looked out Helen's window. 'I'm in the bad books with my sister.'

'I didn't know there was room in her bad books after me.'

Charlie laughed and said, 'One sec,' then went downstairs and out onto the street.

As she set out, she quickly regained the rhythm that was familiar from their emails: swapping indulgent observations and self-deprecating stories they wouldn't dare tell anyone else. This time, she told him about the rave: how Eleanor had come to pick her up, and how she and Helen drove her home together, like parents in the front seat. Mark said she sounded like a veritable damsel in distress, and Charlie said that she hadn't charmed any princes yet. Mark said, very quietly, like he was scared she'd hear, 'That's not true.'

Charlie had stopped at a set of lights. She pressed the button several times. When Mark didn't say anything, she tried a different story: 'And I missed this dinner with Dad, so I could rehearse.'

'Well you got the callback, so that obviously worked out well for you.'

It was quieter now on his end, although it was difficult to tell whether the birds and the cars were hers or his.

'Where are you?' Charlie asked.

'I just got home.'

She tried to imagine his Paddington sharehouse. It would be nicer than hers, but probably smaller, with wide flat showerheads, tiles instead of grass out the back, and a cleaner every other week. All clean and crisp like expensive clothes. She pictured him closing the front door behind him and loosening his tie. It was so mundane it was almost depraved.

'How's work?' she said.

'If we have to talk about my job, I'll hang up. No, but I was going to say: I had dinner with your father once, and I can understand why you might want to miss it.'

'Ha!'

'I don't think he liked me.'

'He doesn't like people. He just "helps" them.' Charlie drew the air quotes with her free hand, and hoped he could hear them.

He must have, because he matched her levity. 'I always wondered whether it was weird that other people also call your father "father".'

'I think he goes by "Reverend". And I'd never call him "father".'

'Too formal?'

'I don't really call him anything, to be honest. We don't speak much.'

'Oh, really?'

'I have my fair share of daddy issues.'

Charlie paused at another crossing, the setting sun loud at her shoulders. *Daddy*, she knew, was goading. It nudged their conversation further from Eleanor, or perhaps closer to her, deeper into the zone of desire and implication.

'That surprises me.'

'Why?'

'I mean I knew he was absent so I probably should have figured, but I always thought a hallmark of daddy issues was, like, low self-esteem.'

Charlie was in the park now. The sounds of the road were distant. And on Mark's end, silence.

'To put it bluntly,' he added.

'And what's your opinion of my self-esteem, Mark?'

'Well, by definition, it's up to you to have an opinion.'

'If you did have one?'

'I know this isn't how self-esteem works, but I guess it didn't occur to me that you could be anything but confident.'

Because nothing whet Charlie's appetite for compliments quite like having already received one, she said nothing, waiting for him fill the silence. She pressed the phone to her ear until it hurt.

'Like, you're obviously very creative, attractive, insightful . . .'

Attractive, sandwiched in there with those other more objective words, seemed to beg the question: Attractive to whom? Everyone? Mark specifically?

'And I would know,' Mark went on. 'I'm a cultured guy.' Just in case he seemed threatening, or too deliberate, Mark always undermined a compliment by making it about him and his own awkwardness.

They laughed then, and Mark seemed keen to get off the phone. Charlie wondered whether he felt he'd overstepped.

On her walk home, he confirmed it.

Her phone vibrated with an email: a retreat to their regular mode of communication.

Charlie found this flattering, perhaps more so than persistent flirting. By emailing, Mark had made it seem important—this friendship that they were both determined not to risk. Also, it was affirming to think that the risk was real—in his head as well as hers—and needed to be managed.

The subject line read: *PS!*

He had written:

> *I'm still thinking about your audition (as your biggest fan is wont to do). I'm sure you'll be amazing and manifesting all the good things etc. but I did wonder: have you ever thought about writing your own stuff? You write so beautifully.*

Even as she typed her response, Charlie didn't know why she was telling him. She'd never told anyone else in her life. But he had that effect on her: he invited vulnerability, and emails were the perfect medium, because she could expose herself in this curated way.

Reading it back before pressing send, she found her own tone spare and stoic.

> *I've only written one story in my life, and telling you what it was is the best way to explain why I haven't wanted to write anything since.*
>
> *I don't know if you know, but when we were younger, we went to a school where my dad taught English. It was very expensive and they took all those national tests very seriously, and they made us practise creative writing in the lead-up. We were given a prompt, and we had to write five hundred words, or something. The prompt was a box, and we had to say what was in it.*
>
> *I'll say at the outset, it's not as dramatic as it will first seem, but basically I described naked women in the box doing things that I shouldn't have known anything about (I was nine at the time).*
>
> *I only knew about them because at lunchtime I sometimes snuck into my dad's office in the senior school. And one time I played on his computer, and saw his most recent tab. So, in*

the scheme of things, it's trivial and even kind of funny. But my teacher was very alarmed, so they did some digging and dad lost his job over it.

What I grapple with is the responsibility of that. I suppose it's why I prefer to act and be other people and tell stories collectively as part of a larger group. Because at the time when I wrote that, I think I knew it was in some sense wrong or shocking. I wanted to write a really adult story so people would think I was clever like my sister and I deserved to be there.

That's all very pathetic and, as I said at the start, melodramatic, but yeah, I'd rather stick to acting.

Mark replied within a few minutes, and said that story was precisely the kind of thing she should write about, and that he would love to read it when she did. He said it was only a matter of time before the world discovered her 'preternatural gifts'.

She hated how much she wanted to believe him.

—

IT WAS HELEN'S second weekend at the apartment, and Eleanor had to go into work on Saturday. When she finished, she promised to meet Helen at a wine bar in Potts Point. It served cured meats, and cocktails with enormous ice cubes.

It had never occurred to Helen that she might date someone who worked in commercial services, let alone experience anything like emotional investment in them. To her, the job of 'business analyst' still sounded fascinatingly dull. She kept asking Eleanor to explain her job, but focusing on the answer was like trying to recall an already-forgotten dream.

In the past, Helen had listened without empathy or patience while friends complained about dating wealthier people. *So, he wants to stay in a hotel for your anniversary? And he's going to pay? What a cunt. No, seriously though, maybe feminism has gone too far.*

Now, however, Helen was realising how much generosity can benefit the giver at the expense of the receiver. Although she knew it probably improved the optics, she found no real comfort in the fact that she and Eleanor were both women. It seemed abstract—not to mention irrelevant—to think of their relationship in terms of histories of oppression. Money was real, and very pressing. She didn't want to be the one who didn't pay for things.

Helen's stomach was sticky after a very small, very creamy plate of pasta and pepper. Eleanor had asked the waitress for the bill, and then used the lull in conversation to look at her phone. When she placed it screen down on the table, Helen spoke.

'So, I know you said I could stay until I found somewhere, and, well . . . it'll be two weeks tomorrow.'

Eleanor blinked at Helen, as if she were waiting for the end of the sentence.

'I haven't found anything yet,' Helen said.

The waitress returned with the bill, which Eleanor accepted with a smile and then placed next to her phone. 'That's okay,' she said, with a dismissive wave. 'Seb loves having you around.'

'Really? He keeps moving my boxes. It's quite passive aggressive.'

'Passive aggression is his love language.'

Helen laughed. 'Well, thank you. I'm very grateful. But I think, while I'm looking for a place, I should start contributing to the rent. Or at least bills.'

Again, Eleanor's response was dismissive. 'We can work it out later.'

An EFTPOS machine was delivered to the table and Eleanor tapped it with her phone, the bill still untouched at her side. Then she placed both hands on the tabletop as if readying to stand and leave.

'No, Eleanor, I need to pay *something*.'

Eleanor removed her hands from the table and sat up straighter while Helen went on. 'I think it's the combination of me living there for free and you and Seb being out all day at work. I feel like I'm some kind of amusement for you. I'm like a kept woman, just waiting around all day for you to come home.'

'That's hilariously unfair.'

Helen leaned forward, her torso across the table. Eleanor's back remained straight. 'I'm just telling you how I feel. It's not a question of fairness.'

'Of course not. Unless the implication is that I'm in some way responsible for those feelings. In which case your feelings are also accusations. Then I'd say fairness comes into it.'

Helen laughed, from shock, at Eleanor's cool hostility. 'I'm saying I want to *pay rent*. To make things *fairer* for you.'

'Sorry.' Eleanor bowed her head, her shoulders slumping. She touched her fingertips to her forehead, her elbow on the table. 'It's just, if you pay rent, then it's sort of, well, what becomes of plausible deniability?'

'What are you talking about?'

Eleanor's voice, which had been dropping throughout her little speech, was now a whisper. 'There will be receipts.'

Helen said, 'Oh,' and nodded, not like she understood but like she was a therapist who could now see Eleanor's problem.

On the walk home, Helen took Eleanor's hand. They were both ideologically opposed to public displays of affection. They had spoken about it before.

For Eleanor, it was because it reminded her of Mark and smacked of ownership.

For Helen, it wasn't about men or women, or about the state of a relationship—it was about privacy. If you liked someone, Helen said, you gave them a version of yourself. That version wasn't for public consumption. In fact, an audience ruined it. You lost something, when you performed a relationship for other people.

But on the way home from the wine bar—a tepid evening, with empty, expressionless air—Helen took Eleanor's hand and gently, privately, so only Eleanor could feel, she squeezed.

Then she said, equally privately—a whisper in Eleanor's ear: 'We need to tell Charlie. This callback thing, it's just an excuse.'

Eleanor sighed, so Helen turned to look at her and was surprised to see her nodding.

Although she would never say it, because she didn't want to seem weak or insufficiently self-loathing, Eleanor was thrilled to hear Helen say *we*. It made her feel like it was normal—or, at least, not uniquely depraved—to be selfish and foolish, and to make mistakes, and to be a bad person, even when she wanted so much to be a good one.

18

THE MORNING LIGHT was crisp; the sun drawing sharp lines around the trees. The record-breaking temperatures had followed them right through February. The sun on Saturday morning had heat that singed your eyes and browned your arms but stopped before it drew real sweat. Eleanor and Charlie were going to the beach. Helen said Eleanor would have to tell her before they swam.

'So the rest of the interaction doesn't seem fake?'

'So she can swim afterwards,' Helen said. 'Wash some of it off.'

'This is like planning a break-up.'

'They're comparable. You're planning to hurt someone.'

'I'll ruin her life, then she can throw herself into the sea.'

Helen laughed, as if Eleanor's last comment were ridiculous. Eleanor laughed too, so they wouldn't have to worry about whether it was, in fact, true.

—

ELEANOR SAID THAT she would drive, because Charlie never did. They met on the street outside Eleanor's apartment and borrowed Seb's car.

At the car park Eleanor pulled up in the furthest row, closest to the cliffs. The ocean spread out beneath them. Eleanor pulled at the handbrake and turned the engine off. The air, immediately, was stifling.

As Charlie reached for the door, Eleanor said in a small voice that she had been burying the whole drive: 'Wait.'

Charlie's hand stilled.

'I have to tell you something.'

Charlie rolled down her window. A breeze entered the car.

Eleanor heard herself swallow. She kept her hands on the wheel and her eyes fixed on the ocean. It was a dark navy. The swell and the wind capped the waves with white peaks.

'What?'

Charlie was applying a second layer of sunscreen. She looked at herself in the visor mirror with detached focus, like she was applying make-up. Eleanor could smell it: a rubbery, pore-clogging smell that never failed to make her feel like a child.

'I'm so sorry, Charlie.'

Charlie rubbed in the sunscreen, circling her cheeks, perfectly rounded atop her smile. 'Sorry for what?'

'It's a bit of a weird situation, and you'll probably want to talk to her as well, but I thought you should hear it from me first. Helen and I are . . . we're seeing each other.'

'What?' Charlie turned to face Eleanor. She had not yet rubbed in all the sunscreen: white strokes on her forehead and down her nose. She might have looked comical, were her expression not so fierce. '*How?*'

'When she moved out, I said she could crash at mine until she found somewhere to live. Seb and I are barely there, to be honest, it doesn't affect us. And she was still paying rent at yours, obviously, so it helped to have somewhere she could just crash for free. And now we're . . . she might actually stay a bit longer. Because we've started seeing each other.'

'You mean you're sleeping together.'

Eleanor removed her hands from the wheel and knotted them in her lap. It felt violating, to talk about Helen that way. Eleanor didn't want Helen to exist like that for other people. That their sex could exist—even as an abstract idea—in someone else's mind tore strips off their privacy. Of course, in Charlie's case, it wasn't just imagination, but memory.

At the thought of Charlie and Helen together, Eleanor returned her hands to the wheel, and squeezed. She itched with the sensation that something had been stolen from her. It was as if Charlie had Eleanor's phone and was scrolling through it, laughing at her messages—the way she expressed herself; conducted her relationships; the stray thoughts in her notes—but wouldn't tell her what she was reading.

'I'm really sorry.' Looking at her sister, Eleanor found it strangely soothing to see how upset Charlie was. She felt nauseous with guilt—a rich, indulgent nausea. 'I obviously didn't think that this would happen. I only just broke up with Mark, as you know. I really wasn't looking . . .'

'You're not in love with her, are you?'

Eleanor looked out to the ocean, seeing nothing.

'Eleanor, please tell me you're not in love with her.'

Eleanor's silence was perfectly articulate.

'I *knew* she liked someone else.'

Eleanor's skin felt extremely hot—not the heat from the car bearing down, but a prickling from inside.

'I went mad with it.' Charlie wiped her face. 'I said things to Helen, really embarrassing things'—each time, her voice broke on *things*—'that I wouldn't have said if I'd known.'

The lie that followed came so naturally, Eleanor felt like it wasn't hers at all. In fact, she was morbidly impressed by it. It was like when she remembered song lyrics, or the full names of people she hadn't thought about in years. Then she'd marvel at her own mind, without claiming any pride in its workings.

'It's only started in the last week or so, after she moved out of Bethel Street. When you both crashed at mine after that rave, she messaged me to say thank you. We got talking, and then she told me about moving out and I joked that she was always welcome to crash at mine again. And then she took me up on it and we both thought it would just be for a few days but . . .'

At Eleanor's use of the plural, Charlie laughed, but made a face to suggest that her laughter tasted vile. 'Well, it's a good thing Seb's gay,' she said.

'What?'

'Helen seems particularly horny for housemates. So, you know, it's good you don't have any competition. Or she'd crash there too.'

Eleanor ignored the slut-shaming by adopting a tone of pointed maturity. 'I'm sorry,' she said. 'I should have told you when she moved in. I honestly thought it would be temporary, and I knew you were upset about her moving out. I really didn't want to make a hard time worse. I thought she'd come and go and you'd never need to know.'

'Well, she came.'

At the crass ease of this joke, Eleanor yielded to temptation and started defending Helen: 'She really cares about you, Charlie. She encouraged me to tell you straight away. She really didn't want to hurt you.'

'Oh, so she was only thinking of me?'

'I'm not saying that,' Eleanor tried to maintain an even tone. 'I'm just saying—'

'Must be nice.'

'What?'

'Not to do anything wrong.'

There was something comfortable—familiar, even—in the rhythm they'd adopted. They were parrying now, with the same cadence that they used to say: *that's mine* and *leave me alone* and *you took the last one* and *you wore my top without asking.*

Eleanor adopted her authoritative voice. It was the tone of their childhood, with world-weary notes to remind Charlie which of them was older. 'Just because you don't *like* something doesn't make it objectively wrong. Helen needed somewhere to live, and I was in a financial position to accommodate that at no real cost or effort. As soon as it turned into a different arrangement, I told you.'

'But you didn't, Eleanor. You didn't tell me.'

'I wanted to wait until your audition was over. I didn't want to upset you. But Helen said we needed to tell you as soon as possible.'

'Well, I doubt I'll get the part, but I appreciate the concern.'

'I'm sorry,' Eleanor said, and she was. For all of it.

Charlie's chin was up at a defiant angle, her gaze trained on the visor mirror. She watched herself speak. 'Look, I'll get over it. Helen and I are still friends. And just because what happened was fleeting, that doesn't mean it wasn't meaningful. To be honest, I find it very hard to wrap my head around the whole thing but, you know . . .' Charlie slapped her hands on her thighs, 'Good for you, I guess. She's a real catch. I mean, I obviously find her attractive.'

Eleanor laughed, but without relief. 'So . . .' She looked back at the ocean, willing Charlie to speak. When she didn't, Eleanor finished with a shrill upward inflection: 'We're okay?'

Charlie shrugged. It looked rehearsed. Like an actor wringing their hands or clasping them behind their back. Charlie's shrug was somewhere to put her indifference when her face was locked: frozen in that self-restraining stare. Eleanor kept watching her. She felt that looking away would be a kind of betrayal. Of Helen, perhaps.

Charlie broke first. She opened the door and the wind raced in. 'Let's go for a swim.'

—

AT THE BEACH, a narrow channel of sea bordered on each side by cement, the swell was huge. Sunbathers cowered several metres from the edge.

Approaching from the car park, the Hamor sisters walked straight onto the concrete—at the far end of the channel they could see a kiosk and a muddy strip of sand. They dropped their bags, stripped to their swimmers and approached the edge, where the concrete wall plunged into the sea. The steps were submerged, and the waves tossed people at the railings, and yanked them back too violently for them to get a grip. Lifeguards stood with their hands behind their backs, holding ropes to pull swimmers in.

'We should jump,' Charlie said.

Eleanor looked at the waves. In the centre, a group of teenage boys yelled over an inflatable donut with pink plastic icing, and flecks for hundreds and thousands. It bucked and heaved. On the other side, a woman clung to the railing, her arms wrapped around it, and her legs flailing behind her. In a pause between waves, she crawled up the stairs on all fours to sit on the cement, panting. A returning wave sprayed her, and she laughed, as if at her own hopelessness.

Charlie jumped.

Eleanor waited for the waves to crest before jumping in after her.

When Eleanor surfaced, water smacked her open gasping mouth. She coughed it out and said, 'It's like a washing machine on spin cycle.'

Charlie headed to the other side of the cement with confident freestyle. There, she trod water, eyeing the railing. Lifeguards gathered. Someone called across the waves. It was difficult to make out what they were saying. Something about a rope. Charlie didn't move.

Eleanor, treading water behind her, said they should swim in to the beach.

When the swell was at its height, Charlie dived under. She emerged, her head bobbing centimetres from the cement and took hold of the railing. With the water receding, she ran up the stairs. At the top, she chatted to a lifeguard. She smiled, and her teeth shone.

Eleanor swam a slow breaststroke to shore. The water had tossed up rubbish, and she could feel seaweed under her swimsuit. She got out, picking her way through coral, an empty chip packet and a discarded syringe, and made her way back to where they'd left their towels.

Charlie was already there, her face shadowed by a book. She did not lower it when Eleanor lay down beside her on the warm concrete.

'What are you reading?'

'It's for book club.'

Eleanor did not ask her to elaborate.

'Eleanor?'

She rolled onto her back. The sun tore through her closed lids. She shielded her eyes with her hand. 'Yes?'

'Why didn't you tell me?'

Eleanor sat up, wrapping her towel around her. She looked at Charlie, who had abandoned her book, spine cracked on the concrete. The pages were damp and curling, as if wet with tears. It took an effort of will to meet her eyes. But Eleanor did, and found them devoid of hostility. She looked curious, like she was waiting to be told a story.

'I think when I said that she could stay, I could already tell that I was, I guess, interested. And then, because I didn't tell you—because, I suppose, I chose to keep the moment for myself—I made it weird. Obviously, there was a very genuine element of not wanting to make a stressful situation worse. But there was also cowardice to it: like, I thought you might never find out. And selfishness. That too.'

This was similar to what she and Helen had discussed. Except it was less honest, more self-loathing, than when she and Helen had composed the explanation together.

Charlie shook her head. 'I meant: why didn't you tell me you were gay?'

'What?'

Charlie just looked at her. She wasn't going to repeat the question.

'I don't think I am.'

Charlie sat up so their eyes were level. Her hair was slicked flat, and her eyes shone gold where they squinted against the sun. She looked formidable. 'You're seeing a woman.'

'And I've been in relationships with men.' Eleanor couldn't account for this defensiveness, even as she scrounged around her past for rebuttals.

'Then why didn't you tell me you were bi, or queer, or whatever?'

'I guess I just like who I like. At the moment I like Helen. I really wasn't trying to keep anything from you. Believe me, it's news to me that I can feel so strongly about anyone at all.' She laughed nervously.

Charlie didn't smile. Instead, she rolled onto her stomach and reached for her book. What she said next was barely audible. 'I was lonely. That's all.'

Eleanor waited a moment, until Charlie found her page, her finger poised to turn it. When she was sure Charlie had nothing else to say, she asked: 'Are you sure you're okay?'

Charlie didn't look up. 'Water off a duck's back.'

—

'WATER OFF A duck's back?'

'That's what she said.'

Helen narrowed her eyes. 'You're sure?'

'Yes, it only happened a few hours ago.'

'You're sure you weren't overwhelmed by the setting—like the sea, and everything?' Seb was vaping on the balcony, listening to their conversation. He'd been out the night before, and had only arisen a few hours ago. A bowl of takeaway udon steamed on the small outdoor table in front of him, and his dry-cleaned shirts for Monday hung over the edge. While they spoke, Eleanor moved the shirts to the couch. They were too precarious for her to bear.

Helen repeated it, sounding it out for new meaning. 'Water off a duck's back.' Then, to herself she added: 'Fuck me dead.'

Seb, who was now leaning on the doorframe, threw his head back and laughed. 'It's not good, is it?'

'Isn't it?' Eleanor's elbows were on her knees and her head in her hands. Helen, sitting next to her on the couch, patted her back.

'She's going to fucking murder you.'

'What?' Eleanor lifted her head to look at Seb.

He nodded. 'Like, in your sleep.'

'I thought she took it well. That's her taking it, like, *admirably* well.'

'Nope.' Seb slurped a thick noodle from the soup. It wriggled and splashed on its way into his mouth. 'It's a terrible, terrible way to take it. She needs to let herself be angry. Now it'll just creep out some other way.'

'Maybe.' Eleanor tried not to shrink from Helen's hand on her back. Her skin smarted with sunburn and her head, dehydrated, cowered beneath a thin veil of pain.

When she'd arrived home, Helen and Seb met her at the door with pre-emptive congratulations. *You did it? Well done. What a hard conversation.*

Eleanor hadn't yet removed her damp swimsuit, let alone showered off the salt. She also hadn't told them what, exactly, she'd said to Charlie. Or that she'd lied. She couldn't tell them, not when they both thought she was so brave. Nothing, in that moment, seemed more important than their approval. Not even deserving it.

Helen's hand stilled on Eleanor's back. 'So now we just take her at her word? I don't need to do any grovelling?'

'Oh I think she'll still expect you to grovel,' Eleanor said. 'Her audition is on Wednesday morning. Maybe get a coffee with her after.'

Seb observed the two women, who sat for a moment in silence. 'Actually, it's a great power play,' he said. 'Like, she's taken the role of the bigger person, so now you're indebted to her.'

Although intended as a warning, Eleanor found Seb's words a comfort. She could not admit it to herself, much less say it to Helen, but it had been a painful stretch to see Charlie as so *reasonable.*

Eleanor's greatest source of pride was her ability to distinguish between feelings and entitlements. Just because someone made her feel a certain way did not mean they necessarily owed her an apology, or a change of behaviour. It was a distinction clarified over the years by contrast with Charlie, who always seemed to suffer, and always understood her own pain in terms of victim and oppressor: if she was hurting, then there must be someone she could blame.

But in the car, Charlie had looked herself in the mirror, swallowed, and demanded nothing. Charlie might have felt—Eleanor could only imagine—rage, jealousy, worthlessness all came to mind. But, as far as Charlie knew, Eleanor had given Helen a place to live, and they'd fallen in love. Objectively, there was nothing wrong with that. And the miracle of it—the graceful intellectual leap—was that these facts (Eleanor was already thinking of them as facts) were invulnerable to Charlie's feelings. They didn't *become wrong* just because Charlie suffered.

Eleanor found it difficult to believe that her sister had such a sophisticated, stable grip on her emotional life. Seb's view made more sense: Charlie was as mad as the rest of them, and, in time, the cracks would show.

—

WHEN SHE HAD lain on the hot concrete by the water and sweated fury—her voice distant and passive—Charlie had tried to be a better version of herself. A calm, go-with-the-flow, happy-go-lucky free spirit who knew that to love was not to own and that, since Helen didn't belong to her, she couldn't be stolen away. An enlightened woman who understood pleasure as just that, and pain as hers to bear alone.

At home, the waves still ringing in her ears, Charlie imagined pulling Eleanor's hair so hard that dark clumps came out in her hands. When they were children, they were always having vicious fights. Chinese burns, scratched faces. It was in this sisterly tradition that Charlie now wanted to gouge Eleanor's eyes out and, when caught, cry: *She started it.*

'Impetuous,' Kevin called it.

Charlie wondered whether he meant *incestuous,* because that was what she'd been thinking.

Mandy was so empathetic that it tipped over from fellow feeling and into self-interest—she never performed better than in the role of Supportive Friend.

'I knew it! I knew it!' she said, in a tone so vindicated, anyone would think she'd been ostracised for her beliefs. 'I thought that whole story about you three ending up at her place was so convoluted.' Mandy spoke as if this was a thought she'd expressed many times before.

Charlie, hearing it for the first time, was still catching up. 'How do you mean?'

'When you blacked out in that bunker and Helen called Eleanor. Like, surely they were already friends then.'

'Kevin called Eleanor.'

Mandy shrugged. 'I just think it's weird that Helen was so keen to get in the car and go to Eleanor's apartment. Like, I love you and whatever, but I would have palmed you off and gone back to the party.'

'Thanks, Mandy.'

Mandy must have seen the tears threatening, because she launched into a crescendo of platitudes, each more supportive and more manic than the last. 'You're taking this so incredibly well. You could not have behaved more perfectly. You're a saint, really. Honestly, if you went on a rampage and shot both of them, I wouldn't even blame you. I'd be like: fair.'

Charlie couldn't bring herself to laugh, but she said, 'Alright, mate,' to show she wasn't taking it all to heart.

That night, however, Charlie opened the Tupperware cupboard and with slow, deliberate movements, like trying to remove a knife without spilling any blood, she took out the old shoebox filled with Helen's 'stuff'.

With a brute conviction that violations were best repaid in kind, she opened the lid, and took the most private, most personal thing she could find.

Helen had left behind one of her film cameras. This was her cheapest and most battered—the one she took to the beach, or a big night out, or anywhere it was likely to get dropped or stomped on.

Picking it up, Charlie was surprised how light it was. The plastic made it feel cheap and insignificant. But opening the flap at the back, and seeing a finished roll of film inside, an unfamiliar electricity crept into her hands, right down to the end of each finger.

Although she could not yet make out the shape of it, she could sense, already, that she had stumbled upon something important.

19

MOST OF THE time—and especially if the show boasted a diverse cast—the people Charlie auditioned for were men.

The most lucrative work she had ever done was for a tampon commercial. The setting was a nightclub bathroom, although they filmed it in a studio, so there were no mirrors, and none of the toilets flushed. Charlie sat on a cubicle closest to the camera so she couldn't see the curation of women who sat alongside her. When the take began, and she looked into the camera, all she could see on the other side of it was the same face, over and over again.

Two of those faces looked up when she entered the audition room. Usually, she could tell if they were seriously interested just from their posture. The keen ones would hold a pen, Charlie's self-esteem existing in the gap between nib and page. The un-interested would look at their phone, and then say something at the end that was so generic it felt pointed. Something like: 'What you're doing . . . it's a lot.'

Today, both men had their fingers interlocked on the desk. They turned to look at the woman who sat between them.

Kathryn Coonan was Helen's favourite director. This fact alone made Charlie nervous. Then there was the fact that she was one of the first female directors at Sydney's biggest theatre company.

And then there were the guest lectures she'd given when Charlie was at drama school.

Unfashionably, Kathryn Coonan hated talking about her career in the context of her gender. In the first lecture, Charlie had made the mistake of starting a question: 'As a female director—'

Kathryn Coonan did not let her finish.

'For me, the joy of directing is that it's *not about me.*' She emphasised each of these words. Like it was very hard to understand. 'In fact, to my mind, that's the point of theatre—of collaboration—in general. It forces you to engage with experiences outside yourself. Can you stage *King Henry V* "as a woman"? Should you?'

Kathryn Coonan had smiled at the patter of fingers and keyboards. How quickly that smile would have faded, had she realised her questions were being typed into Google.

Today, as a director—female or otherwise—Kathryn Coonan was giving off an energy that was more librarian than auteur. Her straight grey hair was tied back in a sensible ponytail, and she pushed her glasses further up her nose to examine Charlie.

They talked through her resumé, the men remaining silent and attentive. Eventually, Kathryn Coonan said: 'When you're ready.'

Charlie read the monologue once. She tried to speak like her sister—with her hands, and each word precise, more clipped and more confident the longer she went on. By the end it was a pleasure just to speak—she felt at once proud of the lines, as if they were her own, and also in awe of them. *Did I say that?* Like talking was a game, and she was so focused on it that it was only afterwards, in silence, that she realised how well she'd played.

When she finished, both men looked her up and down, stopping at the floor. Kathryn Coonan looked her in the eyes.

'Good,' was all she said.

It was enough to make Charlie feel like she'd proven something.

—

CHARLIE KNEW THAT hope could only sharpen her disappointment. Nonetheless, when she walked out of the audition room, it was with an optimistic tread. She had done really well.

Three days ago, this had seemed an impossibility.

The Monday morning after her trip to the beach with Eleanor, Charlie had woken early. She went for a long walk through clear-aired parks, and along bus-exhausted King Street. At eight fifty-five, she stopped outside a store and waited.

Kodak-yellow letters were painted on the glass: *Lights, Camera, Passion.* The attempt at a pun was so lazy it seemed self-mocking. And beneath the silly name, smaller letters read, boldly:

The oldest shop in Sydney

And beneath that, even more boldly:

Established 1955

This jovial exterior—sun on warm glass; silly statements drawn in bright colours—turned out to be deceptive. Inside, the shop was so dark, so seemingly full of secrets, that entry felt like trespass. On the walls, timeless faces stared out of old photos. To get to the counter at the back, Charlie had to slide between several cabinets, each filled with vintage cameras, their lenses dull and dusty.

Behind the counter, the sales assistant ignored her with great care. His face was middle-aged but for a juvenile pout and his thin frame gave him the silhouette of a teenaged boy or a supermodel. He wore a white tank top and several silver chains.

Charlie might have taken a photo of him and texted her sister: *On trend or on crack?* But if Charlie were in the mood to trade personal jokes with Eleanor—or to talk to her at all—she wouldn't have been in this shop in the first place.

She approached the counter and handed over the film from Helen's camera. When she asked whether he thought the film might be damaged, he replied—in a surprisingly high voice—that they'd have to wait and see.

At home, Charlie kept asking her housemates whether they could believe Helen was now seeing her sister. Mandy said no, she could not, the news had literally killed her, and now she was dead of shock. Still, Charlie could feel her interest waning, so she went to her room and called Mark. His phone went straight to voicemail, so she hung up. He called back in his lunchbreak.

She expected him to feel consoled—knowing that Eleanor, too was capable of duplicity. Or at least insulted that she had got over him so quickly. But it seemed as if he were interested in Charlie, not as an instrument to find out about Eleanor, but as the *subject* of the story: a person in her own right. The victim.

Talking about it was helpful. When she'd told the story enough times—of her sister dating her sort-of ex—it acquired a rehearsed quality, like she was reading from a script, rather than reliving an experience.

On Tuesday—one day out from her audition—Charlie decided that she would not revise the monologue. Instead, she looked for casual jobs. She shoehorned her resumé into ever-widening search fields on seek.com. She overstated her abilities as an 'assistant' to television production companies and dental surgeries alike. She called her old manager at a pub in Newtown. She'd quit abruptly so she could rehearse the Ibsen play, but now she told him that she had full availability, indefinitely.

Then, on Wednesday, with a few hours to go before her twelve o'clock audition slot, her outlook changed completely. She received an email with the words *photo* and *film* in the subject line. She saw the notification on her phone, and raced upstairs to open it on her laptop.

Attached to the email was a zip folder containing the scans of thirty-six photographs. From the thumbnails alone, Charlie could tell that Helen's film wasn't damaged at all.

The photos had a grainy, nostalgic quality that was impossible to replicate digitally. Like mythological creatures, the figures in these photos didn't belong to a particular time or place. Even before she opened them in full-screen, she thought she could recognise some of the scenes. Gordons Bay; the backyard at Bethel Street; the stone bunker where Kevin had staged his rave. In each, she could not make out the faces.

One figure in particular caught her eye. A woman's hair, presumably salt-wet, slicked to her head, her face half-turned to the camera. In profile, Charlie could just make out the bump of her nose—it was long, slightly aquiline, just a touch longer than Charlie's.

This was the photo Charlie opened first.

She ran downstairs, her laptop still open, shouting, 'Kevin!' as she went.

'What's up?'

He had been lying out the back, his shirt off, a book by his side and his phone in his hand. He walked into the kitchen with the speed of someone who'd just got out of bed. Charlie stood by her laptop, and pointed.

'Look—I got Helen's film developed.'

'What film?'

'You know she left that box of stuff? There was a film camera in it, so I got it developed.'

'Is that not, like, invasive?'

'*Look*.'

He leaned forward. Charlie increased the brightness on her screen.

Kevin looked up at her. 'Do you find the touchbar gimmicky?'

'What?'

He pointed to her keyboard.

Now Charlie was sure she was being toyed with. She actually jumped up and down. 'Will you look at what's *on* the screen?'

Kevin's smile faltered as he focused.

The photo was of Eleanor, sitting on the rocks at Gordons Bay. She was wearing a navy one-piece swimsuit. Her hair—dry, Charlie now saw—was pulled tight into a bun. She looked over her shoulder, like she'd only just heard the shutter click and had turned, not quite able to catch the photographer in the act.

'You poor thing.' Kevin placed a hand on Charlie's shoulder. 'That must really hurt to see.'

It didn't hurt—not yet. Charlie was still cresting a wave of victory. She had been wronged, yes. But she was *right.* It was a great salve, to think that she was, if maltreated and misused, then at least not insane.

Charlie extended a finger to the bottom right of the screen, where six orange digits were printed in the corner of the photo. 'Look at the date.'

Kevin read aloud: '4 January 2022.'

He exhaled: a long, revelatory *oh.* The final piece slotting into place. 'But that was—'

'Weeks and weeks ago, yeah.'

Kevin pulled Charlie into a hug. He held her for several seconds, before leaning back, looking into her eyes, and asking if she was okay.

Charlie wished it was Mandy who was home, not Kevin, so she might enjoy a less proportionate response. The situation seemed, suddenly, not dramatic at all, just very small and sad.

That was until Kevin's smile returned, and his eyes regained their boyish, teasing glint. 'If they've been seeing each other for weeks, these photos could have been a *lot* worse.'

She closed her laptop, snapping at his fingers.

—

CHARLIE HAD EXPECTED to feel sick, or betrayed. Instead, she felt vindicated—a twist of triumph—to see her worst fears confirmed.

It was with that triumph that Charlie entered her audition on Wednesday at noon. By the time she exited half an hour later, it had doubled.

She checked her phone—adjusting the brightness to the sun—and saw a notification, which, if possible, made her feel even more victorious: *3 messages from Helen.* She opened them immediately.

Hey I hope you went well today.
Crossing fingers and toes for you!!

I wanted to wait until after your audition
because I thought you probably wouldn't
have the mental space for ~ drama ~ but if
you're up to it I'd love to catch up in person
and talk about Eleanor and everything

Have been thinking about you a
lot and really hope you're ok

Their father used to say: there was no correspondence that was not improved by sleeping on it. Like much of their father's wisdom, the Hamor sisters ignored it. Had Charlie slept on it—or even waited a few hours—she might have played her cards differently. She might have spoken to Eleanor first, or to both of them together, or waited for a more dramatic moment with a more fitting setting.

But she was still running on adrenaline, which meant she was in the mood for confrontation.

Are you free now?

—

HELEN OFFERED TO meet Charlie in Walsh Bay, near her audition. It seemed the least she could do, after all the inconvenience she'd caused.

They met at a park just beneath the Harbour Bridge. When Helen arrived, she sat in her car for several minutes. She was trapped in that particular dread inspired by the prospect of a difficult conversation. Wanting very much for it to be over. Wanting even more for it not to begin.

A scream interrupted Helen's thoughts. A toddler, standing by the road. His face was red and wet, and his shrieks piercing. When his mother tried to pick him up, he thrashed until she put him down again.

'Please,' she said. 'Please, we have to go home.'

Helen wound up her window and got out of the car, so she might look less like she was eavesdropping and more like she was just passing through.

As she passed, to her horror, the mother started to cry.

The boy went on screaming. The change in his mother did not register on his face or in his little clenched fists. It was like he hadn't noticed her at all. Helen felt her stomach as a hole, which widened and widened, while mother and son both wept.

She found Charlie seated further up the hill. From there the Harbour Bridge was loud—although so incessant, it quickly became inaudible, like a ticking clock or the hum of a fridge. At intervals, the child's cries rent the air.

They sat together, the ibises silent at their feet, beaks full of rubbish. There was small talk at the start: about Bethel Street, and about the big gig Mandy had coming up.

Charlie mentioned that Helen had left a large box of stuff behind in a cupboard in the kitchen.

Helen, meanwhile, was fretting about the entry of Eleanor into the conversation. She was so busy planning what she might say when they got to that point, she didn't realise that they had already arrived.

Charlie was saying something about getting photos developed.

Charlie's phone was in Helen's lap. It took her a moment to realise what she was looking at.

When she did—when she saw Eleanor's tanned back, a white cross where her Speedos usually sat, and the open mouth, ready with a comment—she pressed the side of the phone and made the screen turn black. The phone seemed heavier then, more like a physical object.

'I'm sorry you had to see that,' Helen said. 'That must have been really shitty, to have to go through those photos like that.'

'The date was what disturbed me.'

Helen clicked the side button again. She handed Charlie the phone so she could unlock it. When Charlie passed it back to her, she zoomed in on the date. It was as she expected: very early January.

This back-and-forth with the phone was too much for Charlie. She raised her voice to compete with a train, which was, at that moment, thundering overhead. 'Eleanor said you only started seeing each other, like, a few weeks ago.'

Had the setting been different—had the bridge not been so loud or loomed so large, and had the child not, at that moment, been wrestled into the back seat with an unearthly cry, and had

Charlie not looked over her shoulder to check that nobody was being abducted—then they might have had a different conversation.

Charlie might have heard Helen gasp. She might have seen that her eyes roved over the photograph not with guilt, but with disbelief.

They might have bonded over it: that Eleanor had lied to them both. They might have laughed even, at the coincidence, that the same photo caught her twice. First, for lying to Charlie about when she started seeing Helen. Second, for lying to Helen about what she'd told Charlie.

But—because of the place, or her mood, or her nature, or any number of reasons—Charlie didn't pay enough attention. So when Helen whispered, 'That's not what happened,' Charlie didn't hear the incredulity. Helen wasn't correcting Charlie's interpretation. She was trying to form her own. *Why did Eleanor say that, when that wasn't what happened?*

But Charlie heard what she wanted to hear. And she responded in an aloof, righteous tone. Taking up arms, as if Helen were being defensive.

'Evidently,' Charlie said, borrowing a favourite phrase of her sister's.

'We didn't do anything that day.' Helen had zoomed out, and was contemplating the whole picture. She didn't look at Charlie. 'We just went to the beach. Eleanor was a bit of a bitch, actually. I was pretty off her. And then I stayed over after that rave, and we got talking again. We didn't start seeing each other properly until a week or so after that.'

'But that was ages ago.'

'I know. I'm sorry.' Helen looked at Charlie now. 'I should have told you much sooner, but I thought you should hear it from Eleanor first. The conversation should've happened weeks ago, though. I'm sorry.'

'We were still living together.'

'I know. We should've told you as soon as we started hanging out. We should've told you right at the start.'

'We lived together. You said you were the one who wanted me in that house. Gordons, Bethel Street: all those places meant so much to me.'

'To me too.'

Helen reached out but Charlie batted her hand away. 'I *knew* you were seeing someone else. I could just tell. And you were gaslighting me that whole time. With my sister. You were my *director* when we met. I looked up to you so much.'

With each of these admissions, Charlie felt smaller and more pathetic. Helen, meanwhile, was nodding in infuriating sympathy and saying, over and over again, that she was sorry.

The whole scene was wrong. Here was Charlie, the abused party, asserting with each line how powerless she was. But Helen—who was older, and had lived in the house for longer, and gave Charlie directions, and was admired by everyone—wasn't acting like she had any power at all. She wasn't defending herself, or fighting Charlie, or insulting her, thereby reaffirming her smallness. Instead, she was looking at her with that curious gaze: looking and looking, her eyes filling with tears, like she hated how much pain she was seeing.

Someone walking past would have seen two young women seated on a park bench, the Harbour Bridge ominous above. Both—light- and dark-haired—crying now, their shoulders shaking, until the blonde one leaned forward, as if in exhaustion, to rest her head on the other's shoulder. They would have seen the slender arms that rose immediately to cradle her, and they would not have been able to say—from watching that tender scene—which of the two had wronged the other.

—

THE ROOFTOP OF Eleanor and Seb's apartment building was empty on Wednesday evening. Helen stood there at eight o'clock, her feet right up against the railing, and looked out across the city. From this vantage the harbour licked the narrow gaps between the skyscrapers. The bridge was a distant curve, like a silver coin half-submerged. And the sky: low clouds at a distance, shot with purple. Everywhere a gentle, fading pink.

It was the sort of view to stretch time. Although it only lasted for a few minutes, it contained all the beauty of a day—of a whole summer.

'Seb and I used to come up here all the time when we first moved in.'

Helen turned to see Eleanor emerging from the stairwell, carrying a bottle of wine and two glasses. She'd changed her work shoes to flats, and moved easily across the rooftop.

'We're lucky there's no one else up here.'

As she approached, Helen saw that the sun spun gold in her hair. Helen smiled at her, and Eleanor smiled in return. She held up the bottle of wine to show Helen, her smile faltering and becoming shy. Like they were being too romantic, or serious: enjoying a wine with a beautiful view. As if they deserved it.

Eleanor placed two glasses on the wooden outdoor table. They tinkled nervously.

'How was your day?'

'I saw Charlie.'

'Oh.' Eleanor stopped pouring. 'How was it?'

Without speaking, Helen eased the bottle from Eleanor's grasp and set it on the table, then took Eleanor's hands in her own. She walked her right up to the railing, and then stood behind her with a hand on each of Eleanor's shoulders. She pulled her closer, until their bodies were flush together. 'It was about as horrible as I could've expected.'

Eleanor raised a hand to meet Helen's, and squeezed.

When Helen had sat on that park bench with Charlie and looked at the photo, she'd made a decision. She could've told Charlie that Eleanor had lied to her too; that she'd wanted to tell Charlie the whole truth from early on, but that Eleanor had insisted on waiting. Instead, she let Charlie say what she'd come to say.

So Eleanor was petty, and when the moment demanded brutal honesty, she'd shrunk from it. So she'd tried to please Helen and Charlie at the same time—to have everyone's love and everyone's good opinion. *But*, Helen thought, *I could have been more involved: I could have told Charlie myself rather than staying at the margins, as if the Hamor sisters comprised the whole picture.*

Helen held Eleanor close, and said nothing about the photo. She just said that Charlie had cried and she'd apologised, and she held Eleanor tighter.

Helen had always thought that if you loved someone, you saw them as they were, in all their infinite complexity. She was always trying to *explain* people: to see their faults and account for them. She'd done it with her housemates—with Kevin, the private school bohemian, whose countercultural tendencies were, on closer inspection, a genuine attempt to author his own life. And with Mandy, the comedian, who needed laughter like a child needs love, and who, like a child, was forever trusting. With Charlie, Helen had failed. To her shame, she hadn't recognised Charlie's weaknesses—that she was not naive just because she was beautiful, but also because she was *young*, and that she wasn't kind and attentive to Helen just because it was her nature, but also because she was in love.

For all these attempts to really see other people, on that bench with Charlie, Helen had decided that love—a devoted, committed love—could also mean closing her eyes.

She saw Eleanor's faults, and she chose to look away.

Right now, with the sun soft and her face buried in Eleanor's warm back, that seemed a natural—even a good—idea.

20

SYDNEY HAD PULLED off one of those taunting days she likes to reserve for special occasions. The sky looked like white noise, and the streets were damp from overnight rain. The sun was noncommittal: a storm unlikely, but possible.

That night, Mandy was performing in the biggest comedy show of her career: a line-up of Sydney's best new comedians. Each of them would be on stage for no more than ten minutes, which, Eleanor said, was how all standup comedy should be performed.

The theatre had a terracotta-coloured facade, which, in the dull grey evening light, looked like pale skin. Overhead, box-office lights warmed the sidewalk. Charlie stood outside, and waited for Helen and Eleanor to arrive.

When Charlie had first suggested they all go together, it was in the spirit of water and ducks' backs. They would try, the three of them, to be friends. After all, Charlie liked Helen, and she liked her sister. Hypothetically, they might have a pleasant time: three girls together.

Now, however, Charlie was anticipating the event like a predator anticipates a hunt. She hadn't heard from Eleanor in the past few days, so she assumed that Helen hadn't mentioned the photo. It seemed that she might yet do the honours herself.

She had asked Mandy several times whether she intended to talk about Helen's camera in her set. It would be strangely flattering, Charlie thought, to have a love life so painful that it fashioned itself naturally into an anecdote. It would be a tortured sort of pleasure: to suffer in a structured, aesthetic way.

Mandy had been sceptical. 'It's a shame there weren't any nudes,' she'd said. 'Now *that* would really be great material.'

Still, Charlie was hopeful. There would be real grace, she thought, in skewering Eleanor so publicly. She'd be frozen—her face in the clutches of a crowd—unable to respond. And even in private, it would be incriminating for Eleanor to interpret Mandy's joke as targeted. Powerless to rebut, or even clarify, Eleanor would be trapped.

Standing outside the theatre, although sober, Charlie experienced a drunken exhilaration. She had proof—evidence!—that Eleanor had lied. Outrage stripped her of inhibition. And as long as the high lasted, lacking inhibitions and having courage felt like exactly the same thing.

—

WHEN ELEANOR AND Helen arrived, the Hamor sisters greeted each other with mutual surprise.

'You're so *early*,' Eleanor said.

Charlie smiled, held out her hands, and said: 'Look at you!'

Eleanor was wearing a pale green double-breasted blazer, over a white t-shirt and matching green shorts. The shorts had a crease down the centre, and a folded hem, which sat halfway down her thigh.

In the shop, Helen had convinced Eleanor that this was an outfit she could 'pull off'. Eleanor wasn't entirely sure that Helen didn't just want the opportunity to borrow it herself—dark chocolate hair and mint suit. But Eleanor knew from experience that she would never feel so desirable as she did at the start of a new relationship. If she were ever going to push the sartorial envelope, now would be the time. She allowed herself to be persuaded, a decision she was less confident of now that the eyes on the outfit were not exclusively Helen's.

Charlie nodded, took her sister's arm, and, at her side, looked her up and down. 'Seriously, this is chic as shit.'

They took their seats—Helen sat in the middle—and talked over the assembling crowd. Charlie was in her fullest charm, that rare state of turning that gift—her sensitivity—outwards: she emoted physically, touching Helen's arm to make a point, and leaning far over to include Eleanor. She was wearing all black, her white hair shocking on top. She looked, to Eleanor, elf-like and gentle.

Just as the evening's emcee was walking on stage, Kevin joined them. He'd come straight from his current job—nobody had asked what it was—and caused a big fuss finding his seat next to Charlie, clad in a bucket hat and high-vis vest.

Mandy's set was third. First was a musical comedy act, by a man dressed as a robot who claimed to find intimacy difficult. Second, a man who was TikTok famous for pouring beers on other people's heads. Eleanor found him inexplicably hilarious. She laughed so hard she had to lean back to stretch her stomach.

Then Mandy, beaming, stood right at the edge of the stage, and held the microphone in two hands like a trophy. She was wearing heeled boots, a short blood-coloured skirt in a very shiny material, and a cropped white top with little puff sleeves that made a mockery of modesty.

Mandy's style of comedy demanded laughter as a way of telegraphing particular political commitments. Some of the stuff Eleanor had seen before was there—jokes about the child modelling industry, and models who are also feminists, and catcalling, and racism in Australia—as well as a long bit on the fad of learning pole dancing for exercise.

As she concluded this last riff, Mandy received her biggest laugh so far. Instead of moving on, she mined the moment, and did the only thing more endearing to an audience than actually being funny. She pretended to stop performing. First, she laughed with them, like she couldn't help it. Then, she pretended to forget whichever joke came next.

Charlie wiped her eyes, and leaned over to say to Helen: 'Real professionals know when to corpse.'

Helen nodded, and Charlie bent around her so she could make the same comment to her sister. Eleanor didn't laugh. She didn't look at Charlie either. Her gaze was locked on the stage, her mouth downturned.

She probably found it overdramatic, Charlie reflected, to call it *corpsing*. As if you died when you broke character.

But for the rest of the set, and for all the comedians that followed, Charlie kept leaning back to glance around Helen at her sister. Mandy didn't end up mentioning the photo, so Charlie's fantasy didn't eventuate. But a version of it—a distortion—played out on Eleanor's face. Instead of the guilty horror Charlie had imagined, she saw a different kind of revelation.

Eleanor—unsmiling, unlaughing—looked furious.

—

AS SOON AS the show ended, Eleanor shot out of the theatre, saying something about the bathroom. Helen went to get a round of drinks while they waited for Mandy to emerge from backstage, and Kevin chased her out, insisting that it was his shout.

After having no luck in the bathroom line, Charlie found Eleanor. She was seated in the bar in the foyer of the theatre—a plastic cup of tap water in one hand, and her phone in the other. She switched to holding the cup between her knees, so she could type with both hands.

'Hey. Is that work?' Panic pressed Charlie's chest, and told her otherwise. Her heartbeat was fast and loud, as if against a low ceiling. Rapidly, she was replaying Mandy's set in her head, scouring it for jokes that might have upset Eleanor. It seemed foolish now, that Charlie had ever hoped for a confrontation. Looking at Eleanor, her posture a question mark, her thumbs furious across her phone screen, Charlie felt at once helpless and responsible, like she was standing on stage and had forgotten her line.

'Eleanor.' Charlie eased into a chair beside her sister. 'What's happened?'

Eleanor was looking at Mandy's Instagram profile. 'It's crazy,' she said. 'I'm probably reading too much into it.'

'Into what?'

Eleanor looked Charlie in the eye, like answers were contained there instead of on her screen: 'Mark's here tonight. I saw him. He's sitting a few rows behind us. And before you say, "he could be here to see any of the comedians," I checked.' She pushed her phone towards Charlie.

'What are you showing me?'

'He follows Mandy.' Eleanor's eyes were wide with her theory. 'And all those jokes she made about pole dancing, and sex work, and . . .'

Charlie's eyes must have also widened, as she followed the thought to its conclusion, because Eleanor grabbed her arm, snatching at an answer.

'For the lovely ladies.' Kevin was suddenly standing between them, his voice louder than his high-vis vest. He placed two white wines on the bar between the sisters.

Helen was right behind him. Seeing their silence, and Eleanor's hand on Charlie, she immediately reached for Eleanor. 'Hey. What's up?'

Eleanor straightened, and returned her phone to the pocket of her shorts. 'It's nothing.'

Charlie turned to Kevin. 'Eleanor wants to ask Mandy if the pole dancing section of her set is autobiographical.'

Kevin's laugh was high-pitched. 'Why?'

In the silence, Eleanor's embarrassment was audible. 'I just thought . . .' She kept looking over her shoulder at Helen, as if delivering an apology. 'Because my ex follows her—not that I care or anything, he can follow whoever he likes. I just wondered whether she knew him.'

'. . . from pole dancing?' Kevin took a sip of wine, and winced. 'That's his vibe, is it?'

'It would be a crazy coincidence, wouldn't it?' Eleanor turned to Charlie and, very softly, as if to prevent Helen from hearing, she whispered: 'I could just ask, I guess? For peace of mind?'

Charlie shook her head again. 'Absolutely don't. Eleanor, I think . . . I think she'd find that very offensive.' And then, because Eleanor was looking at her phone again, now at Mandy's Instagram, and now at her tagged photos, Charlie added: 'It *is* offensive.'

Eleanor turned to Charlie. 'What if you asked for me?'

Kevin answered for her. '*What?*'

'You could do it super casually. Just be like: do you know this Mark guy who follows you?'

'Oh, that's awkward.'

At the sound of a new voice, all four heads turned. The Hamor sisters were still seated at the bar, Kevin and Helen standing at their shoulders. The sisters sat motionless in shock, while the other two shuffled to one side to admit the intruder into their conversation.

How was it, Eleanor wondered, that Mark always looked the same. Perhaps it was those thin wire glasses, or the hair that stopped just under his chin, accentuating his square jaw. No matter where he was—at his desk at work, in bed on a Sunday, or at an Inner West theatre on a Friday night—he looked like such a *lawyer*.

He smiled at them now, and raised his hands in mock surrender. 'Whatever you were saying about me, Eleanor, I'm sure I deserved it.'

Because no one laughed, he tried a more conventional greeting. A second chance at an entrance. He introduced himself to Kevin with a handshake, and then kissed Charlie, Eleanor, and then Helen on the cheek. 'Wow. Helen, I haven't seen you in years.'

Her smile was visibly restrained.

Eleanor, still seated, had her arms crossed. Seeing Mark attempt small talk with Helen, and seeing her loyal hostility, she felt emboldened. 'Mark,' she said. 'I didn't know you were a fan of Mandy's.'

'Oh yeah, she's great.'

'So, when did you, like, discover her?'

Charlie's whisper only flirted with discretion, when she said, under her breath: 'For fuck's sake.'

'What? What is it?'

Eleanor had rounded on her sister, so Charlie turned outwards, as if to an audience. 'This is actually comical.'

Kevin, who wasn't finding the situation funny at all, tried to engage Helen. 'So,' he said. 'How did the move go in the end? You all settled in?'

'Mark,' Eleanor said, 'can I speak to you?'

Kevin persisted with Helen. 'We miss you, you know. The spring has definitely gone out of Petronella's step.'

Eleanor stood up, and motioned to Mark.

'Eleanor, can you just drop it? This is ridiculous.' Charlie grabbed Eleanor, just above the elbow, and tried to pull her back into her seat. The mint green of her suit was smooth. Eleanor shook her off. 'Eleanor, please—'

It was Eleanor's turn to whisper. This one didn't even attempt discretion. It was insect-like in Charlie's ear. 'I'm entitled to the truth.'

'Are you? Is everyone, on principle?'

Now Helen reached into the fray. Her arm on Charlie's shoulder. 'Charlie, don't.'

Charlie shook her off. Her questions grew higher, more strained. She had barely sipped her wine, but her head was spinning. 'Or is it just you, Eleanor? *You're* entitled to the truth. You get to know everything, and decide which bits you'll tell other people.'

'Charlie?' Mark leaned in. 'Charlie, do you think—'

Helen's hand was back at her shoulder. Now she had Mark on one side, and Helen on the other, each trying to pull her back. 'Charlie,' Helen said. 'We don't have to have this conversation right now.'

Charlie took a deep breath, and rolled her shoulders back. Standing resolute, with some of her stage-stillness, she looked at Eleanor. That familiar look that passes between sisters: on the bus, across the playground, at the dinner table. *I have something to tell you.*

'Let's go outside.'

Eleanor followed her sister out, Helen close behind. Mark too tried to follow, but Kevin—who, as ever, was sensitive to poetry—pulled him back, and let the three women retreat alone.

—

OUTSIDE THE NIGHT was surprisingly cool. The hairs lifted on Charlie's bare arms.

Helen was nauseous at the thought of seeing that photo again. And of how Eleanor would react, when she found out about it. But Charlie, it seemed, was determined. When she took a deep breath, Helen took Eleanor's hand, and squeezed.

'It was me.'

'*What?*'

Eleanor and Helen had spoken in unison. But Eleanor's was less a cry of confusion, and more an exclamation. She released Helen's hand, and covered her mouth. It was the thought that had formed when she saw Mark tonight, and saw him kiss her sister on the cheek. How he'd leaned in, brushed her cheek with his lips, and with his hand, the small of her back. How she'd forgotten to flinch.

That thought—that spark that flickered, and now was steady—led her to the next and the next, all the way to the truth.

'Mark was with *me* that night. Not Mandy.'

Helen blinked several times, and closed her mouth, before opening it again. Then, deciding she had nothing to say, she closed it. Eleanor, meanwhile, was unmoving.

Charlie started to speak quickly, without pausing, as if the sound—the smooth flow of her story—might be soothing. But with every word, she felt the tension increase. 'Last November, I had my last shift before I quit to do the play. We finished late, and then we stuck around for drinks. And I saw Mark, in the street. Literally, just bumped into him, wandering around drunk. And he invited me to this apartment they'd rented around the corner, so I went up, and . . .'

Eleanor had turned her back on Helen. Her question, thrust at Charlie, had the force of an accusation. '*And what?*'

'We kissed. That's all.'

Eleanor was shaking her head, as if she could erase something: blur an image. 'I don't understand.'

'Nothing happened. We were both really drunk, and we had this deep and meaningful on the balcony—you know what Mark's like—and we kissed out there. That was it. Then he told you, and you freaked out, so he was like, well, the outcome is the same. I'll let her think the worst of me, if it's easier.'

'Easier? You *knew* it was making me crazy. I told you so many times I needed to know what happened.'

This wasn't the scene Charlie had imagined. She understood why Eleanor had made those wild leaps from Mark's presence at the show, to Mandy's jokes, to some sordid conclusion. It must have been overwhelming—Helen, Charlie, Mark all in one room. But overwhelmed wasn't in Eleanor's repertoire. So instead of feeling, she'd turned to her usual trick, and tried to make sense of the situation. That was all Charlie had wanted, when she took Eleanor's hand and led her outside: to show her how hard it was to sit above and apart and really *see*. How they all made mistakes, and were involved in such a dreadful complex mess—Eleanor included—that there was no sense to be made.

But now Eleanor wore a mask of disgust, and Charlie could see—as only sisters can—what she was thinking. Still trying to make sense of things, Eleanor wasn't looking at Charlie, standing black-clad on the sidewalk, but through her, to Charlie's former self, to those weeks following the break-up, when they'd called and texted every day. Eleanor reached for the past, held it up, and with a devastating look, declared Charlie a fake.

Charlie's voice was growing shrill. A voice that scratched and didn't carry, which she'd never use on stage. Not even in a comedy. 'I hate how close I came to betraying you. But we didn't, that's what I'm saying. We stopped before anything really happened. That's what matters: I turned back. That's why I told you about the emails. I wanted to, like, confess. That I had feelings for Mark, even if we never acted on them.'

'But you did.'

'You're not—'

'I can't believe I have to explain this to you.'

Charlie was so frustrated, she might have stamped her foot. How quickly they'd found the rhythm of their childhood: Charlie shrieking, and Eleanor—just as hostile—calmly interrupting.

'This "nothing happened" kiss,' Eleanor said, 'it infects everything, even those stupid emails. It's not like you and Mark had some special connection.' It was only with real effort that Eleanor didn't put bunny ears around *special connection* too. Although she wasn't conscious of it at the time, she was deriving an unexpected pleasure from Charlie's revelation. It was so easy, after weeks of lacerating guilt, to be back in her old, comfortable position: chastising her sister. 'Those emails were obviously leading to this point. And I would've been a lot more upset about them, if I'd known they were the precursor to basically having sex.'

'We didn't have sex!' Charlie actually stamped the ground with force.

'So? You wanted to. You'd been flirting for so long. This was the natural climax.'

What Eleanor said next, she didn't really mean. But conflict has its own logic: frenzied and associative and snatching at any fleeting thought. And she'd just used the word *climax*. 'It's like telling me: oh we fucked, but don't worry neither of us came.'

Until this point, Helen had watched in silence. Now a laugh slipped out of her, independent of her, and both sisters turned to stare. Eleanor, catching her eye, couldn't suppress a smile.

Charlie shivered, goosebumps all along her arms, as if that laugh was cold and dripping down her neck. She looked at Eleanor and

Helen, and, like a child, saw her mother and her big sister: older, smarter, mocking her with an irony only they could understand.

She swallowed, and blinked back tears. 'After your break-up, I felt sick. I thought, she's such a good person, and I almost betrayed her, of all people. It would've been so typical, your stupid selfish little sister letting you down. Especially when I thought,' Charlie was crying now, and paused to breathe once, deeply, through her tears. 'I kept thinking, she's the best person I know.'

Helen stepped around Eleanor, and put both hands on Charlie's shoulders. They were gentle, and Charlie almost leaned in for a hug.

'We don't have to have this conversation now.'

'What conversation?'

'Charlie, she doesn't know about the photo.'

Eleanor didn't hear Helen, she'd spoken too quietly. But Eleanor could see how tightly she was holding Charlie, and the gentle tilt of her hair, shrouding them both. She felt like her bones had disappeared, realising that Charlie had a secret, not just with Mark, but with Helen too. 'What are you talking about? Charlie? *What conversation?*'

Three women, a tight triangle, and a thinning crowd on the street.

Now both Helen and Eleanor were holding Charlie. One imploring her to speak; the other begging for silence. If Charlie had felt drunk before, she was now suddenly, numbingly sober. She was tired. She was tired of the lies and the secrets and the scrounging; of wondering what other people knew and were thinking, and what they thought about her. So although she'd originally brought it up, because she had a point to prove—a point about hypocrisy—now, when she spoke through tears, she didn't wield the truth. She yielded to it.

'I know about you and Helen. I know you've been seeing each other since the start of the year.'

Eleanor's blood felt suddenly lead-heavy, and her brain like it was being pushed outwards, and would soon seep through her skull. 'That's not true. Obviously, I'd met her before, but Charlie, I promise, it wasn't until she moved in that—'

'That's not true. It's not *true*. It's not possible. You went to the beach together. On the fourth of January.'

Eleanor's first instinct was to dispute the date. She thought back: New Year's Day in bed, the next day at the pool, texting Helen, it had all moved so quickly . . . Eleanor could taste the beer she'd drunk earlier that evening. It was acidic and, for a moment, she wondered whether she might throw up.

'Nothing happened,' she was too distressed to notice that she'd borrowed Charlie's phrase. 'We were just friends then.'

Eleanor hated that reflex—the words that scuttled forth—denying, minimising. She hated that she couldn't apologise to Charlie—not properly—that she couldn't beg forgiveness, but turned instead from her weakest self, growing smaller and more contemptible as she did. Still, she said it again: 'Charlie, I'm sorry, but nothing happened that day. I promise. I should've maybe told you we were friends, but I promise we didn't start seeing each other properly until . . . until later.'

Eleanor looked to Helen for support—a statement, or just a corroborating nod. Instead, with a flash of a septum piercing, and the ripple of dark hair, Eleanor was met with a devastating shake of the head.

'Charlie, honestly, we were just friends.' Eleanor grabbed her arm again, and Charlie shook her off, in one violent movement. She raised her voice to compete with the traffic.

'Here I was, trying to forget what Mark and I almost did to you. I wasn't coping: going out so much and throwing myself at

Helen. I hated how close I came. I kept thinking: Eleanor would never even think about doing something like that to me.'

Charlie's voice cracked on that last sentence. She had almost shouted it. Her hands had been flying, and now, as she fell to silence, she didn't know where to put them. So she crossed her arms over her chest, and stared at her sister, willing her to respond.

But Eleanor didn't speak. She just looked at Charlie right in the eye: a furious stare that was less painful than looking inward. They stayed like that for several long seconds, while Helen watched on.

'I'm going back in,' Charlie said, surprised at her own resolve. 'I just want Mandy to have a nice night.'

As Charlie passed through the swinging doors, Eleanor sunk to the concrete, and leaned her back against the orange-coloured wall. It was night now, and the tiles reflected the street. Eleanor looked out at the restaurants on the other side of the road, all the people eating, and the cars in between. She imagined lying down, and someone—Charlie would be fitting—running her over.

'Can we leave?' Eleanor's head was on her knees. Her left eye was throbbing, right at the back; she wasn't sure if it was her eye or her brain that was causing the pain.

Helen was crouching by her side. 'Sure, I'll just say goodbye to—'

'I need to leave.'

Helen eased one of Eleanor's arms around her shoulders, and lifted her up. The first steps were slow, and people stared until Eleanor removed her arm, and they walked side-by-side.

Stubbornly, the rain held off.

21

IN THE FOYER, Charlie found Mark, right where he'd always been. Hovering in a crowd, waiting for her. Kevin was also easy to spot—at Mark's side in that stupid vest. She stood with the two of them while they politely discussed the show, but she didn't contribute. As was the case when she'd arrived at the theatre several hours ago, Charlie was still thinking about Helen and Eleanor, and that incriminating photo. At first, the photo had been vindicating. It was proof of Charlie's double victimhood: betrayed by both her sister and her friend. In light of the fight they'd just had, Charlie reflected on the twin betrayals: each sister risking the other's happiness, only one going through with it.

Her relief was so strong, it was energising. For months she hadn't let herself think about that night with Mark. It was too horrible to contemplate—they'd come so close. Now, she saw it as part of a wider context: if Charlie had done wrong, if she wanted selfish things, and came dangerously close to acting on them, then she was only as bad as her sister. Strangely, it was from this perspective—not as victim but as almost-perpetrator—that she started to forgive herself.

In this mood, she was able to reciprocate the enthusiasm Mandy had always shown her. Charlie told her, when she emerged, that she was a fucking superstar.

Then the four of them made their way down the road to Mandy's favourite bar. They walked two-abreast: Kevin and Mandy in front, Mark and Charlie behind.

He was tall—taller than Charlie—with a slim frame, and a loose easy gait. He held a long arm out before they crossed, to signal that a car was coming. At the bar, they found a big booth in a dark corner, and they wedged themselves closest to the wall. He kept looking at his drink, and Charlie kept folding her coaster, and when they did look at each other, they struggled to fight a smile.

On the phone, and via email, they'd talked always of other things—each too ashamed to mention it. Even tonight, they talked around it. Charlie was very conscious of her skin, and she had that spine-tingling conviction that they were both, at that exact moment, thinking the same thing. If she looked up, she might see it in his face—the kiss, and what had followed, or *didn't* follow—all that potential, untouched, alive again between them.

At the time, when they were both drunk and smoking on the balcony, his friends loud and brutish indoors, Charlie wanted very much to sleep with him. He was full of compliments, and seemed so open, and if he was predatory, it was only because he pretended to be so vulnerable. Like she had all the power.

When they kissed, his hands were at her waist. Her white tank top was cropped, and as he slid down to her hips, he brushed against her skin. She gasped at the touch.

'Your skin,' he said, alcohol in his breath. 'It's smoother than I could have imagined.'

She loved the way his words ran into each other; how drink made him eloquent. Still, she said: 'We should stop. We'll hate ourselves in the morning.'

He squeezed her hips, and her stomach dropped.

He said, 'I hate myself already.'

She took both his hands in hers, and pushed them away. Perhaps too forcefully, because he raised them, as if in surrender. 'I'm so sorry. Charlie, I'm really sorry. I didn't mean to make you uncomfortable.'

'It's okay. Hey. Are you . . . Mark, are you okay?'

He was crouching, his head on his knees. So she crouched too, and with their backs to the railing, they talked.

He said he thought he probably needed to break up with her sister. Charlie said that he should. 'She's too good for you.'

He laughed, and he tried to nudge her, but he was still very drunk, so he put the whole weight of his shoulder against hers, and she almost fell to one side.

They talked a bit longer, and he asked her, now that they were being frank, whether she really thought he could write, because his greatest fear was that he wasn't talented, just deluded. Instead of reassuring him, she just told him the truth: she knew exactly how he felt. She felt like that all the time.

'I'm so glad, we didn't . . . you know.' He was looking at her now, and she smiled at his tone—like he had been the one to call stop.

He went on: 'That would've all been a bit sordid.'

Then she really did want to stay, because the way he said *sordid* made it sound like he was applying the word to himself—his personality; his weakness—not to the situation, and she wondered whether that was a tactic to weaken her resolve.

But she stood, and he stood too, and with a parting kiss—his lips modest on her forehead—she left.

Perhaps, if she had stayed, that might have been the end of it. But nothing happened, and now they were sitting opposite each other, squeezed into a crowded booth, not talking, but asking each other, with a glance, what might happen next.

Eleanor had Helen. Charlie was comforted by that fact. She recalled her last sight of them: heads bent, all mutual support. And Charlie—it now seemed obvious—had Mark. She'd had him this whole time: in his emails, and his calls, and his confessions and his questions. Mark knew things about her that nobody else did: private, shameful things. And she knew him the same way. And yet, even with that shared fragility, she felt stronger, less exposed, when she was in his presence.

With all of that between them, when he looked at her, and motioned with his head to the door, she had no doubt it was an invitation. He was going, and he wanted her to come too.

As they walked home towards Bethel Street, their conversation leaped ahead. They flew from one topic to another: sentences overlapping, ideas touching. But they walked in the middle of the empty road, at least a metre apart. When a car came, they both ran to opposite sides. Easy and uneasy in each other's company—the way two people are when they sense that their friendship is about to change.

—

ON THE WAY home, Eleanor couldn't stop crying.

While she cried, Helen explained, in soothing tones, because she knew Eleanor liked to have the whole picture, how Charlie knew. She told her about leaving her camera at Bethel Street, about Charlie getting it developed, and about the incriminating photo.

Eleanor turned the conversation to Charlie's other revelation. Of the two, Helen could see why this lie—the one where Eleanor was deceived, not doing the deceiving—was easier to talk about. Although Helen wasn't sure she could think of one without the other. For her, they were intertwined.

'I'm sorry,' Helen said. 'I had no idea.'

'I'm just so embarrassed.'

'You shouldn't be. But I get it. It's humiliating, being lied to.'

'I called her so many times,' Eleanor was looking out the window, even though they were going through a tunnel, and all the glass revealed was her own reflection. 'I told Charlie so many times that it was killing me, wondering who this woman was. She could've put me out of my misery.'

Helen narrowed her eyes, like the situation might clarify, the harder she looked at it. 'I suppose,' she said slowly, 'if he'd told you that he kissed Charlie when they were both really drunk, and they both regretted it immediately and didn't go any further . . . I don't know, Eleanor. You were pretty great about them sending each other those emails. I reckon you could've forgiven a kiss. You know, a drunk kiss. A mistake.'

'Are you saying I should?'

'No! Well, the kiss isn't the point anymore. I think the point is: they didn't tell you. I'm just saying—and this is selfish—but if they *had* told you, you and Mark might still be together.' She picked up Eleanor's hand. 'Which is a scary thought.'

Eleanor moved her hand from Helen's grasp, and covered her face with it. 'God. It's so humiliating. To be *manipulated* like this. Like, he knew I couldn't do it. I couldn't break up with him. So he concocted this fake situation, instead of telling me the truth.'

Eleanor was still speaking outwards, to the window, and her hand was still up around her face. Helen felt she couldn't touch her. So she tried to speak to her in terms she might understand: she tried to rationalise.

'I suppose, that's what people do, when they care about each other. That's why it was so hard for you to tell Charlie about us. And why, when you did tell her, you made it seem like the betrayal hadn't been so deep. Like, as if I wasn't seeing you while I was living with her.'

Eleanor's crying was louder now: shoulders shaking, and a great sticky sniff. Two teenagers at the end of the carriage turned to stare. Through her tears, she managed: 'I didn't know about that photo.'

'Eleanor, I'm not blaming you. I just meant: the humiliation, it's very real. But also, like, Charlie loves you. And you love her. And I think sometimes we lie to people we love, to make their lives a bit easier.' She added, very softly, like the words might have less of an impact if she placed them down gently: 'And this is a bit more cynical, but it's obviously normal, when you've done the wrong thing, to lie so you don't get caught. Or to avoid facing it, if you can.'

When Eleanor said nothing, Helen added: 'I've certainly been guilty of that.'

Although Helen was following their usual rhythm—the personal dramas just the starting point: an example to illustrate a larger principle—Eleanor shrunk from it, as if from an attack. 'Please,' she said. 'I just need a minute.'

A minute became several. They got off the train in silence. On the platform, a used condom—limp and overlong.

Helen didn't want to be one of those couples who fought in the street, so she didn't say anything—not on the walk home, or on the climb up the stairs. But she wasn't surprised, when the door closed behind them, and Eleanor, without turning on the lights, charged around the apartment, as if readying herself for a fight.

The living room had an eerie glow and the apartment opposite studied them closely. Eleanor didn't stop to turn on the lights. First, she called out for Seb, and, hearing nothing, pressed her ear to his door.

Then, while Helen went straight to the couch, Eleanor crossed the room. She sat in Seb's swivel chair at the flimsy desk he'd pushed up against the wall when they were both working from home. Her body was unmoving; wide legs and firm feet, her eyes steady on Helen.

After the cushioned closeness of the train, this new aspect seemed combative. It made the room feel smaller, and the fact that they were sitting in the dark, sinister.

When Eleanor finally spoke, she sounded as hostile as Helen had feared.

'When did Charlie show you that photo?'

'The other day. After her audition. Remember, I told you I'd seen her.'

'You didn't mention the photo.'

'I didn't want to upset you.' It was so simple, it sounded trite.

'I guess your trick worked, then.'

'What?'

Eleanor swivelled: right, and left, then back. Like a pendulum. 'Fucking hell.'

'What trick?'

'Leaving your camera at Bethel Street? What did you think would happen?'

Helen was silent for a moment, in shock. 'I—' she swallowed, and tried to sound less shrill. 'I didn't leave it on purpose.'

'I don't understand why you couldn't just talk to me. If you wanted Charlie to know . . . I thought we were talking. But you went and exposed us in your own way.'

'You're kidding.'

Eleanor had stopped moving. 'I'm extremely serious,' she said. 'It's a huge breach of trust.'

'Why would I leave that camera on purpose? Eleanor, we spoke about when we'd tell Charlie, like, all the time. Actually, it was, like, the main thing we talked about. Why would I go off and just tell her in my own weird way? And how could I know she'd get the film printed? It's so invasive.' She hated how defensive she sounded. Like she was deflecting blame to Charlie. She finished meek, and self-doubting: 'It doesn't make any sense.'

It did make sense: a twisted kind of sense. Helen could see how they'd arrived here. She could follow Eleanor's thoughts from the train up to the apartment, to this darkened room.

The photo wasn't embarrassing because it revealed that they were seeing each other. It was embarrassing because it revealed Eleanor's half-truth: her attempt to be approximately honest—to have what she wanted, without the consequences for wanting it.

So Eleanor, who had lied to Charlie and to Helen, was casting herself as the deceived. But what shocked Helen—what made her flounder, and lose her composure, and struggle to articulate all the ways Eleanor was wrong—was this: Eleanor seemed to genuinely believe it.

She, usually so perceptive, was refusing to see her own role. She was building up this story of Helen's betrayal, in order to mask the true offense: self-betrayal. Of her intellect, and her integrity; of those qualities Helen loved most.

The failure of character, Helen could take. Because she knew already that Eleanor was as flawed as the rest of us. It was the failure of reasoning that brought her to tears. Infuriatingly, they probably looked to Eleanor—in all her determination—like tears of guilt.

Upon seeing her cry, Eleanor didn't cross the room, or reach out. She lowered her voice, so Helen was the one that had to stretch forward, and cover the space between them.

'Maybe you didn't know how to break up with me.'

Helen wasn't sure if she'd heard correctly. 'But, Eleanor, I don't want to? I love you.'

'You say that. But you also said earlier that you think I'm manipulative. And you didn't go this far, but I think *hypocrite* is the other obvious implication.'

It upset Helen to see Eleanor apply all of her intellect and no emotion to their argument, as if to a debate about abstract propositions. Her gestures were measured and non-expressive, like she was delivering a presentation. By adopting this tone, it was as if Eleanor lowered the stakes, perhaps in a functional, but also strangely menacing way. A conversation that didn't involve her personally.

'Eleanor, please—'

'I—please just let me finish. I've behaved terribly. And if you wanted to leave, I'd understand. But maybe, just rip the bandaid? Like, it's already been a terrible night.'

'No, that's not what I want. You're not listening to me.'

'You hate how duplicitous I am. You obviously do. That's why you left that camera for Charlie to find. You wanted me to get caught.'

Helen heard it: the shift that Eleanor had been orchestrating since they got home. She didn't mention *them*—the two of them—getting caught. It was *me.*

Helen stood, and flicked the lights. It seemed silly, suddenly, that they'd sat in the dark for so long. She remained standing, and her voice was loud now—it filled the apartment, with its white furniture, and the black night out the window.

'I don't hate it. *You* hate it. I probably should hate it more, to be honest. But even when Charlie showed me that photo, and she explained why it upset her so much—how you'd lied to her, even though you told me you'd confessed the whole thing—I didn't care.'

She had to repeat that last part, because Eleanor scoffed on *you told me.* Like that proved her point: Helen did have contempt for her, after all.

'*I don't care*, Eleanor. I know what you're like—and I love you anyway. You. Not some idealised version. I even love the bits you don't like about yourself.'

Eleanor whispered very quietly, like she was scared Helen would hear, 'And what am I like?'

Helen was pacing now. 'You're so . . . you're closed. You don't want people to really see you. Like a child covering its eyes, as a way of hiding.' She was so worked up she actually did the mime. 'Like right now. You seem to think self-awareness is some kind of erasure: like as long as *you* see your faults, nobody else is allowed to see them.'

Eleanor closed her eyes so tight, she felt the pressure build against her eyeballs. When she opened them, her whole head was sore. 'Right. That's a pretty damning report.'

'Eleanor, I didn't—'

'No, it's probably all fair.'

Helen sat back on the couch, and looked at her. Silence, heavy with the sense that too much had already been said.

She settled her elbow on her knee, and her chin on her hand. From this pensive posture, she fixed her eyes on Eleanor, in that probing, penetrative way she had that didn't presume an answer, but just looked and looked, until the answer revealed itself. Her voice was very soft, Eleanor had to blink to push back tears. 'Beautiful girl,' Helen said.

Eleanor looked away. 'I think, maybe, we're just clinging to this because we hurt Charlie so much. Like, we have to make it work, to justify it. Like a sunk cost, or something.'

Helen laughed. A grim, dirty sound. 'A sunk cost?'

'Yeah.'

'Is that how you feel?'

'It's how it feels to me, yeah.'

'Right.'

'I think, maybe, you should leave.'

Helen didn't move. Her stare acquired a coldness—her eyes a reflective surface. It occurred to Eleanor, then, that Helen might hate her. 'Why? Do you want me to leave?'

'It's okay. You can go.' Her voice—her own voice—was so soft, it was difficult to hear. Eleanor felt suddenly like she might faint. The room seemed very far away, and the inside of her head—where splotches were forming in her vision—the only immediate thing. 'Please go.'

Eleanor couldn't bear to watch her go, even though that was exactly what she'd suggested—begged for—in that stupid little voice. She couldn't quite believe that she didn't call *stop*, or *wait*, or *please*, even as she sat there, and listened to Helen stand, and pick up her keys, and stall at the door—making all the steps to leave. When the door finally shut, Eleanor flinched, as if at a physical blow.

22

'WE'RE ALMOST THERE.'

As they turned into Bethel Street, Charlie and Mark fell silent. They were walking very quickly now, each trying not to pant audibly in the still night.

She saw the lights first, casting ominous shadows. Then she heard the engine. Before she could leap out of the way, Mark took her arm and pulled her to one side. They let the car slide past, smooth and electric.

Even when Mark let go, she could still feel his touch.

They laughed a little and resumed walking, even faster than before. Charlie took his hand, acknowledging what was about to happen.

'Which number?' His voice was strained.

'93.'

She could see him counting. She did too.

They'd just passed 85.

They were almost running now. Charlie felt like she had jumped from a great height and was in freefall: her decision irreversible, the consequences yet to meet her.

87, 89, 91 . . .

'Charlie?'

Upon hearing her name, Charlie stopped so abruptly that Mark ran into the back of her.

A figure was standing by the front door, small and slight, strokes of hair dark against her shoulders.

'Helen?' Charlie could see she'd been crying. 'Helen, what's happened?'

Charlie rushed forward to open the front gate. As soon as Helen saw Mark behind her, she started to apologise, 'Oh, I didn't realise—'

'No, no. It's fine.'

Mark said something about going. Charlie looked at him with such urgency, he brushed his hair behind his ears, then put his hands in his pockets and looked at his shoes, like he was determined *not* to take up space but had never attempted it before.

'What's happened?' Charlie asked again. 'Is Eleanor okay?'

Helen shook her head, then nodded, then said: 'I think we just broke up. I'm sorry, I didn't know where else to go.'

Charlie babbled, as she fished for her key and unlocked the door and turned on the hallway light. Helen said she didn't want to talk about it.

Charlie told her that she was sorry and of course Helen should stay, and (as if it would help) that she would go get Helen a glass of water.

In the kitchen, she reflected that she really *was* sorry. This surprised her: how much she wanted her sister to be happy, even if it meant having what she couldn't. She drank Helen's water then filled the glass again.

Returning to the corridor, she found Helen sitting at the bottom of the stairs, looking like she'd never moved out. She accepted the water with a weak smile.

'The bed's still in your room.' Charlie stopped herself from saying *old* room. 'You can grab a blanket and some pillows off mine?'

Helen thanked her and stood. Upright on the second step, she was the same height as Charlie. The two women hugged.

Before Helen turned, she looked at Charlie: that infuriating, probing stare. 'Hey,' she said. 'Are you okay?'

Charlie said she was fine, although how she really felt was *callous*, for being here with Mark, now that Helen and Eleanor were apart.

With Helen's footsteps still on the stairs, Charlie felt a hand at her waist. His fingers were tentative—just the tips—but she pressed into him, and the heat from his touch seemed to warm her whole body.

She turned, ready to kiss him and cling to him and to take him in her mouth, tasting all thrilling and destructive.

But Mark removed his hand as soon as she was facing him and reached up to touch his hair. 'Fuck me,' he said, not as literally as Charlie would have liked. 'That must've been weird.'

'What?'

'Helen coming here, after everything she and Eleanor did to you.'

Charlie, in an attempt to skip past the conversation, walked into the living room, turned on the lamp and sat on the couch. Looking up at Mark, who still stood by the stairs, she said with a quick dismissive smile, 'It's okay.'

But Mark maintained his friendship's distance. Only his gaze—unbroken concern—followed her. So she went on: 'I don't know, it's just kind of sad, really, that it didn't work out for them.'

'Is it? Did you want it to work out?'

'At first, no. Obviously. But, after everything they put me through, you know, the least they could do was stay together for more than five minutes.' Her laugh was shrill and met without a smile. Instead, a slow, grave nod.

'Yeah, that must be really tough.'

Because the couch was starting to feel like a therapist's, Charlie shuffled up—right to the edge—to make room for Mark. 'We don't need to talk about it.'

'Of course not,' Mark nodded knowingly, as if she had in fact talked about it and revealed something deeply personal.

Charlie crossed her legs and felt a pressure against her skin from the inside, like something was trying to claw its way out.

Just when the silence was becoming unbearable, Mark said, 'I can't imagine how it feels for them. I mean, when you and I'—in the dim lamplight, she saw him blush, and although Charlie was already very hot, she felt her own cheeks redden—'I felt so guilty.'

He looked at her then, not with concern, but with a gaze so penetrating that when he swallowed, his Adam's apple moving up and down, Charlie felt her mouth go dry. 'And all we did was kiss,' she said.

At last he moved towards her: a brutish sort of lunge, so clumsy lurching that she almost recoiled.

But before he could reach the couch there was a flash of brown and a high, comical sound, which she realised, only later, must have come from him.

Mark was still, his hands on his head—not, for once, to tend to his hair—but as if he were being held at gunpoint. 'What the fuck was that?'

At Charlie's feet, Petronella sat, ears aloof and nose twitching.

Mark followed Charlie's eyeline and, seeing the bunny, started to laugh. 'I'm so sorry. I thought it was a rat.'

Charlie picked her up, feeling her little heart sputter beneath her palm. Her fur was soft and Charlie pressed her cheek to the crest of Petronella's head and rubbed it back and forth.

She walked through the kitchen out to the back of the house. In the yard, she returned Petronella to her coop—her bum planted squat on the grass, the rest of her following.

Back inside, Mark was still standing by the stairs.

'Let's go to my room,' Charlie said.

Mark, embarrassed perhaps by the pitch of his own scream, followed a conservative distance behind.

When they'd closed the door behind them, they smiled at each other, awkwardly, to acknowledge the sound coming from the next room. Helen on the other side of the wall, crying—quietly, she probably thought—but loud enough for Charlie and Mark to make out each individual sob.

Mark shrugged. 'We've all been there.'

Charlie laughed, because she felt the way he wanted her to, when he made that face: eyebrows up and gaze down and out. Like he was hers to toy with, to break or to complete.

Feeling more confident now that they were, at last, sitting side-by-side, Charlie went on: 'Have you cried like that recently?'

'No, not recently. I've been feeling immensely guilty, obviously. But that didn't involve much crying. Weirdly, it kind of helped to know that Eleanor held me in such contempt. It was, like, pleasurably self-flagellating. Like I deserved it.'

They were perched at the edge of the bed. While he spoke, his hand inched across the doona between them. With every tiny movement Mark seemed less concerned about his betrayal of Eleanor and more about its repercussions—how it made him look, and how it might bond him and Charlie.

His hand had almost traversed the distance between them and his voice was softer, like it was coming from further back in his throat, when he said: 'It's hard to talk about, because it was a really shitty time, to be honest. I haven't . . . I actually haven't slept with anyone since. I just had so much headnoise. But I think, now . . . I think . . .'

Then, and only then, did he touch Charlie: the tips of his fingers grazing her bare thigh. 'I think I'm ready to try again.'

'Mark—'

There was something about the pressure of his fingers on her leg that now felt—although it was the lightest brush—forceful. Frozen beneath that heat, she suddenly realised that she and Mark had both been working towards the same point all night. She, with her desire to skip past talking and get straight to touching. And Mark, with his insistence that they pause for a while and swap emotional intimacies. Instead of ripping off her clothes, he had stripped slowly and lain before her: his ego naked and weighty in her hands.

She wasn't even sure that he'd done it consciously—he, who was such a mystery to himself: who wanted to be a writer but not to write; to have power, but not to relinquish the option to be pitied; to be sensitive, and not like the other boys who don't talk about their feelings. But he was also looking at her now like he wanted to fuck her, and he'd manoeuvred her into this position where she felt, suddenly, like she had to—like he was powerless, and she, through tender touches, and opening herself, could be the one to help him.

And how easy it would be. All she had to do was match Mark's personal confession with her own. She could tell him how hard it was to hear Helen crying: how she was still a little bit in love with her. Then he would hold her and comfort her and they would be back in the familiar rhythm of their emails and they could go on like that forever: trading intimacies and thinking highly of themselves for being sensitive enough to deserve them.

She recognised all this with such immediate clarity, it was as if she had always known. A truth she had long hidden from herself:

that Mark was only able to manipulate her, because she relished his attentions.

His hand was still on her leg. He moved it to her face, and gently cupped her chin.

This time, when he asked if he could kiss her, Charlie didn't smile or make a joke or reveal anything personal.

She just said: 'No.'

—

ON SATURDAY MORNING, Eleanor moved through the apartment with a sense of inevitability, as if she had already dreamed the scene.

She found it empty.

It was several hours later that Helen made contact. She wanted to know when would be a good time to collect her things. Then she added:

> *I think we both need space. I'm conscious there wasn't a lot of closure. If you want to meet to talk about anything, I'm here.*

In her response, Eleanor matched Helen's tone: considerate, articulate. They both behaved perfectly. Like they were trying to prove to themselves that they were not the kind of people who broke up because of a failure to communicate.

Eleanor sent her texts from bed: curtains closed, a punishing darkness. She felt like her insides were seeping out through her pores. She was empty, and at the same time heavy. Moving—even just to the door, or to the window—seemed as abstract and impossible as moving to another country.

It had been a little over four months since Mark broke up with her. No break-ups in twenty-five years, and then two in quick succession. Last time, she had set about getting over it as if she were working to a deadline. Now, any attempt to move on felt like regression. She was back again, sadder and more alone. Except this time, she thought much less of herself.

She didn't eat, except for at eight in the evening, when she went to the corner store and bought a cup of mi goreng with three sachets of flavouring, each a wildly different colour. Seb was out, so she boiled the kettle in peace, and then took the steaming cardboard cup to bed. She hoped Helen was enjoying her space.

—

ELEANOR CHECKED HER phone and found nothing from Helen. Just three missed calls from her father. It was Sunday morning now. She'd gone to bed early, thinking that sleep, at least, would make the time pass faster.

She waited until eight, and then called her father back. She tried three times.

Trust him not to answer, she thought. Just when she was in the mood for a sermon.

Because she couldn't stop crying, and because she didn't want Seb to wake up and see her and ask questions about her weekend or her feelings or Helen's whereabouts, Eleanor decided that now would be the perfect time to take herself for a swim.

She took Seb's car keys off the kitchen counter, and sent him a text.

It was raining again. A drizzle now: the sky soft, the streets slick. Her eyes itched, and her stomach was uncomfortable, stretching a finger up towards her throat. Eleanor gripped the wheel with both hands, and tried to ignore these physical sensations, with an effort so great it only accentuated them.

She stopped at McDonald's before she was out of Potts Point, and ordered a hash brown on the self-service screen. In the queue, she and the other customers stared at each other with lazy curiosity. Most of them were heavily clothed in the previous night: smoke-smelling, large pupils. She ate the hash brown back in the car, the hot crust scraping the roof of her mouth. When she finished it, the wheel was greasy.

Before pulling out into the traffic, Eleanor selected a history podcast that purported to—in twenty-two minutes—'explain' the Taliban. She thought it might give her some perspective.

Eighteen minutes later—her thoughts un-diverted from Helen—she parked at one of Sydney's most dangerous surf beaches.

The beach was deep and not very wide, with a short slab of sand, and a heavy, concrete sky. In the rain, the beach was unpatrolled. Today, there was a single figure at the far end. He walked with his shoes in his hand, and steered clear of the sea. The waves didn't break in a line—they attacked each other from opposite ends and dumped right on the shore, seemingly at random, like frontline soldiers falling under fire. They coughed up seaweed as they fell. It bled onto the shore.

Eleanor watched through wind-squinted eyes. It looked like the perfect place to have an epiphany. It was violent and beautiful and everybody on the planet agreed that nature was good for your mental health.

With a careful tread, and shoes in hand, Eleanor walked out onto a wide flat rock at the north end of the beach. From there she could see the curve of the coast, sheer cliffs biting into the ocean all around the headland. Her friend, meanwhile, had put his shoes on and was walking away from the sea.

She wished she were the type of person who could just take off her clothes and let the water have her. For one thing, she'd need to have a different body, or a different relationship with her current one. She was basically happy with it, but—not looking like a model or an actor (or her sister, for that matter)—she would be mortified if anyone saw her. It's *frolicking*, Eleanor thought, if a beautiful person does it. For everyone else, it's *having an episode.*

Aside from the danger of being seen, there was the risk of a rip. Eleanor wished she could just wade in, gasp at the cold, hold her breath, put her head under, swim a few strokes, float, swim harder, try to put her feet down, fail, swim harder still, plant her feet, wade with great effort, collapse panting on the beach, and think, after all that, *What a dangerous thing to do.* Instead, she stood on her rock holding her white leather sneakers, studied the scene and identified a rip. Diving in would be attention-seeking and indulgent, because she had responsibilities to other people, chief of which was to stay alive and not cause any more grief.

Also, she was scared—scared of a rip, scared of what other people thought of her, scared of having no power, scared of being judged, and of not being the one to do the judging. It was all she could do to stand still and stare at the sea, and think about its vastness, and how objectively small she was in comparison, and wonder that she never, ever—not even now—felt small or insignificant. Even when she hated who she was, and wished she were different, she was still the centre of her own thoughts and actions.

Eleanor turned, the waves raging at her back, and picked her way along the rocks. She towelled her feet before putting her sneakers back on—anxious not to get any sand in Seb's car.

She was halfway home when her phone rang. She had developed a high, clear headache, like her brain was attached to strings and was being yanked out of her skull. Seeing the caller ID, she pulled over, so she could focus.

Her father spoke as soon as she answered. 'Charlie? I was in church. Is everything okay?'

'It's Eleanor.'

'Sorry, Eleanor.'

'I was just returning your call. From last night?' Eleanor closed her eyes, and felt as if her body were rocking, so she leaned her head back against the seat. Even hidden behind clouds, the sun was hot and precise in her right eye. Her father took several seconds to respond. 'I was at a funeral yesterday. Did I call you?'

'Yes.'

'Was it late?'

'Like, ten?'

His reply was whispered, which made Eleanor wonder whether other people were in earshot. 'I might have had a bit to drink.'

'Okay, well, crisis averted.' Eleanor's voice achieved that customer-service pitch which is at once friendly and inhuman. 'It was good to speak to you, Dad, and I hope your funeral went well. Not *your* funeral—'

'Not yet, anyway.'

'But you're well? Health-wise?'

'Oh yes. Like a peach. Now I'd better let you get on, because I'm needed somewhere in a few—'

'Wait, Dad.' Eleanor was surprised at her own panic. 'Who died?'

'Sorry?'

'The funeral. Whose was it?'

'A parishioner.' His diction, which was slightly theatrical, confirmed to Eleanor that he was in the presence of an audience. 'She was a lovely lady. We're very sorry to see her go.'

'Give her my condolences.'

'I'm not sure she needs them, but I'll pass them on to the family.'

Eleanor laughed. 'Of course.'

'Everything okay, Eleanor?' He said this like a joke, as if it were ridiculous that Eleanor might not be okay.

'Oh, you know, just falling apart. But otherwise okay. Bye, Dad. Good to chat.'

'All my love.' That last part sounded sincere, and was almost cut off by the speed with which Eleanor hung up.

Eleanor felt foolish then for thinking that he might have needed her. Or that he might have known how much she needed him. It seemed the saddest most obvious thing in the world—that people changed, and also didn't.

23

'I'VE BEEN WONDERING when you'd show up.'

'Same to you—evidently.'

Eleanor was standing in the hallway outside her mother's apartment. She had been there for so long that her phone had started to bore her, and she was now almost fifty pages into a book from the communal library in the front lobby. She folded the corner to mark her page, and stood back so her mother could open the door.

Mary walked straight into the apartment, and placed her bag on the kitchen bench. Without asking, she filled the kettle, and pulled two mugs from the cupboard. Her movements were exact, and the mugs clanked onto the bench with something like reproach.

Eleanor realised then, under the yellow kitchen light, that her mother's anger was personal. As someone who lived for other people's praise, few things were quite so potent as her mother's disapproval. It made Eleanor feel like she had no right to exist, perhaps that she had never really existed at all, except when people lied to her and said that she was doing well. Her mother poured the boiling water with a frown, and Eleanor's insides turned to liquid and dripped out her feet.

Mary bobbed the teabag up and down: loose skin on her hands, knuckles bulging around her rings. She looked, Eleanor thought, exhausted.

When she realised her mother was waiting for her to start, Eleanor said, 'I feel dreadful.'

'I gather this is about your sister.'

'Did she tell you?'

'She didn't say anything about you. She just said she was upset about some girl.'

So Eleanor told Mary the story about the girl. Not the whole story. That big sister instinct—to protect and not to dob—pulled her up short of the truth. She said that she had fallen in love with a woman, and lived with her briefly, and that Charlie had loved her too—that she, Eleanor, had known this, on some level, from the start, and done it anyway. And she said that Charlie knew the whole time, who Mark had cheated on her with, so they'd both kept secrets. Which, Eleanor said, wasn't an excuse. Just some context.

When she finished, she didn't dare look up. She stared at her milky tea.

'Jesus,' Mary said. 'If all this happened with Charlie and her theatre friends, I'd say they have too much spare time. But, Eleanor . . . you're a busy woman.'

Eleanor knew it was intended to be funny, but in her current mood, she could see no humour in a joke at her expense. It just seemed depressing and true. Her head fell into her hands. From that position, she heard her mother, but couldn't see her face.

'I must say, I've been worried about you for a while.'

'Since when?' Eleanor's voice was muffled through her hands.

'You know, it's funny. Recently, just this year, I've thought you looked happier than you have for a long time.'

Eleanor lifted her head. 'So you've been worried for a long time?'

'Certainly since you started with Mark, yes.'

Her mother said this so calmly, staring into her tea, it was as if it were obvious. But Eleanor was struck by it. It had always been a consolation to think that however badly she treated other people—Charlie, even Helen—there were some people whom she was incapable of hurting. Her mother, she now realised, was the example she always clung to. It was because she wanted soothing—to think that she, as opposed to Charlie, was *the good child*—that she said: 'And I'm meant to be the one you don't worry about.'

Her mother looked her in the eye and gently, with a sad smile that acknowledged what Eleanor wanted to hear, let her daughter down. 'I worry about both of you,' she said. 'Always.'

Eleanor smiled defensively. 'Always?'

Her mother smiled too, but it was a smile that claimed to know better—to see more—not a smile of amusement. 'So, what's she like?'

'The opposite of Mark.'

'In that case, I can't wait to meet her.'

Eleanor thought she was laughing, but when her mother said, 'Oh, sweetheart,' she realised she was also crying.

Eleanor let her mother hug her.

'Gosh, two heartbreaks in four months.'

'One heartbreak,' Eleanor corrected.

'Maybe I should try going out with a woman. See what all the fuss is about.'

Eleanor laughed, and wiped her nose with the back of her hand. 'Don't force it, Mum.'

'It's not unheard of,' Mary said. 'Late-onset lesbianism. A lot of women at work gave up on men after their first or second marriage. And they seem very happy.'

'It's not like taking up golf when you're retired. It's part of who you are.'

Mary sat back, so she could study Eleanor from a distance.

Under that loving, critical gaze, Eleanor said, very quietly: 'Do you think I'm a terrible person?'

'Oh, Eleanor, no.' Mary reached across the table and touched Eleanor's wrist. Her hand was clammy from the tea. 'From what you've said, though, it sounds like you might have behaved a bit terribly.'

Eleanor raised her head and smiled weakly.

Mary ran her thumb in gentle circles across Eleanor's skin. 'But I'll always think you're not terrible. And I'm an extremely low bar. Even if you murdered someone, I'd still think you were worth visiting in prison.'

'I'll keep that in mind.'

'I'm just saying, I'll always love you. Even when, uncharacteristically, you haven't made me proud.' Mary smiled. 'How's this tough love going for you?' She was still holding Eleanor by the wrist. Now, she gave it a little shake. 'I expect a lot from you, you know that. So I think I'd be letting you down if I said: *You're perfect, everything's okay.* We both know you can do better.'

Eleanor moved her tea to one side, placed her arms on the table, and let her forehead touch the wood. She really didn't want to cry again. Her last hope, she thought, was to take this well. Dry-eyed and reasonable. Like criticism improved her, rather than breaking her into infinitely smaller pieces. With her eyes closed, her head bowed, and her voice muffled by the wood, she said: 'I think I need a career change.'

Her mother laughed and stood to stack their mugs in the dishwasher. 'Like what?'

Eleanor turned her head so she was facing Mary. 'I don't know. The public service. Like, helping people. Or what you do.' She sat up now. 'I could work in aged care strategy or something.'

'That seems like an overcorrection.'

'I just want my work to be *for* something. Other than me, you know?'

Mary sighed, and sat back down. This time, her gaze contained some disappointment. 'I think,' she said, her eyes set at a wistful distance, 'I think life can be for other people, Eleanor. Loving someone else might seem like a small achievement, in the scheme of things, but I'm not so sure that it is . . .'

Her mother sounded so uncertain—her voice trailing off at the end—that Eleanor let her sit for a moment in silence. She had seen a change in her mother's face: the softening around her eyes and mouth, the tears that threatened. With the strength of instinct, like a cry in the dark, she pulled her back. 'Mum?'

'Mm?'

'How did you know?'

'What?'

'That Charlie and I were fighting. You said she didn't mention me.'

With a barely perceptible shake of the head, Mary's mouth hardened: a sadder, straighter line. 'Darling,' she said, 'when Charlie has a problem, she calls you. She always has. If she's calling me, you *are* the problem.'

They both laughed then: the same laugh, through the same bow-lipped mouth. A brief moment of harmony, broken by a text buzzing on Mary's phone.

Mary stood up to read it.

'Charlie's at the door.'

—

WAVERLEY CEMETERY WAS so beautiful, it almost wasn't fit for purpose. A sloping green hill, sheer cliffs, white tombstones petty against the relentless sea. Looking back at it from further up the headland, the cemetery was a patterned patch of fabric—crucifix flowers on a clean green print. Perhaps at night it was eerie, with the moon ghostly on the water, and the waves a fervent whisper, but while the sun was up it was as sombre as a theme park, or gelato in a waffle cone. On sunny days, locals ran along its rim, their activewear sparse and tight. The sea was green and navy and, where it reflected the sun, a piercing white. All you could see, even in the names fading on the tombstones, was life.

Just inside the cemetery's stone gates, the Hamor sisters sat. They were in the last few weeks of daylight saving, when the sun set late and each pink evening still felt like a second chance at the day.

'Have you heard back about the audition?'

Charlie shook her head and ran her hands through the grass at her feet. 'Not yet. They're taking their sweet time, so it's not looking good to be honest.'

'I'm so sorry.' With her *sorry*, Eleanor claimed responsibility. Not sorry that it happened, but sorry for her own hand in it. Only someone who knew her well could have heard the difference.

'It's really not your fault,' Charlie said. 'That photo was an asset. I was feeling, like, high on confidence at the time.'

'Really?'

'Yeah, well. It's nice to have your suspicions confirmed.'

Eleanor had not yet looked at her sister. Their conversation had been conducted out to sea. Now, she turned her head so she could stare at Charlie's profile. Her own face, but prettier. For several seconds, Eleanor didn't speak. Charlie twisted a fresh blade of grass around her finger and pulled it tight until it snapped.

'I'm sorry, Eleanor. I've been so selfish.'

'It's okay.'

'Please let me say it.' Charlie took a deep breath. She was sitting cross-legged, her hands resting on her knees, and she held herself with such theatrical stillness, Eleanor braced herself for a long speech.

'I like attention too much.'

Eleanor laughed, shocked how quickly that sentence had ended.

'I'm serious!'

'You sound like Mum.'

'Seriously, Eleanor. I have to start finding validation internally.'

'Now you sound like a therapist.'

'It's not wrong though. Like, that's what the whole Mark thing was about. And you're right, I knew from the start where he was going with it. That's why it was so flattering. It's pathetic, really, that I respect myself so little. I wasn't thinking about you at all. I just thought about how he made me feel.'

Eleanor was silent for a moment while she contemplated her sister. Usually, when Charlie criticised herself, it was in a pleading tone: begging to be contradicted, her shows of vulnerability only ever the cue for someone else to pet her and tell her she was perfect. Today, however, Eleanor found Charlie contemplative. Her comments seemed egoless. Like she was looking at an artwork and trying to understand it. So Eleanor didn't correct her, or console her by drawing prettier pictures. She just nodded slowly to show she was listening. Eventually, Charlie continued.

'I kept telling myself we were just good friends, and that we hadn't actually crossed a line. But I think I knew deep down that we'd already crossed several—that it wasn't fair to you. That's why it had to be such a big fucking secret.'

Eleanor couldn't help herself. 'I thought you didn't tell me because it was "easier" for me to make up my own hairbrained version.'

Charlie shook her head. 'I did believe that, I think. Like, that's how I justified it to myself. It's so much easier to tell yourself you're lying for a good reason. But it's not that complicated. I knew I'd done the wrong thing, and I didn't want to get caught.'

That phrase—*get caught*—sounded like Helen's, and Eleanor couldn't hear it without being back in her apartment, alone, hating herself for telling Helen to go. She started to cry. 'Sorry. I'm a wreck at the minute, Charlie.'

It wasn't until her sister said it that Charlie realised how totally she wanted it to be true. It wasn't the apology that moved her. *A wreck.* The frailty of it all.

Her older sister, who had good marks and good jobs, and arrived on time and walked a step ahead to school, who laughed when her mother was snide or frank, who always had the wry reply, who was flat and affectless, even when people let her down—when her father left or didn't show or came back suddenly without warning—that Eleanor was, at twenty-five, in her own words, wrecked.

It spoke to a deep, inarticulate, half-remembered part of her. A young girl looking up to her older sister, reaching but never touching, sitting at the same table but asking her to explain the joke.

'Hey.' Charlie put a hand on Eleanor's knee. 'Everyone's a mess from time to time.'

And she provided an example, although it was difficult to hear, because her sister spoke at the exact same time.

One: 'Mark came home with me on Friday.' And the other: 'Helen and I broke up.'

Charlie responded first. 'I know.'

'How?'

'She's back at Bethel Street.'

Eleanor squinted into the wind until her eyes were almost closed. Charlie watched her, waiting for her to speak. Several seconds passed.

'It's because of me, is it?' When Eleanor didn't reply, she repeated herself. 'Eleanor, is it because of me?'

Still Eleanor said nothing.

'Don't feel like you have to break up because of me, okay? Because I don't need that. I'll get over it. Really, I will.'

'No that's not . . .' Eleanor was rubbing her eyes again, although she had stopped crying. 'That wasn't the reason.'

Charlie went on. 'I've been trying not to speak to her about it. And, to be fair, she hasn't brought it up. Obviously, it's awkward for me in the middle. But it does seem . . .'

'What?'

Charlie held Eleanor's gaze. 'It just seems like you really love each other.'

'I think it's for the best.' Eleanor stretched her legs out in front of her, and in that big-sister tone, which ends one subject by beginning another, she said: 'So.'

Charlie knew what was coming.

'What happened with Mark? Did he give you some attention?'

'No. Nothing happened.' Charlie heard her own voice—high and defensive—and laughed. It seemed absurd, suddenly, that she was telling the truth. 'Literally nothing. We just talked.'

Eleanor laughed too. All this lying and sneaking around, only to end up where they began.

'I wanted it to,' Charlie said. 'I was really keen. But he can be a bit self-pitying or something, can't he?' She didn't need to look at her sister. She could feel the judgement irradiating. 'I know, I know. Coming from me.'

'I know he's self-pitying and whatever, but I'm starting to pity him too,' Eleanor said. 'I told so many people he cheated on me with a sex worker.'

'Really?'

'I mean, Seb was the first person I told.'

Charlie smiled. 'So half of Sydney knows.'

'Mark would've known I'd do that too. I actually think, in a strange way, he kind of did me a favour by not correcting my worst assumptions.'

'Yeah, I guess it's helpful to be able to see him as the bad guy,' Charlie said. 'Like, being a victim is easy.'

'He's been rudely considerate, hasn't he?'

'Why can't men be worse?'

'I know! They're the worst!'

They were both laughing now, and they both knew the reason.

However different Eleanor and Charlie were, they were still, and always would be, capable of thinking the same thing at the same time. You can't grow up with someone—stitch your character from common threads: childhood, home, family—without forming similar patterns. So they both knew, without needing to articulate it, where their thoughts had turned.

'He drunk called me last night,' Eleanor said.

'Oh, I'm so sorry.' An apology that claimed no responsibility. In sympathy, Charlie pulled out her phone. 'He does that to me all the time.'

Eleanor took it and looked at Charlie's call log. She scrolled for several seconds. When she looked up, it was in disbelief.

'You always pick up.'

'Yeah, well. I try to. It's sort of something small I can do.'

Eleanor kept holding Charlie's phone. The screen went dead in her lap.

Maybe it was the combination of constant churning sea, and weary graves, that made everything seem complex, or maybe it was because the sun was setting and she was very tired—but for a reason she didn't understand, and never would, Eleanor realised, with so much conviction it was as if she'd always known, that she couldn't know everything. And, too, that she didn't need to understand people—like Charlie, like her parents, like Helen—to love them wholeheartedly.

Charlie, watching her sister's steady stare out to sea and the serene curve of her mouth, wondered whether she was having an episode, or some kind of epiphany.

'I know it's a lot to ask,' Eleanor said, 'I know it's selfish of me, but you do . . . God this sounds so sincere and melodramatic—'

'What? Just say it.'

'You do,' Eleanor's voice was so tiny, the waves and the wind almost drowned her out, 'forgive me? Don't you?'

Although Charlie had tried to give it before, it meant something totally new, now that forgiveness was requested. Like love requited, forgiveness requested—and now granted—*changed* things.

Charlie's words were action when she said: 'I do. Of course I do.'

At the same time, they reached their arms out to each other and said: 'Lollies you.' In that embrace, Charlie begged for what she had just granted, and Eleanor gave it.

The sun was setting, and the two sisters formed a single silhouette. The curves of their backs tapered to a pale point with Charlie's bleached-blonde head. From a distance, they might have been another gravestone.

24

ELEANOR WAS RUNNING late. When she arrived at the theatre, a bell was ringing with the intensity of a siren, summoning the audience to their seats.

Eleanor took one last look at the view: water black like a phone screen, and lights sparkling on the bridge. She took her coat off and bunched it under one arm. Already, she was sweating.

In the theatre, she slid into the empty seat. On her left, her mother. To her right, her father, who had driven down for the occasion: Charlie's first show at the Sydney Opera House. Or, as Eleanor had called it so many times her phone now autocorrected, *the Sydney Fucking Opera House!!*

Eleanor craned her neck, and looked at the rows behind her.

In the four months since they'd broken up, Charlie had been patient—Charlie was always patient—and let Eleanor know any time there was an event that Helen was likely to attend. These were usually plays. Tonight, however, there was nothing of Helen. No flashes of black hair. Not a single dimpled cheek.

Her mother, watching her, leaned across Eleanor to include her father as well, and whispered, 'I thought I saw Mark back there.' She pointed. A man in a white shirt, no tie, with thin wire-framed glasses.

Her father shook his head. 'His hair isn't ridiculous enough.'

They all laughed, although Eleanor's laugh was more in sympathy—without the old vindictive thrust. Looking across the auditorium at all the suited men who dressed and held themselves like Mark, she didn't see him at all.

Then the stage lights rose, the play began, and from its first moments, Eleanor felt a calm descend.

A crowd frozen on stage. On cue—a cue the audience could neither see nor hear—they started to walk. Each had an individual route; no one interacted. But the simple sight of twenty people moving at once—cells in one large organism—caught Eleanor's breath.

For the rest of the show, she didn't think of Mark, or Helen, or anyone except her sister, and even then, only when she was on stage.

It was—while it lasted—the most captivating thing: a world that Eleanor wasn't in; real outside of her, where people suffered and struggled, and loved one another. Where everyone was connected, and each affected the other.

When the lights rose an hour later, she blinked, and struggled to shake the stage off. It was almost a shock to look around and remember she was seated in a crowd.

She cast her eyes around once more for Helen, although this time with an easy, curious stare. Her problems seemed small, all of a sudden, and the solutions close at hand.

Eleanor leaned first to her left, then to her right, telling her mother then her father that she was going to get some air.

Washing her hands, Eleanor scanned the bathroom mirror. Heartbreak had made her superstitious: she anticipated Helen in all the sentimental places—beaches, pools, bathrooms of theatres.

Eleanor stood in the line at the bar, and looked at her phone.

'How are you finding it?'

It was fortunate that Eleanor had not yet purchased a drink, because she jumped so violently that any liquid would have ended up on the floor.

Helen was wearing a white muscle t-shirt tucked into white wide-legged jeans, and her Doc Marten Mary Janes with long white socks. Her arms were expressive, like brushstrokes. On the bar, she had placed—of all things—a white hat. Eleanor swallowed. A hat. At *night.* In a theatre? Hair that didn't look stupid when the hat was removed. If it wasn't Helen—if anyone else in her life were pulling off that hat—Eleanor would say they could get absolutely fucked. As it was, Eleanor was reminded that her own outfit only looked good when it was obscured by her coat. The coat that was now minding her seat.

'I'm loving it, actually.'

'Really?'

They looked at each other, and with her look, Helen asked several other questions.

Was it too simple, or too trite, to say that the play had moved her, or touched her, or that she felt elevated in the presence of something beautiful? Instead, she said, 'Put it down to my sentimental education.'

'Have you warmed to theatre in general, or just—'

'No, no. I wouldn't go that far. I just think this play is excellent. And Charlie's amazing in it.'

'Isn't she?' Helen smiled now, and drew those articulate hands into the conversation. 'And she just gets better and better in the second half.'

'Oh, you've already seen it?'

'I went to the dress rehearsal. "Another pair of eyes" type thing.'

A bell, and the swelling movement of the crowd in the foyer, confirmed that the play was resuming and they should take their seats. Helen motioned to the door with her thumb. 'Maybe we should . . .'

Whatever warmth they had found in talking about Charlie, it faltered now. Helen's smile grew tight and polite.

'Helen, I should have said, I wanted to call or something . . .'

Mortifyingly, Eleanor had to repeat this, because an usher approached them, and Eleanor had to shake her head and tell him not to worry, and then guide Helen to a chair in the corner. When they were sitting down, the seats stiff beneath them, Eleanor said, with a bit more bravado, 'Sorry, I was just saying: I should've called you. Or messaged, or asked to meet up or something.'

Throughout her little speech, Helen had been staring at her: long and unbroken. Now, she looked away, with a shake of her head. 'It's okay.'

'No, I should have said sorry. I am.' Eleanor was speaking faster, as if she could hold Helen to the chair. 'I really regret saying that, about you leaving the camera for Charlie to find. It was obviously just . . . I was so upset. It was petty and spiteful.'

'I don't know. It was pretty insightful.'

They both heard it: the accidental rhyme. Helen smiled first. Then they were laughing, and Eleanor relaxed her grip on the arm of her chair. They smiled at each other, shyly, like they were scared to admit that they were having fun.

Helen pulled her hair back so it fell behind her shoulders. As she ran her hands through it, she spoke—softly, not like she was making a point. 'I don't think I did it on purpose. I definitely wasn't conscious of it. But I do think, maybe, I wanted us to be found out. I was exhausted.'

Eleanor's voice was quiet too. 'I was only ever ashamed of myself.'

'I know.'

Eleanor's throat tightened around her next words. 'I behaved terribly,' she said. 'The whole time.'

'Don't beat yourself up too much.'

'No, I might start to like it.'

Helen gave her a look which registered, physically, in Eleanor's skin. Then she felt an urge to reach out, because that look was sad as well as longing—it clarified what they'd lost.

'The doors are closing.' The same usher from before, standing stern above them.

They both jumped up. Eleanor was conscious of the room shrinking around them. Crowds, like a rising tide, pushing towards the doors. She was finding it difficult to breathe.

'Well, it was good to see you,' Helen concluded weakly.

They hugged, then, the brush of other bodies around them. It only took a moment before Helen was gone, replaced by strangers.

It was exhilarating, Eleanor later reflected, to want something so much that you knew what to do—that you acted on instinct and not in accordance with type, and analysed it later. At the time, she made no attempt to understand herself, or explain herself, she took one step, knocked someone's bag, heard a gasp, and seeing a white sleeve, grabbed Helen's shoulder.

'Helen, wait.'

They were at the front of the line, right before the doors, where the crowd was closest. Eleanor worried about her breath on Helen's face. She whispered, and tried not to move the air. 'Do you want to just . . . keep talking?'

'Now?'

Eleanor turned her back on the doors and dragged Helen with her. She ignored the usher, who threw his hands up in exasperation and started to close the double doors.

'But what about Charlie?'

'I'll come back another night. She'll understand, when I explain it.'

The bell had stopped ringing. Empty and silent, the foyer still felt too small—filled with Helen's probing eyes, her slow deliberation.

'She's forgiven me for worse.'

Eleanor had said it as a joke, but Helen didn't laugh. She let the comment sit, refusing to make light of it. The longer she said nothing, and just looked at Eleanor, the more their silence meant.

For a moment, a different world—where new starts exist, and they could be together—trembled within reach. Eleanor's bow-lipped smile quivered with a promise so subtle that only Helen could see.

A promise, perhaps, to change.

ACKNOWLEDGEMENTS

MY THANKS:

For their support of me personally, to my parents Karen and Peter Reid; to my aunt Maureen Ryan; to Patrick Still, and to all my friends, in particular, Joseph Baine, Caitlin Lee and Ruth Ritchie.

For their support of this novel, first to my publisher Robert Watkins, for seeing what was good in this book before I could and for making it better. Also to Ali Lavau and Rebecca Hamilton for their wise editorial comments. And to my friends and first readers, Tom Davidson McLeod and Luca Moretti, for their generosity and insight.

For their support of my writing, to everyone at Ultimo Press, especially to James Kellow, Emily Cook, Brigid Mullane, and Katherine Rajwar—thank you for your tireless work and for always making me feel like part of the team. And for their faith in me, to my agent Fiona Inglis and to everyone at Curtis Brown, especially Benjamin Paz.

And finally, for the ideas: what these characters learn from experience, I learnt from other people. I drew particularly heavily on two works: Harry Frankfurt's *Reasons of Love*, and Martha Nussbaum's *Love's Knowledge: Essays on Philosophy and Literature.*